WELCOME TO BOMB ING HAM

RHONDA LYNN RUCKER

WELCOME TO
BOMB
ING
HAM

RHONDA LYNN RUCKER

PELICAN PUBLISHING
2019

*The word "Pelican" and the depiction of a pelican are
trademarks of Arcadia Publishing Company, Inc., and are
registered in the U.S. Patent and Trademark Office.*

Library of Congress Cataloging-in-Publication Data

Names: Rucker, Rhonda, author.
Title: Welcome to Bombingham / Rhonda Lynn Rucker.
Description: New Orleans: Pelican Publishing, 2019. | Summary: In 1960s
  Birmingham, Alabama, nonviolent activist Shirley Dupree tutors Earl B.
  Peterson, whose grades plummeted, threatening his college scholarship,
  after his mother's death by a Ku Klux Klan bomb.
Identifiers: LCCN 2018050221| ISBN 9781455624928 (hardcover : alk.
  paper) | ISBN 9781455624935 (ebook)
Subjects: | CYAC: Race relations—Fiction. | Nonviolence—Fiction. | Ku
  Klux Klan (1915-)—Fiction. | Bombings—Fiction. | African Americans—
  Fiction. | Birmingham (Ala.)—History—20th century—Fiction.
Classification: LCC PZ7.1.R8278 Mig 2019 | DDC [Fic]—dc23 LC record
  available at https://lccn.loc.gov/2018050221

Printed in the United States of America
Published by Pelican Publishing
New Orleans, LA
www.pelicanpub.com

For Marvin Smiley
and for all the others who also marched

The author's husband (in glasses), James "Sparky" Rucker, and friends marching in the 1960s. (Photograph by Terry Moore, from the author's collection)

Chapter 1

The man held the bomb in his arms as a mother might hold a baby. When the Pontiac hit a pothole, it momentarily propelled the weapon out of his grasp. He rescued it and glared at the driver.

The car eased up to a curb. Windshield wipers stopped and headlights darkened. The man climbed out, tucking the bomb inside his coat. Shivering, he walked hunched over toward a bungalow. Pulling the device from his coat and a flashlight from his pocket, he dropped to the ground and crept under the porch. It was pitch black. A musty odor of decay filled the air. He crawled on his belly for several feet, using elbows and knees. Water dripped from the brim of his hat onto his hand as he fumbled with the flashlight and pushed on the switch. Nothing. Great time for batteries to go dead. Using his thumb, he pressed harder.

Bull's-eye. It worked. Something ahead scurried through the damp leaves. He aimed the beam of light toward the noise—nothing except cobwebs, an empty beer can, and the concrete foundation. After advancing a few more feet, he inspected the weapon and traced the wires to the detonator cap, which was plunged deep into a stick of dynamite. Everything was intact. The rain increased for a few seconds, beating on the porch above him, then slacked off again.

The man placed the weapon on the ground, then crawled in reverse. He thought of a crab he had once seen burrowing backward in the sand of a riverbank. His head hit the porch, producing a meteor shower in his field of vision. He waited for it to clear, then continued his trek. Reaching the edge of the porch, he turned off the flashlight and stood under the eaves.

The driver was waiting, holding two gasoline cans, his pale complexion flushed pink with the frozen air. The men worked together, spilling the contents under the porch. "Happy Thanksgiving," the driver mumbled, screwing the lid on the empty can.

Walking back to the car in the drizzle, they glanced around—nobody. The motor turned over, and the Pontiac eased its way onto the road, disappearing into the mist-shrouded night.

Chapter 2

It was a bitch growing up in Birmingham. Unless you were white. And Earl B. Peterson wasn't white.

He was reminded of that fact every time he drew a breath. It wasn't so much the everyday insults—sitting in the back of the bus or stepping off a curb when a white person passed. Earl B. had become numb to those slaps in the face. It was the bigger things that really stuck in his craw. Like the cross burnings and beatings he heard about happening under cover of darkness. But that stuff was just child's play compared to what happened during his senior year of high school.

Most of the time, Earl B. focused on football, mainly to keep from thinking of the problems in Birmingham. He loved the sport. His fall performance on the gridiron had attracted the attention of college recruiters, even the ones at Alabama A&M. He fiercely followed their games and planned to wear one of their maroon and white jerseys next year.

But on this particular Saturday night, A&M had just lost in overtime by one touchdown. It had put Earl B. in a bad mood. He turned off the radio and stared out the back window into the dripping-wet darkness. The gloomy weather made it all the more appealing here in the armpit of the South.

Mama was cutting up onions and peppers at the kitchen counter. "Your clothes ready for church tomorrow?" The ceiling light cast a golden halo around her face, accenting her high cheekbones.

"I don't know." *And I don't care.* That was the last thing on his mind as he slouched against the window. The water made a plunking noise as it dripped from the edge of the gutter.

"They're having dinner after the service," his mother said. "I'm getting some food ready to take."

"So they talked you into cooking a free meal again?"

The expression on her face told him she caught his sarcasm. "They actually asked Grammaw, but she has to work late tonight. So I offered."

As far as Earl B. was concerned, his mother had no reason to be so cheerful. He turned his gaze back to the murky outdoors.

She picked up the cutting board and scooped the onions and peppers into the skillet. The sizzling noise startled him. Their sweet, sharp smell filled the air. "Something wrong, child?" Mama asked.

Earl B. felt her eyes on him. It was a question he had heard too many times during the past year. Yes, he wanted to scream, plenty wrong! But he didn't answer.

Wiping her hands on a rag, she turned the skillet off, then walked over and put her arms around him. He smelled her familiar fragrance, the scent that meant home and comfort. "What's the matter?" she pressed.

His jaw grew tense. She had no answers. He had no answers. There was no reason to dredge it all up again. "Nothing. Nothing at all."

"Is it 'cause A&M lost?"

Let it drop. His fingers gripped the windowsill as he let out a frustrated sigh. "Just wish football season wasn't almost over."

"You wouldn't wanna be playing football in this mess anyhow." She gave his shoulders a squeeze. "Besides, we got Thanksgiving and Christmas coming up." Mama tried to hug him again, but he squirmed away and headed for the doorway. She went back to the skillet. "Well, I'm gonna finish this up and then go to bed. See you in the morning."

"Night," Earl B. mumbled. He wandered down the hall and unbuttoned his shirt. Stretching, his knuckles hit the top of the bedroom doorframe. He ran his fingers through his tight curls. His classmates made fun of his hair. And his brown skin, too, which had a golden cast to it, almost bronze. The guys at school came in all shades—some light, some dark, and everywhere in between—and they all got teased.

After putting on his pajamas, Earl B. slipped into bed and listened to the pellets of rain beating down on the roof. He thought about his father. Unlike everyone else, Earl B. believed he knew what might have happened to his dad, but he tried to shut out those uncomfortable ideas.

Memories of his father continued to haunt him. One rainy afternoon, Dad had come to his bedroom with two umbrellas saying, "Come on, boy, let's go for a walk." They'd wandered around the neighborhood and talked about everything from school and football to his father's job.

These thoughts kept Earl B. awake a long time that night. Gradually, they turned into a dream, and the dream became a nightmare. He was once again walking with his father, when he sensed someone behind them. Turning around, he saw people in the distance, floating above the sidewalk. This would have been enough to upset anybody, but these were not your ordinary, run-of-the-mill people he'd expect to see in his neighborhood. They were dressed in long white robes and hoods, making them look like ghosts.

Then things got more bizarre. Earl B. was now walking alone. His father had disappeared. "Dad!" he yelled, looking around. No answer. "Dad, where'd you go?" The phantoms were drifting rapidly, gaining on him.

One of the ghostly figures yelled, "Better run like hell, nigger!" He pulled a sawed-off shotgun from the front of his robe.

Earl B. bolted. The others cackled. He glanced behind, craning his neck as he tried to run faster. The man pulled the trigger.

It sounded like an explosion—a huge one. Earl B. woke up. The next moment, he heard an earsplitting scream. His eyes began stinging. He realized the blast hadn't been the gun in his nightmare. It had been real—something in his home.

Sitting up in bed, Earl B. scrambled out of the covers and ran barefoot from his room. The smoke in the hallway was so thick he couldn't see. A violent coughing fit came over him, leaving him gasping for breath.

Through the murky air, toward the front of the house, he saw fire. The sight sent a hair-raising message through his body. His mother's bedroom was that way. The back door of the house was nearby, but in the opposite direction.

"Lillian! Earl B.!" It was his grandmother's voice, coming from the front of the house, followed by a barrage of coughs. Then silence.

Earl B. ran toward her, but his progress was agonizingly slow, with him feeling his way down the hallway and using the blaze as a beacon. As he drew closer and peered through the haze, he saw a hole in the front wall of the house, with flames outside, licking up from the seared wreckage that used to be the front porch.

Something sharp stabbed the sole of his foot. He limped along until another convulsion of barking coughs overwhelmed him. Earl B. was drowning in dust and smoke.

Taking another step, he stumbled over a body on the floor. "Grammaw!" he hollered, kneeling beside her. No answer. He called her name again, shook her, then put his hands on the sides of her face. Still no response.

"Grammaw, wake up!" he croaked, then broke down into another coughing fit. The dirty air was overpowering him. Earl B. grasped his grandmother's ample body around the waist, lifted her, and staggered through the cloud of smoke toward the back door. Fumbling for the doorknob, he almost dropped her. His eyes stung. Trying not to breathe, he hoisted her body over his shoulder, then opened the door and stumbled outside, drinking in gulps of fresh air. He lowered her to the ground and bent over panting.

"Esther!" Mrs. DuBose, the next-door neighbor, ran toward them and cradled Grammaw in her arms, but her eyes didn't open.

Sirens pierced through the smoke and early morning darkness, sending an alarm through Earl B. He rushed around to the front of the house, still gasping and coughing. The firemen were unpacking their hoses. Flames engulfed the front porch, blocking the entrance. But his mother's bedroom window was shattered. Jumping up, he grabbed the sill, then lost his hold and fell back to the ground.

"No!" a man shouted.

Earl B. jumped up again and grabbed the sill. *It's just a chin-up,* he told himself. He did them all the time in the gym at school. But the window ledge wasn't as easy to hold as a bar, and he lost his grip again.

Someone grabbed him from behind. "Don't go in there." It was Mr. DuBose's voice. He was surprisingly strong for an older man. Earl B. broke away from him, but Mr. DuBose caught him again. This time, another set of arms also held him.

"Let me go!" he yelled, struggling against the two men. "My mother's in there!"

"You can't go inside. You'll die," Mr. DuBose said sternly. "Let the firemen get her."

Still struggling, Earl B. watched the firefighters douse the flames on the front porch. One of them entered the house. Several seconds went by, but it seemed like hours. Finally, the fireman reemerged, carrying Earl B.'s mother. He lowered her to the ground, examined her, shook his head, and rejoined the others.

"Mama!" Earl B. bellowed. The two men loosened their hold, allowing him to break free. He ran to his mother, who lay motionless, with a gaping, bloody wound on the side of her chest. "Mama!" He grabbed her face and tried to arouse her, but she didn't respond. Cradling her in his arms, Earl B. sobbed. *No. This isn't happening.* He squeezed her hand and shook her shoulders, but her limp body fell back to the ground. Laying his head on her chest, he wept. Lights flashed around him. Voices called out, but he couldn't understand the words. He didn't care. All he knew was something horrible had happened. After a while, someone slid his mother's dead body out from under him, leaving Earl B. to collapse facedown on the grass.

A man grabbed his wrist, then laid his fingers on Earl B.'s neck for a few moments. "Boy, you okay?"

Lifting his head, Earl B. looked into the eyes of a fireman.

"Talk to me," the man said. "You okay?"

"Do I look okay?" Earl B. barked.

The man shook his head and walked away.

Earl B. laid his head back down on a broken board. Time passed. Maybe five minutes, maybe five hours, he didn't know.

Mrs. DuBose roused him from his grief. "Child, you all right?" The voice he heard was far off, like he was under water and she was calling to him from land. "Earl B.?"

He looked at her. She had dark skin, almost blue-black in color, and kids sometimes made fun of her. "Grammaw?" he asked, his voice cracking.

"I think she's okay. Come on over and see her."

His grandmother was still lying on the ground where he had left her. Her eyes were open, but confusion was etched on her face.

"Grammaw?" he said, feeling a wave of relief. "You okay?"

She responded with a cough. He helped her sit up. Putting his arm around her shoulders, he felt her body trembling. Or maybe it was his own body.

The police took their time arriving and left before the others finished. Earl B. hadn't expected any help from them anyway. Dad used to tell him to watch out for the cops, because most of them belonged to the Klan. In any decent town, the police would be there, roping the house off as a crime scene. But not in Birmingham.

The fire truck pulled away. Sitting down on the grass, Earl B. found a splinter the size of an awl tip in the sole of his foot. He yanked it out. His grandmother was now wandering through the mess in the front yard, picking up picture frames, shoes, and other items. "I can't find it," she muttered over and over.

Standing up, Earl B. picked up a piece of guttering that had landed near the fence. What should he do first?

"Your mama and I were real close, child," Mrs. DuBose said, turning to leave. "Let me know if you need anything, you hear?"

"I will." Earl B. glanced around. A sea of black faces stared at the house. Some were crying.

"I can't find it." Grammaw was nearby, searching on the ground and wiping her eyes with a handkerchief. Her silver hair, usually up in an elaborate French twist, hung loose down to her shoulders.

"Can't find what?" he asked, stepping over pieces of splintered wood.

"Calvin's picture."

"Grandpa?"

"Yeah. You know the one, don't you?"

Yes, he did. A large portrait of his grandfather had hung in the front hall. "Maybe we'll find it, Grammaw. Maybe during the clean up." He knew it was a long shot.

She leaned over to retrieve a shard. "My coffee cup," she mumbled.

A shiny object caught Earl B.'s eye, something almost hidden under a board. He picked it up and ran his finger across the smooth surface. It brought back long-ago memories.

"Lord, have mercy," his grandmother said, turning over a piece of wood in her hand. "Came off the dresser in the front bedroom."

Earl B. was still fingering the flat, oval stone in his hand. It looked like a green and black spider web trapped inside a milky, white gem. Somehow, it had survived the blast. He slid it in his pocket.

Grammaw, who stood hunched over in her bright yellow and blue nightgown, was now weeping. The entire neighborhood still gawked. Earl B. guided her into the house away from the crude stares and put his arms around her. They stayed that way until her sobs grew quieter, then he helped her into a chair.

Returning to the front yard, Earl B. carefully stepped through the rubble and gazed at the front of the house. The porch was gone, its pieces scattered throughout the yard. Dad had given the whole house a fresh coat of paint about two years ago, a peach color his mother had carefully chosen. The front windows were shattered. Most of the house still stood, but the bomb had blasted a huge hole in the clapboard siding. The front of the house had been gutted, like a jack-o'-lantern on Halloween. That was exactly the way his chest felt right now—hollow and empty.

Now, he knew firsthand why people called this town "Bombingham." Earl B. had heard about bombings. Hell, he heard about them all the time. But why did it have to happen to *him?* As if his family didn't already have enough problems trying to make it without Dad's income. The bomb could have been thrown from a car or planted somewhere near the porch. No matter what had happened, somebody was responsible. Likely a Klansman. Definitely a cracker.

His throat tightened. The emptiness he had felt only a few moments ago was now replaced with a wave of nausea rising in his chest. His muscles tensed up, first in his jaw, then his neck and shoulders. Earl B. bent over and let out a fierce scream that came from deep within, a scream that had been building a little at a time from seventeen years of humiliation and abuse. He didn't care if people heard. Let them stare. Someone had bombed his home. Killed his mother. And somewhere, somehow, he would get his hands around the neck of the man who had done it.

Chapter 3

January 1963

"You should play baseball instead of football at A&M," Asa told Earl B. The two friends were walking along Sixth Avenue. "They could use a good pitcher right now."

"I'm not interested."

"But you're an ace pitcher. I bet your fast ball is ninety miles per hour. Think of what it would be like to—"

"I said I don't *want* to," Earl B. snapped. Asa was forever trying to talk him into playing baseball in college.

"Okay, okay."

They stopped at an intersection. The western sky, at first filled with pink and purple clouds, darkened into oranges and browns as the sun slipped farther over the horizon, draining the colors away.

Asa changed the subject. "You've been to a mass meeting before, right?"

Earl B. sighed. No, he hadn't. The truth was his dad, who had been active in the movement, hadn't wanted him to get involved. Too dangerous for kids, he had said. Grammaw was now in charge. It hadn't come up, but Earl B. suspected she wouldn't approve. She was even more skittish than his parents had been.

"Did you hear me?" Asa pressed.

"I heard you," Earl B. said. "You know I don't like churches."

"You don't like *anything.*"

"If it hadn't been for your constant nagging, I wouldn't be here now."

"Don't get all bent out of shape about it. What's wrong with you, man? You never want to do anything anymore."

Earl B. pressed his lips together. No use answering a question like that. Asa meant well, but he was sometimes clueless.

"And you're so touchy," his friend continued.

"You'd be the same way if your house was bombed."

Asa's mouth opened, then closed.

"I don't even know who did it," Earl B. continued. Lately, he'd been living in a fog. Things happened to him, and he had no power to control anything. "There's nobody I can go after. Just some Klansman. That doesn't exactly narrow the field of suspects. Not in Birmingham."

Asa lowered his voice, taking on a gentler tone that irritated Earl B. even more. "That's why you should get involved in the movement. You could fight back."

"Right," Earl B. said sarcastically. "Those people don't fight back. They lie down and let white people roll over 'em."

"No they don't. Look at Montgomery. So many people quit riding the buses it forced the city to change."

"I'd rather find the guy that killed my mother and make him die a slow and agonizing—"

"Stop!" Asa's arm flew out in front of Earl B. "Look ahead."

A crowd had gathered in front of the church, including a long line of figures parading in white robes and hoods.

"Klan!" Asa whispered.

"Yeah." Earl B.'s neck stiffened. "Come on." He took a few steps. Asa didn't follow. "I don't know."

Earl B. glared at him. "Remember, this was your idea. I didn't even want to come to this thing."

"I know, but . . ."

"Come on." Earl B. led Asa toward the church. He wasn't about to let a bunch of bullies tell him what he could or couldn't do. In spite of the marching Klansmen, black people were still entering the building. As the two teens approached, the end of the line of hooded figures passed in front of them.

Asa froze and grabbed his arm.

Following his gaze, Earl B. saw a folded piece of paper on the pavement ahead. "Where'd it come from?"

"The last guy. It fell out of his robe."

At that moment, the figures halted and prepared to turn around and march back toward them.

"Let's go!" Earl B. took off. In one fluid motion, he leaned down, grabbed the paper, and rushed toward the front stairs with his friend trailing.

They reached the steps, where a crowd had gathered in front of the door. "Man, I see why A&M wants you," Asa said. "You're fast."

People stood in the church doorway talking, forming a bottleneck. Earl B. shot an uneasy glance back toward the line of marchers. The last Klansman had fallen behind and was pacing back and forth, crouched over, searching the sidewalk.

"He's looking for it," Earl B. muttered.

The Klansman turned his gaze toward him and the paper in his hand. Behind the mask, the man's icy stare sent a shiver down his spine.

Then it was over. The man raced back to join the others. By now, the entrance to the church was clear, and Earl B. turned to go inside.

"That was creepy," Asa said as they entered the foyer. "I don't mind saying those people scare me."

"Most of 'em are cowards."

"Bold words, considering what they did to your house." Asa pulled him aside. "What's the paper say?"

Earl B. glanced at it. "Looks like propaganda. That and a list of addresses."

Asa motioned for him to follow. "Come on. We're late." Walking into the sanctuary, they were swallowed up by powerful singing:

> *Woke up this morning with my mind stayed on freedom*
> *Hallelu (Hallelu), Hallelu (Hallelu), Hallelujah . . .*

The place was packed. The song ended and a Miles College student was introduced. Earl B. stuffed the paper back in his pocket, then followed Asa up an aisle to some vacant seats.

"Bull Connor's up to his old tricks again," the young man shouted from the podium.

The crowd grew restless, and several people yelled out.

"We're proposing a renewed boycott," the speaker said. "Or *excuse me,* selective buying campaign!"

The audience laughed and cheered.

"And we'll extend it right up through the Easter season!"

Several more speakers came to the podium, including Asa's father, who was pastor at one of the local churches. Earl B.'s attention wandered. His mind kept going back to the piece of paper in his pocket. He pulled it out and studied it, but the words still didn't make sense.

As he put it back, the congregation stood up and sang "We Are Soldiers in the Army." But the speakers weren't finished. Rev. Wyatt Tee Walker discussed his ideas for a spring campaign in the city. Finally, Rev. Fred Shuttlesworth took the pulpit. Until now, Earl B. had only seen him on television. A few years ago, when the preacher had tried to enroll his daughters in an all-white high school, a mob had chain-whipped him. Though he had miraculously survived, the attack had stirred up the black community. As Shuttlesworth spoke, more people responded, and he gathered momentum. By the time he ended, people were on their feet, with their arms crossed, holding hands, and singing "We Shall Overcome."

"So what did you think?" Asa asked after the meeting ended.

"Ain't much different from church," Earl B. mumbled.

Asa shook his head, and the two threaded their way through the crowd and exited the building. Their breath formed clouds in the cold air.

A young white woman approached them on the stairs.

"This is Rachel Cohen," Asa said, introducing them. "A friend of mine from ARC."

"ARC?" Earl B. asked.

"Alliance for Resistance and Change," said Rachel, holding out her hand.

Earl B. halfheartedly shook it. He had heard about white people who attended these functions, stirring up trouble. A young black man in a crown-style kufi hat stood next to her.

"Cornell Huff, Earl B. Peterson," Asa said. "Cornell started ARC."

"It's for young people who want to work in the movement," Cornell added. A jagged scar ran along the left side of his face.

"Wanna help out?" Rachel asked.

"I don't think so." Earl B. didn't appreciate them pressuring him to join.

A black teenage girl approached the group. "Hey, Asa," she said, with a little wave.

He nodded to her. "What's up?"

Earl B. raised his eyebrows, wondering if something was going on between the two, but Asa only gave him a sheepish grin.

"Who's your friend?" the new girl asked.

Asa introduced them. Her name was Shirley Dupree.

She mumbled a greeting and took Earl B.'s hand into both of hers and held it gently. It didn't last more than a moment, but the feeling lingered. It made him uncomfortable in front of Asa, but he didn't seem to notice. Out of the corner of his eye, Earl B. sensed someone watching them. He turned and saw the robed Klansman looking at him from across the street—the same one who had dropped the paper.

Earl B.'s attention was drawn back when he saw Shirley and Rachel wander off together. By now, Cornell had also left.

"Ready to go?" Asa asked.

"You know her?" Earl B. gestured toward Shirley.

Asa shrugged. "She's my cousin."

"Oh," Earl B. said, laughing. He had seen Shirley at school before but hadn't met her. She was the last person he expected to be involved in the movement—one of those honor roll students, the straight-A type that teachers liked to use as an example when the other ninety-eight percent hadn't done so hot on a test.

Glancing across the street, Earl B. noticed the Klansman had disappeared. He followed Asa, who inched his way down the stairs through the crowd, but his thoughts kept returning to the piece of paper in his pocket. As soon as he had a chance, he wanted to examine it more closely. Maybe it was the look in the man's eyes, but something told Earl B. the information was important.

Chapter 4

Boarding the bus, Earl B. pulled out the piece of paper he had retrieved from the Klansman.

"So what's it say?" Asa asked, leaning toward him.

Earl B. turned it so they could both read the typewritten words:

Hark, Citizens of the Invisible Empire
Here Yesterday, Today, Forever!
For Knights are Riding in the Dark.

59	*35th Ave. N.*
321	*2nd St. S.*
109	*Jefferson Ave. SW*
30	*Court G Alley*
81	*7th Ave. N.*
130	*4th Ct. N.*
348	*29th Ave. N.*

"You think those are places they meet?" Asa asked.

Earl B. stared at the list. One thing immediately jumped out at him. "No," he answered.

"What makes you say that?"

"My street's on here. Second Street South. But my address isn't 321."

"Yeah, I guess the Klan wouldn't exactly be meeting in your neighborhood."

Earl B. scanned the list, looking for other familiar streets. "I'd have to find all these places to know what it is."

"You aren't really thinking about doing that, are you?"

"Look at you!" Earl B. stared at him in mock amusement. "You're awfully weak-kneed for someone in the movement." Asa's expression made him regret his words. Earl B. had been nasty to him all day with his sour mood and wisecracks. Asa had been a constant ally, even to the point of clearing debris in his front yard after the bombing.

"You want to come over and see the house?" Earl B. asked.

"Sure," Asa said. "Is it done?"

"Everything but the painting."

They got off the bus and walked toward Earl B.'s home. Approaching the front yard, Asa slowed his pace, then stopped. "Wow," he said, his eyes full of surprise. "That's some seriously fine work."

A satisfied feeling rose inside Earl B. The house still needed painting, but other than that, the repairs were done. Of course, he knew about all the corners he had cut to save money, but overall, it looked good. Almost as good as before the bombing.

"How'd you do that, man?" Asa's voice interrupted his thoughts.

"Big Ben helped," Earl B. admitted.

"Mr. Ross?" Asa said, referring to their science and chemistry teacher at school.

"Yeah. He took me to the lumberyard and showed me how to do everything."

Ben Ross, known as "Big Ben" to most of the community, was a solid man in both character and stature. With his imposing figure, he easily stood head and shoulders over the rest. He had married Earl B.'s Aunt Ella. Though she had died long ago, Big Ben still considered himself part of the family. He had never been able to stomach the name Uncle Ben, so he insisted that his nieces and nephews call him by his nickname.

"I don't know if I would've liked that or not," Asa said. "That man can be scary."

Earl B. almost smiled. His uncle had a gruff exterior, and most students assumed that's all there was to him.

The two friends went up the walkway and entered the house. Grammaw glanced around the corner. "Earl B.? Where you been?" she asked in her husky, alto voice. The old woman stood at the kitchen table, thumbing through a stack of mail. She was dressed up, complete with her Sunday hat, in colors loud enough to wake up the students in Mr. Baugus's study hall.

"Hello, Mrs. Mathes." That was the thing about Asa—he had perfect manners. It made the rest of the kids look bad.

A smile crossed Grammaw's face for a moment. "Hi, child." Then her scowl returned as she looked at her grandson. "Where you been?"

Earl B. and Asa threw glances at each other.

"We were just looking at the front of the house, ma'am," Asa said. "It looks great."

Grammaw barely glanced at Asa before returning her gaze to her grandson. "Big Ben said he's gonna bring a batch of paint over here today or tomorrow." She threw a piece of mail down on the kitchen table and locked eyes with Earl B. again. "I just got in from Bible study five minutes ago. You two weren't out there goggling at the house then."

Bible study. His grandmother was holding down two jobs and somehow she managed to make it to Bible study. Earl B. decided to give up their little tug-of-war. "We were at the mass meeting."

Her voice rose. "The mass meeting? After what we been through?"

He didn't respond.

"Listen here. I don't want you going to no more of them. You hear?"

Earl B. felt his jaw tense up. Asa was shifting his weight from one foot to the other.

"Answer me."

"I'll go where I want to."

She pointed a finger at him. "Don't you be getting mannish with me." She yanked off her hat and grabbed her coat from the chair. "No more mass meetings. You hear? Answer me."

"I hear you."

Asa cleared his throat and turned to leave. "Well, I better be going. See you."

Grammaw and Earl B. hollered their goodbyes, then she hobbled down the hall with her hat and coat in hand.

Filling a glass with ice water, Earl B. stared out the window. As far back as he could remember, Grammaw had always been afraid. Afraid of the Klan. Afraid of everything. At the dinner table, she and Earl B.'s father had often argued about his civil rights work.

"You better watch it," she'd say, "or them crazies'll come after you."

"They'll keep coming after us as long as we let 'em," Dad would answer.

"Keep up with that attitude and you'll go to your grave a young man."

"You gotta die sometime. Might as well make it worth something."

Usually, about that time, Mama would interrupt and make them stop squabbling.

In those days, Earl B., who was young and stupid, had always taken his father's side. He was dumb enough to believe his dad was really changing the town, making things fair for black people. Earl B. was even proud of his father, and he wondered why others, like his grandmother, were so spineless. But now he knew neither of them had been right. Dad was wrong for thinking he could change things. And Grammaw was wrong to be afraid.

Earl B. turned on the kitchen radio. A saxophone played. Sipping his drink, he listened as the song ended.

"King Curtis, the king of the rock 'n' roll sax, here on WENN. And you've got Shelley the Playboy, the Mouth of the South—"

"Turn that thing off!" Grammaw hollered, returning to the room. "You need to do your homework."

Earl B. switched it off. He went through the stack of textbooks on a chair.

Grammaw shuffled to the sink and turned on the faucet. "You get supper?"

"Yes," he lied, throwing his Algebra II book on the table. He sat down and flipped through the pages.

At the kitchen counter, Grammaw set up the coffee pot for the morning. "I'm heading off to bed." She moaned and put one hand on her lower back. "Old Arthur's got me, bothering me something awful."

Arthritis, Earl B. wanted to say. *It's called arthritis.* Watching her disappear down the hall, he noticed a heaviness in her step that hadn't been there before the bombing. After spending all day at the hospital as a nurse's aide, she had a reason to be tired. On top of that, she worked odd hours at the church, cleaning up after their almost daily events. It took both jobs to make up for the loss of Earl B.'s parents. Long ago, he had quit trying to keep up with her schedule.

Earl B. got up and fixed a bologna sandwich. Lately, he had eaten enough bologna to scare off a field of pigs. He was sick of it, but it was clear Grammaw didn't feel like cooking. Pitching the meat package back in the refrigerator, Earl B. took a bite out of the sandwich and returned to the radio. He turned the volume knob down, then switched it back on.

A commercial played. He changed the station. Another commercial. Earl B. turned the dial almost all the way to the right. Occasionally, he could get a good Chicago station at night. Big Ben had explained it in science class a couple of years ago. He called it "skip" and said you could sometimes get stations across the ocean. Listening carefully, Earl B. slowly turned the dial back and forth. No luck. He turned the radio off, sat back down, and finished his sandwich.

Flipping through his math book again, Earl B. found the section Mr. Miller had discussed in class that day. He made it through the first paragraph before realizing he hadn't comprehended anything. His eyes read the words, but his brain wasn't paying attention. Starting over, Earl B. tried again. Nothing. He couldn't concentrate. The fog had descended upon him again. It was a constant problem, dogging him in most classes. He was hopelessly behind in algebra.

Earl B. stared at the page until his eyes crossed. He had never liked school, especially math. But studying hadn't been much of a problem until the bombing. His grades had always been acceptable. Even good enough for an Alabama A&M scholarship, which had come as a surprise. For a while, Earl B. had thought he wasn't going to college at all.

After Dad disappeared, Mama had sat down at the kitchen table and talked with him.

"I'm sorry, child, but we can't afford college," she had said. "Not with your dad gone. Without his income, we just can't do it."

"That's all right," Earl B. told her. But he didn't mean it. Her words hit him in the pit of his stomach. His dad had wanted him to go to college, so he had always assumed it would happen.

"I've talked to the principal about it," his mother said later that week. She put her hand on top of his. "And there still might be a way."

The expression on Earl B.'s face must have showed his disbelief.

"Now, don't go getting an attitude. It'll only get in your way."

Earl B. shrugged. Something in his throat kept him from speaking.

"Don't lose heart." She squeezed his hand. "You've got to believe in a miracle, child."

Sure enough, two weeks later, Coach Richards had called him into his office and told him he was the top contender for a football scholarship. "It's yours to lose," the coach said. "Just keep on doing what you're doing. Your grades are decent. You're bound to get it."

Back at home that evening, Earl B. told his mother.

"I told you, I told you, I told you!" she cheered, grabbing his hands and dancing around the living room. The radio was on, playing "The Twist." He laughed and danced with her, not even caring that Grammaw called them two crazy, flea-bitten loons.

Propping his elbows on his math book, Earl B. put his head in his hands and shut his eyes. His mother's face was still clear in his memory. Would it always be? He thought about that day in the kitchen, when he'd looked out the window at the rain. She'd put her arm around him. Now, he wished he hadn't squirmed away.

Reaching into his pocket, Earl B. pulled out the spiderweb gem he had found in the front yard and ran his finger over the smooth surface.

The bombing had changed everything. Even the world looked different to him now, as if life had gone backward, from a color movie to a black-and-white one. It had looked that way earlier today at the mass meeting, when the pair of eyes, framed by a white hood, had stared at him. Perhaps that man had bombed his home. If so, Earl B. had someone to pin the blame on, a specific guy he could go after, not just some unknown Klansman lost in the bowels of Birmingham. All he had to do was find him.

Chapter 5

Earl B. stopped in the hallway when he heard Grammaw's hushed voice.

"Tell me, how's he doing in school?"

A long pause followed. Was she on the phone? Then Earl B. heard a man's voice.

"There've been a few problems. Why?" Big Ben—that's who it was.

"He sits around, don't study no more. Says mean stuff," Grammaw said. "I'm worried about him."

"It's been a few weeks, but I did talk to him."

"If anything, it's gotten worse."

Big Ben grunted. "I'll see what I can do."

Earl B. walked into the living room.

"Hey there, child," Grammaw said, showing some surprise. She had on her pink and orange housedress. "Big Ben brought a mess of paint for the front porch. And he's *giving* it to us! Ain't that nice?"

His uncle held up a can. "My cousin owns a store and they couldn't sell this green color. Tahiti lime, they call it." He chuckled.

Earl B. glanced at it. The color didn't resemble anything that could have come from an exotic South Pacific island. Instead, it reminded him of the stuff Grammaw vomited after her gallbladder surgery.

"Did you hear about that bombing last night?" Grammaw asked, looking at Big Ben.

"Over near Miles College? Sure did."

"They was talking about that at the hospital today," Grammaw said. "I ain't even had a chance to look it up yet." She gestured toward the newspaper on the coffee table.

"I been looking into these bombings." Big Ben set the paint can down on the welcome mat. "Went over to the *World* office. There've been over fifty of 'em in this town since World War II."

The *Birmingham World* was the local black newspaper. It was just like his uncle to do that kind of extra homework. In class, he was always telling them to ask questions and do the legwork to answer them.

"Several of 'em were churches," Uncle Ben said, "but there were lots of homes over on Dynamite Hill too."

Previously all-white, Dynamite Hill was a favorite target after black families began moving into the neighborhood.

Grammaw shook her head. "I don't know what this town's coming to."

Big Ben hooked his thumb around the strap of his overalls. They were so large it must have taken a bolt of cloth to make them. Having grown up on a farm, his uncle preferred his comfortable, railroad-striped bibs to the stiff clothes he wore at school.

"Anyway," he said, looking at Earl B., "I put the other cans in the shed, along with a couple of paint brushes and some old drop cloths."

"Thanks," Earl B. muttered.

"Something wrong?" Big Ben walked closer.

Earl B. tensed up. How could his uncle even say that, after the house had been bombed? Besides, Big Ben had his own history, his own problems. The two of them had spent many hours together working on the house. That's when they had really gotten to know each other. His uncle had told him stories, and . . . well, let's just say that the man had been through a lot. Earl B. knew things about him most adults didn't know.

Big Ben shot a glance at Grammaw, and she disappeared down the hall.

"Heard you been having some problems with school."

Earl B. didn't answer. He resented people talking about him behind his back.

His uncle put a hand on his shoulder. "You want to talk about it?"

A hard lump of anger rose inside of Earl B.'s chest. He lowered his gaze and tried to control himself. Big Ben might be the only person around who could understand him. But if Earl B. talked about it, he'd lose it and go off the deep end. "Just leave me alone," he managed to say, his voice cracking. He turned away from his uncle, forcing him to drop his hand.

"Well," Big Ben said, pulling his keys out of his pocket, "let me know if you change your mind." He paused, and when Earl B. didn't respond, he said, "See you later."

At the window, Earl B. watched him walk away. Why did he treat his uncle like that? If it hadn't been for Big Ben, he'd be living in the projects right now. The house wouldn't have been repaired. Earl B. traced his finger along the edge of the window his uncle had helped him install. Parts of a sticker were still attached to the new glass. The man wasn't even a blood relative—he was an uncle by marriage. He had simply seen a need and responded. Earl B. hated himself for saying mean things to people like Big Ben and Grammaw and Asa, people who were just trying to lend a hand. He hadn't been like that before the bombing.

Nearby, the newspaper still lay on the coffee table. Earl B. picked it up and scanned it, searching for the article on the bombing near Miles College. He found it buried on page four. A house had been hit the day before, one rented by college students.

Dropping the paper, Earl B. went into the kitchen and turned on the radio. He sat at the table and opened a textbook.

"For the hundredth time, turn that thing down!" Grammaw hollered, entering the room. "You got a perfectly good radio in your bedroom if you want it that loud."

He stalled, pretending to write something on his homework paper. Grammaw started doing the dishes.

The song on the radio ended. "You've got Shelley the Playboy, the mouth of the South, here on WENN!"

Earl B. got up from his chair.

"Listen, folks," the deejay continued. "I hope you were at the big party on Monday night. The Reverend Shuttlesworth hisself came down from the Queen City to talk about the big plans for Birmingham. If you missed it, shame on you! But stay tuned for the latest scoop, 'cause—"

Earl B. turned down the volume, then moved the dial toward the right and went back and forth a few times. He found it—the Chicago station, playing Mary Wells. He sat back down, using his pencil to drum out the beat on his math book.

The phone rang. "Who on earth would be calling at this time?" Grammaw asked, grabbing a towel. "Can you get that?"

Earl B. rose from his chair.

"I hope it ain't Bessie DuBose again," Grammaw muttered. "She's always trying to talk me into going to a mass meeting. That woman's about to run me crazy."

"Hello?" Earl B. said, turning the radio down more.

No response.

He tried again. "Hello?"

"You were at the mass meeting." It was a husky male voice.

Earl B. went into the hall, stretching the phone cord as far as it would go. "Who is this?"

"I saw you there," the man said, taking a few raspy breaths. "You got something of mine."

Several seconds went by. "Who *is* this?" Earl B. repeated. He couldn't even tell if the person was black or white.

"Ever heard of the Klan?"

Earl B.'s breath caught.

Click.

"Hello?"

No answer.

Earl B. hung up. His mouth was bone dry. Grammaw had disappeared into her bedroom. He sat down at the kitchen table and stared at his open algebra book. Reaching into his pants pocket, he pulled out the paper dropped by the Klansman. He unfolded it and read the part at the top again. *Citizens of the Invisible Empire.* Obviously the members of the Ku Klux Klan. *Here Yesterday, Today, Forever!* Probably just one of their slogans. *For Knights are Riding in the Dark.* That phrase had a more sinister meaning—maybe the lynchings, beatings, cross burnings, and bombings?

Bombings. His eyes went out of focus as a new thought came to him. Hearing a shuffling noise, he quickly slid the paper under his math book.

Grammaw returned, wearing her robe. "One of your friends?"

It took Earl B. a moment to realize what she was talking about. "Yeah," he lied. "Uh, Grammaw?"

"Hmm?" She picked up a copy of *Jet* magazine in the front room.

"Besides our house," he said, rising from his chair, "what other bombings have there been?"

"Lord, have mercy, child." She walked back with her magazine in hand. "What makes you ask a fool question like that?"

Earl B. dug a biscuit out of the breadbasket and munched on it. Sometimes, she would answer him if he didn't respond.

"I don't know," she finally said. "Like Big Ben said, bombings've been going on since the end of the war."

"I mean recently."

"Why're you asking?" She took a few more steps toward her bedroom. "Is it 'cause of the one yesterday?"

"Yeah. Just wondering."

"There's been a slew of 'em lately. Bethel Baptist was in December."

"Where's that?"

"Collegeville. You know, where Reverend Shuttlesworth used to be." She thumbed through the magazine in her hand, then headed toward the hallway. "I'm going to bed. My feet are paining me something awful. I got a long day tomorrow."

Earl B. opened the drawer of the telephone table and pulled out the phone book. Flipping to the *B*s, he found Bethel Baptist—it was on Twenty-ninth Avenue North. Glancing up to make sure Grammaw hadn't returned, he slid the Klan paper out from under his algebra book. There it was. Twenty-ninth Avenue North. The street was listed sixth on the paper, but its number didn't match the address of the church.

He got the newspaper from the living room, opened it to the article, and located the address of the house near Miles College. Picking up the Klan sheet, Earl B. found what he was looking for—Court G Alley. That meant bombings had occurred on three of the streets on the list, counting his house. One matching street name could have been a coincidence. But not two. And definitely not three. Earl B. was now convinced of one thing. He held in his hand a list of Klan bombing sites.

* * * * *

Before falling asleep that night, Earl B. tried to remember the eyes of the Klansman who had dropped the sheet of paper. He was probably the one who had called him on the phone that evening. He could have also bombed his home.

Whoever the guy was, Earl B. aimed to find him. The possibility of catching up to the bomber breathed new life in him. When was the last time he'd felt truly alive? That was easy—when he'd made that incredible run on the gridiron last fall.

Earl B.'s mind drifted back. Carl Washington, the quarterback, had just called the play, and the huddle broke. Earl B. stood behind Carl and waited for the count. They'd be lucky if this plan worked. They had done it so many times, the defense would be expecting it. But with fifty seconds left and the game almost lost, they had to try. Still, seventy-one yards was a lot to hope for. Carl bellowed out the count. The snap came on two, and Earl B. charged forward. The defensive player saw him and broke to one side. Earl B. mirrored him, then slammed into his body, driving him to the ground.

Meanwhile, Carl was still poised with the ball, but he had nowhere to throw. The receiver wasn't there. Nobody was. Earl B. darted through a hole, then turned to look at Carl over his shoulder. A big linebacker had broken free and was heading toward the quarterback. At the last second, Carl threw a bullet pass. Earl B. caught it and blew past a defensive corner, who was left in the dust. Charging diagonally across the field, Earl B. crossed the fifty. He sensed another player nearby and cut toward the sideline. Thirty. As he turned to head toward the end zone, the guy was still hot on his heels. Push, push, push, past the ten . . . five . . . zero!

The crowd roared. A second later, Earl B. was tackled from behind by his own teammates, who bowled him over and buried him under several hundred pounds of wild, crazy-happy players. He about suffocated before they climbed off and let him stand. Carl even slapped him on the back and said, "Well done, my man." That was saying something.

Earl B. rode that good-mood feeling a long time after the game. In the morning, Mama had the *Birmingham World* spread out on the kitchen table for him to see. "Listen to this," she said, her face beaming.

"What's that?" he asked, pulling two pieces of bread out of the toaster.

"An article about the game."

He carried his plate to the table and looked over her shoulder.

"Listen," she repeated, then read from the paper. "'But the *real* star of the game was the fullback Earl B. Peterson, who did a superb job of keeping the quarterback open, occasionally blocking more than one player. And when the last play was about to crumble because the receiver had been blocked, Peterson stepped in, caught the pass, and scored the winning touchdown.'" Mama turned and put her arms around him. "Oh, sweetheart, I'm so proud of you."

Earl B. stood stiffly as she squeezed his arms to his sides. If he hadn't been feeling so good about the game, he would have turned away. Then she held him at arms' length, her eyes brimming with tears. The spiderweb gem, a moss agate, hung around her neck as a pendant, and the colors brought out the amber of her skin. Mama had the kind of face people paid attention to. Not because she was pretty, although most people thought she was. It was because she always had a determined look that said, "Don't mess with me." But that hard, strong-minded appearance had melted now, and her expression made him embarrassed but pleased at the same time.

A tear escaped and ran down her cheek. "I wish your daddy could . . ." Her voice cracked and she didn't finish.

Lying in bed, Earl B. felt one of his own tears fall from his face to the pillow. He glanced at the clock. Midnight. Ever since the bombing, he'd had trouble sleeping.

The Klansman's eyes flashed before him, and his train of thought abruptly shifted. The possibility of revenge was exciting. Earl B. desperately wanted to find him. But first, he had to answer some questions. Do some research, some legwork, just like Big Ben always said. He needed to figure out who the guy was and where he lived.

But what would Earl B. do if he found him? Killing the guy would land him in the pen—or worse. He'd have to take him out without anybody knowing. Do it by stealth. And do it when the Klansman least expected it.

Chapter 6

On Monday morning, Earl B. sat in English class as Mrs. Delaney droned on about grammar. Like he was supposed to care. To his right, Asa sat two seats away with his eyes locked on his English book. For a moment, he had a slight smile on his face. *Suspicious.*

Mrs. Delaney was writing on the board. Earl B. slipped a piece of bubble gum into his mouth and slumped down in his seat. He was tired. He always felt tired. Not able to concentrate anymore, he was falling further and further behind in his schoolwork.

Asa turned a page. Earl B. looked more closely and noticed something inside his English book—maybe a magazine? His friend moved it slightly, and Earl B. then saw a grim figure—Doctor Doom. Now he knew why Asa had been smiling. A Fantastic Four comic book.

The teacher had her back turned, writing on the board again. Earl B. blew a bubble. Some movement at the window caught his eye. He glanced outside and saw a little boy, perhaps four years old, swinging on a man's arm. Earl B. used to do that with his dad. He thought back to his last conversation with his father.

"Baseball practice starts in a few weeks," Earl B. had said. "Coach says I need new cleats." In his hand was an old pair Big Ben had given him.

Dad's nose was stuck in the newspaper. It was obvious his thoughts were a million miles away.

"He says these don't fit, and one of the spikes is loose. See?" Earl B. wiggled it.

His father looked up. "I can't believe it. They put my name and address in here."

"What?"

"This article tells who spoke at the meeting," his father said, looking displeased. "My address."

Earl B. waited. He knew his dad had been helping out with mass meetings, trying to get Negroes registered to vote. "Dad, about these cleats—"

"Leave 'em on the coffee table. I'll take a look. Maybe I can tighten that spike."

"But they're small. Coach says I need new ones."

He folded the newspaper and sighed. "Okay, son. We'll go this weekend."

And that was it. Those were the last words he'd heard his father say.

The next day, Mama held supper because Dad was late. Nothing unusual. Earl B. sat at his desk, working on a history paper, as the aroma of good food drifted into his room. His stomach growled.

He glanced at the clock above his desk. Six forty-five. Down the hall, Mama was on the phone. Her tone made him uneasy. Something was wrong. Earl B. got up from his chair and entered the hall. That's when he smelled it. The pork chops were burning. Mama hung up the phone, then muttered, "Damn!" He'd never heard her cuss before. Hurrying to the kitchen, he saw her pull a skillet off the stove and set it aside.

"What's wrong?" he asked. "Where's Dad?"

She glanced at him, then grabbed a metal spatula and began scraping the bottom of the skillet. "I don't know." Her voice was strange and high-pitched. "They said he never showed up at work today." She gave up scraping and dropped the spatula.

A chill passed through Earl B. Mama pulled two more pots off the stove and took a pan of half-baked biscuits out of the oven. She picked up the phone again and dialed, her hand shaking. Earl B. knew it would be a long time before they ate dinner. But he no longer felt hungry.

In retrospect, it all made sense, like a puzzle finally coming together. But Earl B. pushed that thought away—the hows and whys of his dad's disappearance were too unnerving.

"Earl B., can you tell me?"

His neck jerked around, and he looked at the front of the classroom. The teacher's question brought him back to reality. Mrs. Delaney was looking straight at him. "Ma'am?" Earl B. said, hoping she would repeat the question.

"You weren't listening, were you?"

Earl B. blew a bubble and let it pop. She hated gum.

"Come up here, young man, and spit that mess into the trash can." Mrs. Delaney started writing on the blackboard. "Show me where the subordinate clause is in this sentence." There was an eruption of suppressed giggles in the classroom.

He shuffled to the front and spit out the gum. Mrs. Delaney handed him the chalk. Earl B. had studied subordinate clauses last year, but that was a long time ago. Taking a chance, he circled a group of words.

"That's right," said Mrs. Delaney, looking disappointed. "Now can you tell me whether it functions as a noun, adverb, or adjective?"

This was more difficult. Earl B. stared at the board, hoping for inspiration. There was a knock at the door. Carolyn Owens, who worked as a student assistant in the office, came in the room and gave the teacher a note. While Mrs. Delaney was reading it, Carolyn flashed a smile at Earl B. and winked. Then she flipped her long, shiny hair back with one hand and walked toward the door. It wasn't the first time she had flirted with him. Carolyn was on the cheerleading squad, so he had seen her during football season. He decided to ask her out sometime.

"Mr. Peterson," Mrs. Delaney said, her mouth drawn into a tight bow. At first, Earl B. thought she had seen the interchange between Carolyn and him. But the teacher was merely holding out the notice she had just been given. "It appears you've been given a reprieve. Mr. Richards wants to see you in the gym."

Earl B. took the note, gathered his books, and left the classroom. So Coach Richards wanted to see him. Maybe it was about colleges and football scholarships again.

Two girls approached from the other direction, giggling behind their hands. Avoiding eye contact, Earl B. forged ahead, taking one long step to their three. Even after they passed, he still felt their upward gaze. *Stupid freshmen.*

Heading into the empty gym, he had an uncomfortable thought— maybe Coach had already heard about the F he'd made on his Algebra II test. Earl B. slowed as he heard someone talking inside the office.

". . . major attitude problem, always going around with a chip on his shoulder," a man said.

Earl B. recognized the voice. *Mr. Miller.* His math teacher was talking to Coach Richards. Earl B. hid along the wall outside the door.

"He's been going downhill since December, really," Mr. Miller continued. "It hit him hard. He's a different person since it happened."

"I suspected something all along." It was Coach Richards's voice this time. A chair scraped on the floor. Coach was getting up. "Anyway, I've sent for him, so he should be here any minute. Thanks for coming. It's more understandable now."

Another chair scraped the floor, and Earl B. backed away, ducking behind the equipment room's door.

"See you later," Coach bellowed, as Mr. Miller's rapid footsteps echoed in the gym.

Hearing the chair again, Earl B. waited a couple of minutes before easing out of the equipment room. To make the coach think he had just entered the gym, he crept around to the doors, pushed one open, and let it close. Then Earl B. walked toward the office, making sure his footsteps could be heard.

Coach looked up and rose from his desk chair. "Peterson, what's up with algebra?" That was Coach Richards for you. Straight up and to the point.

His mouth tightened. "I'm not doing so good, sir." *Understatement.*

"Your math teacher says you flunked your test."

Lowering his gaze, Earl B. tried to think of a response. A paper clip lay on the floor near his right foot. He kicked it and watched it slide several inches like a hockey puck.

"These grades are important, Peterson. You don't want to blow this opportunity. Up to now, you've been the top contender for that football scholarship."

Here it comes again. Another lecture. Sticking his hand into his pants pocket, he fingered the spiderweb gem.

"Most kids would love to have your talent." Coach walked around his desk to come closer. "You always had trouble with math?"

Earl B. shrugged.

"What happened with algebra in the fall?"

"I made a C."

"Well . . . that's not great, but it . . ."

"Made a B in math last year," Earl B. said, lifting his gaze.

"Look, Peterson, believe me." Coach put his hand on his shoulder. "I know what you're going through. But if—"

"You don't know what I'm going through." The words came out before Earl B. could stop them.

Coach's expression hardened, and he dropped his hand. "Maybe I don't, Peterson. But I'm certain of one thing you don't seem to understand. If those grades don't come up—"

"I don't need algebra to play football," Earl B. spat. "Grades don't matter."

"Grades *do* matter, young man. And you better figure it out, or you won't get a scholarship at all. Alabama State won't even want you. And A&M will give that scholarship to Carl Washington."

Earl B. turned and stomped out.

"Come back here!" Coach barked. "We're not done talking."

Increasing his pace, Earl B. charged out the gym door into the hall. He kept going toward the front of the school, then went outside and jogged down the sidewalk. At Sixth Avenue, he turned, heading west. Dodging two women going the other way, Earl B. picked up speed and sprinted for a while. Gasping for breath, he slowed to a jog again, his sides heaving.

"Damn," he growled. Earl B. was mad at himself for losing his temper with the coach. It would only make things harder for him. But he couldn't stand adults who always thought they knew everything. They wouldn't admit that a black kid—even a straight-A student—still ended up working on an assembly line. Teachers made it sound like you could be an astronaut or the next president of the United States. False hope was cruel. The only thing college could buy Earl B. was a few years' delay in a lifetime of hard labor or factory work.

Turning right on Second Street, he headed north. A constant headwind made the winter air seem even colder. Earl B. ran by a vacant lot, a few small houses, and a church. Bare trees stood silhouetted against steel-gray clouds. Later, he'd probably get in trouble for his behavior, but that didn't matter now. He needed to get away from everybody and try to get control of himself again. But that was the problem—Earl B. couldn't control himself. It didn't make any difference how hard he tried. He couldn't study, sleep, pay attention in class, or concentrate on anything except the bomber.

Now, Earl B. was on his own street, approaching his house. This morning, Grammaw had reminded him that he hadn't painted it over the weekend. Another failing on his part.

Inside, he collapsed on his bed and pounded the mattress with his fists. Something tightened like a vise deep inside him. It made him want to cry. But he didn't, and that made the feeling worse. Things were disappearing from his life. Not meaningless stuff like a wallet, a radio, or a car. Earl B. had lost his father. Then his mother. And now he was losing football.

His thoughts traveled back to the night of the bombing, then to the marching Klansman. Feeling spent and exhausted, Earl B. fell asleep with these images ricocheting throughout his head. He dreamed he had cracked the code in the Klansman's bombing list. Now knowing when and where the next attack would take place, Earl B. found the target, a church, and sat in its backyard. Hidden behind a barrier of tall weeds, he watched for the thugs. A car cruised by, then came to a stop. A man got out, holding something in his hand, then dropped to the ground near the porch and fumbled with the object. Earl B. crept toward him, coming from behind, then ambushed the guy, knocking the device out of his hand. The man recovered his wits and strained against him, saying, "You're gonna die!" His husky voice matched that of the guy who had made the threatening phone call.

Wrapping his hands around the man's neck, Earl B. squeezed, compressing his airway. Strange sounds came out of the guy's mouth.

The key to the bomber's identity was right there in front of him—their faces were inches apart. But the more Earl B. concentrated on the man's appearance, the more blurred everything became. "Show me!" he screamed. The bomber's body faded, until Earl B.'s hands were squeezing nothing but air. He awoke from the nightmare with his whole body trembling.

"I had him!" Earl B. wailed. "Right in front of my eyes." He climbed off his bed, opened the top drawer of his desk, and pulled the Klan paper from under a tray. Earl B. sat on the bed and studied it. The list was his only clue, but it might be all he needed. If only it weren't encrypted. He already knew three of the seven places. Earl B. just needed to find the other four. Heading down the hall, he got the phone book and looked in the *Yellow Pages* under churches. Most of the names weren't familiar. His own church wasn't even there. Many couldn't afford to be listed.

Closing the book, Earl B. decided he'd have to find the streets himself. He would be systematic about it—go through the list and look on each road for possible bombing sites. Searching all the way up and down each street could take a long time. But Earl B. was determined to do it. And he'd start this weekend.

Chapter 7

Slamming his locker shut, Earl B. headed down the hall, dodging the excited, end-of-day students. They acted like they didn't know they lived in the cesspool of the universe. Asa passed him without speaking, as if avoiding him.

Earl B. called out his name and caught up to him. "What about Saturday, man? You going with me?"

An uneasy look came across Asa's face, and he kept walking. "I don't think so."

"What? Come on." Yesterday, Earl B. had told him he was sure the Klan paper was a list of bombing sites. "This is important. We need to check out those addresses."

"But I work at the ARC office on Saturdays."

"You can get out of that for one day, can't you?"

"I don't want to get involved in that mess."

"Come on. You aren't afraid, are you?"

Asa shook his head. "You're asking to be lynched, getting mixed up with the Klan."

"All I'm doing is looking around on Thirty-fifth Avenue. How's that going to get me lynched? Come on, man. Go with me."

"Did you not listen to a word I said?" Asa stopped and faced him. "You have no idea what you're getting into. Don't you realize if they figure out what you're doing, you'll be finished?"

"Fine." Clenching his jaw, Earl B. tried a different tactic. "I'm going whether you are or not."

Asa let out a long sigh. "All right, I'll go, but just this once. I'm not chasing after every place on that paper."

Earl B. felt his body relax. "All right, thanks. Be at my place by eight thirty."

"In the morning? On a Saturday? You're crazy!"

"I want to catch the bus right after Grammaw leaves."

Asa lumbered away, muttering something unintelligible.

Earl B. headed toward the chemistry classroom. For some unknown reason, Big Ben had requested an after-school meeting. Earl B. wondered if Coach Richards had told his uncle about his behavior two days ago, when he had stormed off from the gym. Yesterday morning, Coach had called Earl B. back into his office and dressed him down, but fortunately, nothing more. Then, in the afternoon, things had gotten worse when Big Ben said he was arranging a math tutor for Earl B. Did his uncle not realize how humiliating that was? With his luck, the tutor would be somebody like Luther Pennington. Besides being the biggest slide-rule-wearing nerd this side of the Mississippi, that guy had a mouth the size of Moby Dick. It would be all over the school before the first tutoring session—Earl B., football star and dumb jock, needs a math tutor!

Approaching the classroom, he heard the sound of soft voices. Earl B. peeked inside the open door.

"Ah, there you are!" His uncle stood, then dragged an extra chair near his desk and gestured toward it. "Have a seat."

Shuffling inside, Earl B. noticed he wasn't the only student in the room. He glanced over to see who it was and his heart stalled. A girl. Earl B. had been so worried the tutor might be Luther Pennington he hadn't considered it might be a girl. And it was the same student he had seen at the mass meeting, the one talking to Rachel. Earl B. sat in the chair next to her.

Big Ben folded his hands on top of a huge stack of disorganized papers on his desk. "Not sure if you two already know each other . . ." His voice trailed off as he waited.

She turned and gave Earl B. a tentative smile. Definitely not Luther Pennington.

He realized his uncle was staring at him, expecting an answer. "Kind of," he said, shrugging. Seeing her up close was different from seeing her at school or at the mass meeting. She wasn't exactly ugly.

In fact, if he hadn't already known she was the brainy type, he'd say she was easy on the eyes.

"Shirley Dupree, Earl B. Peterson," the teacher said, nodding to each of them in turn. "Shirley's a senior also and a top-notch science and math student."

He glanced at her again, but she had dropped her gaze to her lap, where a stack of books lay. Was it a pretense, or was she really modest? From her white, freshly ironed blouse to her coiffed hair, she represented the high-class, power-performance students, the ones way beyond his reach. Most of them rated football slightly one notch above egg throwing.

Big Ben continued, "She's offered to spend a little time helping you with Algebra II."

Nice to be worthy of her attention.

The teacher spoke again, this time directed at Shirley. "Earl B.'s actually my nephew. He's taken a few knocks lately. He's a good student—probably just needs a little encouragement to get back on track."

Earl B. glanced at Shirley, who was now lining up the folders and books in her lap so the corners were even. The edge of her sleeve was frayed, contrasting with the Ruby Dee image her face portrayed. Maybe she wasn't as upper crust as he thought.

"Sound good?" Big Ben asked, looking back and forth between them.

Earl B. didn't know what to say—and also didn't care. "Sure," he finally said, then as an afterthought, glanced at Shirley. "I mean, if it's okay with you."

"That's fine," she said. Earl B. realized she hadn't spoken until now. Her voice was soft and smooth, with dark undertones. In fact, if the skin on her face could talk, that's what it would sound like.

"Okay," said Big Ben, rising. "I'll leave it to you two to decide on a time and place. I might suggest Kelly Ingram Park or the Smithfield Library." He walked them to the door.

The two stood in the hall for a few moments, neither one speaking. Earl B. glanced at her a couple of times, wishing she would take the lead and suggest a time and place. Then they both turned their attention toward the approach of a chattering group of cheerleaders rounding the corner.

"Well, look who's here," Carolyn Owens simpered, switching her gaze back and forth between Shirley and Earl B. "Did y'all miss the bus?"

Neither answered. The other girls stopped in the hall and became spectators.

Carolyn fingered the sleeve on Shirley's blouse. "Where'd you get this thing? Thrift shop?" One of the other girls giggled.

"At least I don't pander to the white people, shopping at their department stores," Shirley snapped.

"Did I mention my father won't be seeing yours much anymore?" Carolyn continued, unfazed by her remark. "They're giving him day shift. Your dad's still working nights, ain't he?" Carolyn laughed, flipped her hair back over her shoulder, and walked away, with a string of cheerleaders trailing behind like ducklings. Earl B. watched her leave. So this was how girls fought. He preferred an old-fashioned fistfight to this kind of nonstop, underhanded sniping.

Shirley avoided eye contact with him. "I need to go to my locker," she said, taking off down the hall. He followed, not knowing what else to do. The thought crossed his mind that perhaps she didn't want to tutor him any more than he wanted to be tutored. Maybe his uncle had pressured her to do it.

Reaching her locker, Shirley fumbled with the padlock. "Who's your algebra teacher?"

"Mr. Miller."

"I had him for geometry." She opened her locker and rummaged through some books and papers. "I thought he was fair."

Great, Earl B. thought. *She won't cut me any slack.*

She stood and faced him. "So . . . a tutoring session?"

"Look, you don't have to do this if you don't want—"

"Mr. Ross wants me to," she said, cutting him off. "Besides, he said it would look good on my college applications." She closed her locker.

How unselfish of her.

"How about Sunday afternoon at two?" she asked.

"I guess," he said, still rattled over her response. "Where?"

"The park?"

He nodded. "All right, see you then." Earl B. walked away. He had lost sleep over this meeting, and the whole ordeal had lasted less than twenty minutes. Yes, he had gotten his wish—the tutor wasn't Luther Pennington. It was a girl. And not one of those chattery, blabbing types who would spread it all over the place. Instead, she was a self-centered snob. One thing was for certain—he wasn't looking forward to Sunday's study session. Seriously, what was Big Ben thinking, pairing him with her?

Earl B. walked out of the school with a strange feeling inside, as if something were about to happen. He didn't know if that something was going to be good or bad. But whatever it was, he knew it would involve Shirley Dupree. And it had nothing to do with algebra.

Chapter 8

Asa showed up early Saturday morning, before Grammaw left for work.

"There's grits left," she said, holding the pan. "You want some, Asa?"

"No, thank you, Mrs. Mathes." He stood near the kitchen table with his coat still on.

"You two are up awfully early." Grammaw threw a suspicious glance at Earl B, who was sitting at the table. "Got something planned today? The house needs painting. It's supposed to be warm enough this afternoon."

"I could help paint the—" Asa stopped short when he saw the expression on Earl B.'s face.

"You gonna answer me?" Grammaw said, her eyes still fixed on her grandson.

Earl B. scraped the last bit of grits from his bowl before he answered. "I'll do it sometime."

She put her hands on her hips and walked toward him. "I want it done this weekend. Today. It's clean and ready, the weather's good, and you've put it off too long."

Asa turned away, walking toward the living room.

"I'll do it when I want to," Earl B. drawled.

"Don't you be sassing me, boy," Grammaw snapped. "I heard you been mouthing off at school, too."

"Where'd you hear that?"

"None of your business. And I better not hear it again." She put on her coat and grabbed her purse. "I mean it, now. Get that painting done." With that, Grammaw went out the door.

Earl B. took his bowl to the sink.

Asa followed him into the kitchen. "Why don't we just do the porch today?"

"No!" Earl B.'s tone made his friend jump.

"Come on, man," Asa pressed. "We can look on that street another time."

"Obviously, it wasn't *your* mother who got killed."

Asa turned away and sat at the table. Earl B. unfolded a city map and reviewed the streets. Then he threw on his brown jacket and checked the pockets. A pencil, a notebook, and the Klan paper were all inside. Stuffing the map in with the rest, he went out the door with Asa following.

On the bus, the two had to sit in separate seats. Most of the riders sat silent, stone-faced, sleepy and not ready to socialize. The bus still reeked of sweat from the evening before. He stared at a stain on the back of the seat in front of him. Maybe Coke . . . or coffee?

Earl B. was just behind the movable board designating the "colored" section. An elderly white woman sat in front of him, her back bent into a question mark. The dandruff in her beehive hair suggested it needed a wash. Earl B. could see the side of her wrinkled face as she stared out the window. She winced each time the bus braked or bounced.

Across from her sat a well-built white man who was completely bald except for a few wiry, feral hairs. His egg-shaped head reminded Earl B. of Elmer Fudd. Dressed in a suit and tie, he perused the morning's *Post-Herald*.

Two black women behind Earl B. were chatting. From their conversation, he could tell they rode together regularly.

The question mark woman rose, grasping the nearby pole. The brakes screeched as the bus slowed and pulled to the side of the road. It jerked to a stop, propelling the woman diagonally into the aisle. The bald man shot up and reached out, grabbing her shoulders, breaking her fall. His massive hands held her tightly while she regained her balance.

"You okay, ma'am?" The man's voice was thick as sludge at the bottom of a riverbank. Earl B. noticed he was missing the index finger on his right hand. Only a short stub remained.

"It's my blood pressure," the woman said, attempting to extend her stiff neck so she could look her rescuer in the face. "Sometimes it's high, and sometimes it's low." With her hand she patted the bald man's arm. "I'm fine, now. You're a nice man. Thank you." She held on to each seat as she walked to the front and disembarked.

The bus went a few more blocks, stopping at Thirty-fifth Avenue. Earl B. and Asa got off. For a moment, they stood on the sidewalk, surveying their surroundings. The bald man exited at the front of the bus, then went into a phone booth on the corner to make a call. The sun was out, burning off the morning chill.

Asa pointed east on Thirty-fifth Avenue. "That looks like a bunch of factories."

"Yeah," agreed Earl B., unzipping his jacket. "Let's start the other way."

They headed west. The numbers decreased, so they had chosen correctly. Earl B. pulled out the Klan note to make sure. Fifty-nine was the number listed before Thirty-fifth Avenue. The addresses on the houses, however, were in the thousands. At this rate, they'd never get to fifty-nine.

Judging from the people in yards, Earl B. could tell they were in a black neighborhood. Farther down the street, the first church steeple rose. Drawing closer, he jotted down its name, First Baptist Church, along with the address number. No people were around, and the parking lot was empty. He knocked on the door. No response.

Not two blocks away was another church, the Gospel Believing Baptist Church. Earl B. wrote down the name and address number. There was one car in the parking lot. He knocked, but nobody answered.

Farther on, there were a few stores sprinkled amongst the houses. Continuing their westbound trek, they passed a shoe repair shop and a grocery. They were almost to a barbecue place on the corner when Earl B. noticed a police car coming toward them, slowing as it approached. Every fiber in his body reacted automatically. Along with an adrenaline surge, his hands came out of his pockets, as if they were pulled by something. Always have your hands visible, his dad used to say, whether you're in a store or dealing with a cop. Years of warnings had made it an ingrained habit. Even without looking, he felt the cop's eyes on him.

"Oh, man," said Asa, his voice tight and anxious.

"Don't act nervous," Earl B. said through gritted teeth. "They'll think you did something wrong."

"I can't help it."

"Follow me," Earl B. said, making a split-second decision. He abruptly turned into the parking lot of the barbecue place.

"Where are you going?" Asa asked, but he followed.

Earl B. chided himself for turning too quickly. His father had always told him sudden actions made you look guilty. Behind them, he could hear the police car braking and turning. His mouth felt like cotton. "Come on," he told Asa, walking as fast as he could without appearing to run. Cutting the corner at the intersection, they ducked behind a fence dividing the restaurant from the backyards of houses. Glancing over his shoulder, he made sure they were no longer in the cop's line of sight. He dove behind a large brush pile in a yard, with his friend following. Soon after, the cruiser crept by.

Kneeling on the ground, Asa tried to change position.

"Don't move," Earl B. spat out.

Asa froze. They both stayed in awkward, crouched positions, with the brush pile between them and the cop. Realizing his arm might be visible, Earl B. remained still as a lamppost, aware of every breath and heartbeat. The motor was now idling, the cop apparently willing to wait them out. Earl B. knew they had done nothing wrong. Well, nothing illegal. But in Birmingham, it didn't matter—being black was against the law.

Earl B.'s right leg went numb, especially around the ankle. His body pitched forward, then backward as he overcompensated. Just when he could hold out no longer, the car moved, this time faster, until it was gone. The two boys sat on the ground in more comfortable positions and waited to make sure the cop wasn't coming back. Earl B. pulled out the map. They still had some westward distance to cover.

After a few minutes, they walked back out to Thirty-fifth Avenue and headed farther on, past more houses. Earl B.'s eyes were drawn to every passing car to make sure it wasn't the police. Ahead, they saw another church, High Praises Community Church. Drawing closer, Asa said, "Hey, I know about this one."

"What do you mean?"

"My dad knows the preacher. They've been at mass meetings together."

Earl B. wasn't surprised since Asa's father was a minister. "Does that mean you know him?"

"I've met him, but I don't know if he'd remember me. You're not going to talk to him, are you?"

"Why?" Earl B. was now watching a black man heading toward a car on the other side of the church parking lot.

"If my dad finds out about this whole thing, I'll be toast, that's why."

"Then don't follow me." As Earl B. hurried after the gentleman, he regretted his angry tone. After all, he had strong-armed his friend into coming on the trip in the first place. It was a wonder Asa still hung around him.

"Sir!" Earl B. called.

The man turned and looked at him, now holding onto the car door.

"Sir, may I talk to you for a minute?" Earl B. said, drawing near.

"What do you want?" the man asked, his voice betraying some annoyance. He had a head full of white hair.

"Are you the minister at this church?"

"Why? What do you need?"

"I'm not asking for help."

"What is it?" he asked, looking at his watch. "I got to be somewhere."

"This church might get bombed."

The man's mouth opened slightly, but he didn't say anything.

Pulling out the Klan paper, Earl B. explained, trying to speak above the rumbling cars going by on the main road.

Sometime during the explanation, the man pushed the car door closed. Afterward, he held out his hand. "I'm Reverend Cartwright, the minister here."

"Pleased to meet you, sir." Earl B. introduced himself and they shook hands. Asa was still hanging back, near the sidewalk.

"Now, son, I appreciate what you're trying to do," the preacher said. "But fifty-nine ain't our address." He pointed to the Thirty-fifth Avenue listing.

Earl B. explained about the other bombings. "I don't know how those numbers are related yet."

"And there are two other black churches on this street," the man persisted.

"I know," Earl B. said, his voice rising a little. Then he added, "Sir." The preacher's stubbornness was getting on his nerves. "But they aren't fifty-nine either."

Reverend Cartwright shook his head. "And you don't even have a date."

Earl B. tried a different tactic. "But sir, don't you want to keep the people in your congregation safe?"

"Of course, but you expect me to lock up the church from here on out? And that's on a maybe?"

"But three of these places have been hit."

"I understand." The man now sounded even more hardheaded. "Look, son, if you think I'm running from the Klan, think again. We get at least one bomb threat every week or two here. I ain't closing down the church because of that. That's what they want. If I do that, they've won."

"But sir—"

"Bethel Baptist was hit three times. *Three times.* And they don't close down."

"I'm not asking you to close down permanently. I'm just—"

"Thanks," he said, opening his door. "But I ain't gonna do it." He got in the car and took off.

Left alone in the parking lot, Earl B. jotted down the church name and address. He was collecting possible targets, but if nobody was going to listen, what was the point? Returning to the sidewalk, he joined Asa. "Stupid, ignorant jackass," Earl B. muttered.

"I heard what he said about bomb threats," Asa said.

"So?"

"That's true. My daddy says they get 'em at his church all the time."

"I don't care."

Earl B. pulled out the map, studied it, and continued west. Asa followed him. Neither of them said much. Before long, the houses were farther apart, set back from the street. Then the road ended.

"Did you say the number was fifty-nine?" Asa asked.

"Yep."

"These numbers were all in the thousands."

"No kidding," Earl B. said sarcastically. He took a deep breath and let it out slowly. He had to quit snapping at his friend.

The boys turned around and went back the way they came, passing all three churches.

At the bus stop, Asa halted. Earl B. kept walking.

"Aren't we going back?" Asa called after him.

"I'm going this way."

"But the numbers are going up." Asa ran, trying to catch up. "There's no way—"

"Shut up!" Earl B. barked. This whole thing wasn't working out the way he had planned. They'd walked a long way and hadn't figured anything out.

"Tell me again," Asa said. "Why are we doing this?"

Turning to face his friend, Earl B. gave him a cold stare. "*Because. They. Bombed. My. House.*"

"I'm starting to worry about you, man," Asa said, his voice rising. "This stuff is making you crazy."

Earl B. was too angry to answer.

"Don't you see?" Asa asked. "It's eating you alive. It's all you ever think about anymore. It's going to kill you if you keep—"

A loud motor rumbled behind them, interrupting Asa. Earl B. shot a halfway glance backward. He stiffened.

"Police?" asked Asa, his eyes glued straight ahead.

"No," said Earl B., walking at a brisk pace. "But just as bad. A car full of crackers."

The vehicle cruised up beside them, and someone rolled down a window. "Hey, niggers. What are y'all doing, looking so neat and clean?" Laughter followed. Earl B. kept his gaze forward and continued walking on the outside, with the strangers rolling beside them. "Boys, y'all too clean to be niggers." More laughter. "We'll have to fix that."

Something struck the arm of Earl B.'s jacket. Asa cried out, then ran. Earl B. quickened his pace, but didn't run. The pelting continued. One struck the side of his face, and something wet and gooey ran downward. Eggs. Earl B. veered off to the side, away from them. They gunned the motor and took off.

Anger coursed through Earl B.'s veins. He wanted to run after those guys, grab each one, and pound their ugly faces with his fist. Leaning over, he put his hands on his knees and tried to calm down.

Asa turned around and trudged toward him. "Yuck," he said, wiping the slime off his jacket with a handful of leaves. "Just so you know, I ain't going on any more of these trips of yours."

"Good," Earl B. said, looking at his clothes. "At least you only got hit once." His left side was covered in egg. He pulled out his dirty handkerchief and wiped the goo away.

"Let's go back to your house," said Asa, turning west.

Earl B. glanced around, then followed him. They were in an industrial area, without any visible numbers. He pulled out the map and perused it as they strolled. "We're not far from Collegeville, where Bethel Baptist is."

Asa nodded. "Reverend Shuttlesworth's church."

"Someone said he's not there anymore."

"Yeah," Asa said, "went to Ohio. My mama's always talking about moving up there."

The leftover mess on Earl B.'s face had dried into a tight, smelly mask by the time they reached the bus stop.

Back at the house, the two boys rinsed their dirty clothes in the bathroom, and Earl B. found an old jacket Asa could wear. Afterward, they sat at the kitchen table drinking iced tea.

Asa rose. "It's only one o'clock, and it's nice outside. Why don't we paint?"

"I'm not in the mood."

"Your grandmother'll be upset."

"I don't care."

"Is the stuff in the shed?"

"I don't know." Earl B. knew perfectly well where it was, but he didn't want his friend pressuring him to work.

Asa walked out the door.

Earl B. ran a finger on the outside of his iced tea glass, drawing figures in the droplets of condensation. He was sick of everyone bossing him around. Grammaw. Big Ben. Even Asa. And pretty soon—tomorrow in fact—that tutor girl would be doing it too. Shirley. He could tell she was the type who lived to tell people what to do.

The ladder clanged outside. Earl B. got up from the table and went out on the porch.

Asa handed a paintbrush to him.

Earl B. hurled it away, and it sailed into the next-door neighbor's yard.

"What's up with you?" asked Asa.

Instead of answering, Earl B. sat on the front porch and watched his friend climb the ladder and paint. It was pleasant outside, warm for February. After a few minutes, Earl B. got up, retrieved the brush from the neighbor's yard, and started painting on the other side.

The two boys worked all afternoon and into the evening, mostly in silence. Earl B. thought of the time right after the bombing, when Asa had helped clean up the mess. After that, Big Ben had cut boards while Earl B. climbed a ladder and nailed up the wood siding. One conversation with his uncle had particularly stuck in his memory.

"Son, I'm just saying you gotta roll with the punches," Big Ben had said. "You can't let it eat at you. If you do, they win."

"Easy for you to say," Earl B. shot back, gripping the hammer with a tight fist. "Your mama wasn't put six feet under by a Klansman."

Big Ben put down his saw. Slowly and deliberately, he removed his work gloves. "Come down from there, boy." His voice was stern.

Earl B. almost refused, then thought better of it. He climbed down the ladder and stared at Big Ben, waiting for him to speak.

His uncle pointed to a lawn chair. "Sit down and listen." After he obeyed, Big Ben said, "I don't usually talk about this, but I'm gonna tell you something."

This was going to be a waste of time. Earl B. could tell.

"I grew up on a farm in southern Georgia," Big Ben said.

With chickens and hogs and cows, Earl B. thought. Everybody in school made fun of his uncle's upbringing.

"All the other Negroes in our parts were sharecroppers," Big Ben continued. "My folks were lucky. They owned land. The Klan didn't like that. They burned crosses and tried to burn our crops, then our house."

His uncle paced back and forth in front of Earl B. as he talked. "My daddy was gone to town one day to pick up supplies. I was eight and my sister was six. Dad always went to the next county 'cause the people in our stores overcharged when they saw him coming. So he was gone all day. Them Klansmen knew it and came to our house."

Big Ben took a ragged breath and let it out. "Mama was in a . . . delicate . . . condition. Expecting a child. She saw them coming and was afraid they might set the place on fire again. She sent us to hide down in the creek bed in the back of the house and told me to take care of my sister. Next thing I knew, Mama was screaming. I crept up behind a bush and saw them dragging her out of the house. Had their way with her, then hanged her and sliced her open. The baby dropped to the ground. They trampled it till it was dead. Poured gasoline over Mama's body and set fire to her. They left everything in the front yard for Daddy to find." He swallowed. "So yeah, son. I guess you could say my mama was put six feet under by a Klansman."

Chapter 9

Earl B. grabbed his algebra book and headed out the bedroom door. It was Sunday afternoon, the day of his first tutoring session. He had ten minutes to make it to the bus stop.

Grammaw sat in her living room chair, holding a magazine. She looked at Earl B. over the top of her reading glasses. "So you say you're going studying, huh?"

He was tired of talking about this. "Yes, Grammaw. I'm studying with someone at school."

She raised her eyebrows. "This wouldn't be a girl, by any chance?"

"I don't have a girlfriend. We're doing algebra." Why couldn't she accept the truth? Women's intuition. What a joke.

"Got your key?"

"Yes," he said, stuffing his hand into his pants pocket to check.

"Well, you make sure you get back here at a reasonable time."

Earl B. headed out the front door, then turned around and went back inside. Grammaw stared at him.

"Need a blanket," he mumbled.

Grammaw's voice rose. "A blanket?" Her eyes were wide.

Earl B. snorted. "To sit on. At the park."

She got out of her chair. "You ain't taking one of my good ones." He followed her down the hall. Looking back over her shoulder at him, she muttered, "Since when do boys care 'bout their clothes? I knew this had something to do with a girl."

As Grammaw rummaged in the cedar chest, Earl B. checked his watch. Now he only had five minutes. If he missed this bus, he'd have to wait another forty minutes, which would make him late.

That might not be a bad thing. Spending an entire afternoon with that tutor girl wasn't his idea of fun. Her words kept coming back to him: *Besides, he said it would look good on my college applications.* What a jerk. In spite of that, her first smile made Earl B. desperately hope he had somehow misheard her remark.

Grammaw held up an orange plaid blanket and shook her head. "I don't know. This one might be . . ." Digging deeper in the chest, she pulled out a brown, wool blanket with a couple of holes in it and handed it to him. "Here."

"Thanks." He grabbed it and headed toward the bedroom door.

"Earl B.?" she hollered.

He froze and turned to face her. *Now what did she want?*

"Thank you." She smiled. "Thanks for finishing the house. It looks really nice."

"No problem." Earl B. hurried down the hall and out the front door. The blanket trailed behind him like a cape as he ran down the steps and headed to the bus stop.

He got to Kelly Ingram Park ten minutes early. Spreading out the blanket, Earl B. opened his algebra book and tried to look busy. But he was so far behind, it would be impossible to catch up. This was going to be bad. Really bad.

His eyes crossed as he stared at the book, his pencil poised over the paper. Earl B. glanced at his watch. Five minutes after. A man in a three-piece suit came out of the side door of a church and passed by on the sidewalk. Nobody else was around. Maybe he'd get lucky and she wouldn't show up. Earl B.'s gaze drifted back to algebra.

"Sorry I'm late." It was Shirley, dressed in a winter coat and gloves. She had walked up behind him.

"Too busy filling out college applications?" Earl B. muttered, before he could stop himself.

A puzzled look crossed her face as she sat down. "Pardon?"

"Nothing."

"Thanks for bringing a blanket." She leaned over his paper. "Which assignment are you working on?"

Earl B. hesitated. She didn't sound selfish. Or rude. And her eyes looked so dark and warm. Now he regretted his little charade. He haphazardly flipped through the pages of the book, shrugging his shoulders. "Not sure."

Shirley looked confused. "Did Mr. Miller give you homework?"

He pulled out his assignment sheet and handed it to her.

She glanced at it, pulled off her gloves, then grabbed the algebra book and flipped through it. "Are these all of this month's assignments?"

Earl B. nodded.

"How much of this have you done?" Shirley's facial expression changed, making her seem older. Much older. For a moment, he saw what she would look like at fifty, with gray, wiry hairs framing her face.

The silence stretched out. This wasn't going well. She was clueless. "I ain't exactly done . . . ," he began.

"Haven't done what?" Shirley asked.

Was she correcting his English? Like a parent? Or worse, a teacher? "I *ain't* done *no* homework this semester." He put emphasis on the words *ain't* and *no*—just to see what her reaction was. Earl B. got what he was looking for.

"No homework at all?" Her face looked just like Mrs. Delaney's last year when a rat had run across her feet during English class.

Earl B. laughed. He couldn't help it.

Shirley didn't. "You're joking. The month's almost over. You haven't done any homework?"

"Nope."

"How do you expect to pass the class without doing assignments?"

Earl B. didn't answer.

Shirley flipped backward through the pages. "Okay," she said, in a business-like tone. "Maybe if we start at the beginning of the section you're in now . . ." She trailed off, finding the first lesson. "Let's look at these examples first, so you can use them as a guide." Shirley walked him through it, then said, "Now, see if you can do the first problem."

He did it, then put his pencil down. It was simple enough. But Earl B. didn't know why they were wasting time on problems he wasn't going to turn in.

Next, she helped him through several homework problems. They weren't so difficult. He just needed someone to help him focus, to keep his attention from wandering. Earl B. had to admit she was good for that.

Afterward, Shirley closed the book. "Once you get started, you don't seem to have much problem with the work."

He shrugged.

"I sometimes help a friend of mine with algebra. She has a lot more trouble understanding the material than you do, but she manages to get decent grades."

"Sorry I don't live up to your expectations," he said crisply.

She ignored his remark. "Mr. Ross told me you were a football player?"

"Yeah." Earl B. pulled his knees up to his chest, rested his arms on top, and ducked his head inside, wondering where this conversation was going.

"Are you hoping to play in college?"

"Yeah," he said. No need to give the gory details.

"So . . . last semester," she began, "your grades were okay?"

"I passed."

"You played football and didn't have any problems?"

"Did okay till the end." Uninvited memories of the bombing flashed through his mind.

"The end?"

His jaw tightened. "End of the semester." Earl B. thought about saying more, but it really wasn't any of her business.

"You hope to get a football scholarship?"

"I pretty much got one."

Her eyes widened. "What? Where?"

"A&M."

"But surely they won't let you keep it unless you keep your grades up."

Does she think she's telling me something I don't know?

"So that's the problem, isn't it?"

"This stuff is useless," Earl B. said. "I don't need it to play football."

"You aren't gonna play football all your life. You'll need a college degree and a job afterward."

"Doesn't matter if I have a college degree or not," he mumbled.

Shirley's voice rose. "Excuse me?"

"School doesn't matter. I'll end up on an assembly line whether I have a degree or not."

"That's not true of everybody. Who's to say you won't be the first Negro broadcaster in football?"

Earl B. rolled his eyes. This girl was crazy.

"Or the first Negro mayor of a city? Or the first—"

He snorted, interrupting her list of firsts.

"You can laugh all you want, but it's true." A determined look came across her face. "I'm not going to let anybody else tell me what I can or cannot do."

"So what's that?" he asked sarcastically. "You gonna be the first Negro to win a Nobel Prize in math or something?"

"I'm going to be a biochemist."

"A what?"

"A biochemist. Somebody who does research, developing new medicines and things like that."

Earl B. couldn't keep a look of surprise from coming over his face. "And you think Birmingham's gonna let you do that?"

Her mouth tightened into a thin line. "Not the way it is now, but I'm trying to change that."

He shook his head and laughed again. "Girl, you got a lot to change."

"It's better than just sitting around complaining." Shirley's tone was serious. "You ought to come to the mass meeting tomorrow night. If you heard some of those people speak, you'd change your mind. When I heard Reverend Shuttlesworth at St. James Baptist—"

"I've been to one, thank you very much," scoffed Earl B. "Churches. A lot of talk and no action."

"Maybe that's true for some. But others are banding together and putting pressure on white businesses."

"They're all alike," he shot back. "They preach all this nonviolence stuff. Turn the other cheek. That doesn't work."

Shirley frowned. "Okay, have it your way."

Earl B. slid his algebra papers inside a pocket folder.

She gestured toward it. "Let me show you something. Take out a blank sheet of paper."

He hesitated, wondering where this was going. Was it extra homework? He wouldn't put it past one of the honor roll types. Those kids probably did extra homework for fun on the weekends.

"Come on," she said with the hint of a smile. "It won't hurt, I promise." Her anger seemed to have evaporated and her expression made him melt.

Earl B. pulled out a sheet of paper. "Okay."

"Write down three phone numbers. Any three'll do."

He raised his eyebrows. Was this some sort of joke?

"You can't think of three phone numbers?" Shirley asked.

Realizing she was serious, he wrote down three—his own, Big Ben's, and Asa's.

"Done?" she asked, reaching for the paper. "Give me one minute."

Earl B. glanced at her several times as she studied the paper. Her shoulder-length hair was turned in a flip, and he liked the way her dark skin contrasted with her blue coat. He regretted not doing his work before this session. In spite of her selfish remark the other day, her interest in helping him seemed genuine. But he had made it difficult for her.

"Okay," Shirley said, handing him the paper. It had been less than one minute, he was sure of it. She closed her eyes, then proceeded to recite the three numbers. She nailed them. Opening her eyes, she gave him an expectant look. "Well?"

"Weird." Earl B. shook his head. So she memorized numbers for fun. Not exactly homework, but still. For a moment, she looked hurt. He laughed, trying to make her think he had been kidding. "What's that about?"

Her face relaxed a little. "Just a game I've played since I was little." Shirley took the paper back, tore it in half, then wrote a number on the blank part. "My phone number," she said, handing it to him. "If you get stuck on homework, call me." He took it and she slipped the other half in her purse.

Back home that evening, Earl B. pulled out the Klansman's paper and tried once again to make sense of it. Surely, there was a mathematical code he wasn't recognizing. He dug out his pajamas and started undressing for bed with the numbers still bouncing around in his head. Emptying his pockets, he found the slip of paper with Shirley's phone number and tossed it on his desk. It landed on top of the Klan note. As Earl B. stared at it, a new idea came to him. Shirley was a math whiz. Could she decipher the list of bombing sites? If she learned he was stalking the Klan, however, she would no doubt disapprove. But something else told him Shirley was clever enough to crack that code.

Chapter 10

Mr. Miller sat at his desk and peered at Earl B. over the top of his glasses. "You probably know why I called you in here."

Earl B. glanced down at the test in his hand. "My grade, sir?" A big, red C-minus adorned the top of the page. He had now met with Shirley two times. In the second session, she had helped him through three assignments. His test grade was certainly much better than the Fs he had gotten earlier in the semester.

"Yes, a C-minus." The teacher paused, maybe for effect, and took off his glasses. A frame was perched on one corner of his desk that held a picture of his family. His wife wore glasses and had her hair pulled to the back of her head. She was light-skinned with a few freckles on her face. Two small sons were also in the picture.

Nice to know some people have families.

"I realize I said you needed a C or better from now on in order to pass the class," Mr. Miller continued. "But this is cutting it close. Too close for comfort."

"Yes, sir."

"I understand you are being tutored."

"Yes, sir."

"Mr. Ross said it's Shirley Dupree."

"Yes, sir." Earl B. wondered if he should have brought a recording of his voice.

"How's it going?" He chewed on one end of the earpiece of his glasses. "Is that working out?"

Staring into Mr. Miller's stern, dark eyes, Earl B. realized *he* had been responsible for any problems. Shirley was better than some of his teachers. "She's a good tutor, sir."

Mr. Miller waited for him to say more, but when he didn't, the teacher continued. "I had her in class. An excellent student, very studious. She has ambition."

Ambition. Maybe that's what he had lost. Earl B. craved some of that energy. He needed a reason to live.

"Now, you've been through a lot, and I'm willing to work with you on this."

Earl B. remembered what Shirley had said about the teacher. He was "fair."

"But you need to snap out of these doldrums you're in," Mr. Miller said. "I can't just give you these grades. You have to earn them."

Yeah, he knew that already.

"But besides making sure you get the most out of the class," the teacher continued, "I've got Coach Richards breathing down my neck. He wants to make sure you get that football scholarship. Until now, nobody doubted you would . . ." His voice drifted off, as if he thought better of finishing. "Anyway, am I making myself clear?"

"Yes, sir." Earl B. glared at the man. "You don't want Coach Richards breathing down your neck."

Mr. Miller's eyes widened and his expression hardened. "Listen," he said, leaning forward, "I don't like your attitude."

Earl B. continued staring, his lips pressed together.

"I don't ever want to hear you mouthing off like that again." The teacher put his glasses back on and pointed toward the door. "You're dismissed."

Leaving the room, Earl B. walked into the vacant hallway. School was over and his bus had already left. He could walk home or wait for a later bus. Earl B. decided to walk since he needed to let off steam.

The sky was gray and overcast, matching his gloominess. Reaching Sixth Avenue, he turned and headed toward Titusville, his own neighborhood. The conversation with Mr. Miller replayed in his head. He shouldn't have made the smart-aleck remark. After all, the teacher was just trying to help. It had come out of Earl B.'s mouth before he even realized it. Why couldn't he control himself anymore?

Turning right on Second Street, he headed north. A young woman approached him, going the opposite direction, pushing her baby in a stroller. Her eyes kept darting at him, as if she was afraid he would nab her baby. Earl B. was used to whites doing that sort of thing, but not his own people. Maybe he should snatch her ugly baby and take off.

After a few more minutes, his house came into view, freshly painted and puke-green. Yes, it was all in one piece now, but putting himself back together was more challenging. He still felt gutted.

His home was drab, just like the rest of the world. Weeds were sprouting, overtaking Mama's bed of daffodils and tulips in front. Grammaw, working two jobs, didn't have time for that kind of thing. No matter. The flowers would probably be gray this year. Or puke-green.

Next door, Mrs. DuBose's garden was weed-free, fertilized, and mulched. The bulbs had sprouted, ready to bloom any day. Her husband had spent the biggest part of his life slaving away at Sloss Furnace, making some white guy rich. Everyone in town called that a good job. What did Mr. DuBose have to show for it? Nothing. Earl B. had watched enough people grinding away in a meaningless nine-to-five factory job. He didn't want that kind of life.

Inside the house, Earl B. found one lone biscuit left in the breadbasket. Munching on it, he headed to his room and collapsed on his bed, feeling dull and lifeless. Mr. Miller had told him to snap out of it. Gee, thanks. Like it was that easy.

Lying on his back, he thought about the Klan note. Two weeks had gone by, with no more bombings, no harassing phone calls, and no egg attacks. But he hadn't forgotten—Earl B. still aimed to find the guy. It was his one and only goal, and the idea constantly nagged at him, growing like mildew in Mississippi. Nothing else seemed to matter.

Later that afternoon, his grandmother came home. She had gotten off from work earlier than usual. Pretty soon, the aroma of good food filled the house. No bologna sandwich for supper tonight. It reminded him of the old days when his mother was always home.

After a satisfying meal of meat loaf, green beans, and mashed potatoes, Earl B. cleaned up his bedroom. No, scratch that. He moved things around a little—just enough to keep Grammaw from nagging. Gathering a handful of dirty clothes, he stuffed them into a drawer. His old baseball cleats lay on the floor, their metal spikes pointing upward. Earl B. threw them on the other side of the bed, where she wouldn't see. On his desk lay a stack of school papers. Buried underneath was the Klan paper, notebook, map, and moss agate—the contents of his pockets on the day he had been egged. Opening a drawer, he scooped everything inside.

His algebra book, still lying on the floor, reminded him of all his unfinished assignments. Earl B. picked it up, and it felt as if it weighed a hundred pounds. Groaning, he pitched it back on the floor. "Not tonight," he muttered.

Pots and pans clanged in the kitchen as Grammaw did the dishes. Somewhere along the line, he dozed off. The phone rang, bringing him out of a deep slumber. Hearing the drone of his grandmother's voice, he turned over and tried to sink back into oblivion.

Outside his window, a solitary bird sang. But it was the tone of Grammaw's voice that caught his attention. Something was wrong. Earl B. tried to ignore it and go back to sleep. If there was a problem, maybe it didn't involve him. Besides, he was tired of problems. Tired of everything.

Then there was silence—Grammaw was no longer talking. Earl B. had almost drifted back into a comfortable haze when he heard footsteps, then a knock on his bedroom door.

"Earl B.?" Grammaw asked.

A creaking sound told him the door had opened. He groaned but didn't move.

"You already asleep, child? It's only nine o'clock."

He grunted.

"That was Bessie DuBose on the phone. There was a bombing this evening."

The remark penetrated his brain fog. "A bombing?"

"Yeah."

Earl B. raised himself up on his elbow. "Where?"

"She didn't say, but Joyce Smiley got hurt. You know, Asa's mother?"

"Hurt?" Fully awake now, he sat up on the side of the bed.

"Something hit her in the leg. Bessie said it's pretty bad."

Another bombing. Earl B. put his head in his hands.

"You all right, child?" Grammaw sat beside him and put her hand on him.

Earl B. automatically recoiled, squirming away from her touch. "Don't do that," he snapped, then immediately regretted his reaction.

She stood up and her voice turned cool. "Well, I just thought you'd want to know. They're doing surgery right now. She's over at Hillman."

Grammaw walked out the door. She was his closest relative now, and she cared for him. Why couldn't he stop being mean to her?

Needing to organize his thoughts, Earl B. pulled out a blank sheet of paper, sat at his desk, and carefully copied the seven numbers and streets from the bombing list, leaving room for notes. So far, the Klan had hit three sites. He wrote *my home, Miles College,* and *Bethel Baptist* next to those. Four other sites remained. Asa's father was the preacher at Mount Zion Baptist. Was that one of the four?

Earl B. rose and went out into the dark hallway. His grandmother's bedroom door was closed—she must already be reading. He went to the telephone table and dug out the phone book. Flipping through the pages, he found Mount Zion. It was on Fourth Avenue West. Back in his room, Earl B. checked the list of bombing sites, but the road wasn't on there. Tomorrow, he would track down Asa and ask a few questions.

* * * * *

The Negro wards were in the basement of the hospital. Earl B. wound his way through the bleak corridors. Finally locating the area, he wandered among the beds until he saw Asa.

"Hey!" his friend called, rising from a chair.

Earl B. answered as he approached the bed. Mrs. Smiley was in the far corner in the back. She was asleep, in a hospital gown, with her left leg in a cast. Another woman sat nearby knitting.

"This is Mrs. Cartwright, my mother's friend," Asa said.

After introductions, the woman nodded, then resumed her knitting.

Mrs. Smiley, who was usually strong and spirited, looked weak and vulnerable in the hospital bed. A few moments of awkward silence passed as Earl B. glanced back and forth between Asa and his mother. "So what happened?"

Asa opened his mouth to answer, but Mrs. Cartwright beat him to it. "Honey, she was in the wrong place at the wrong time, that's what happened."

Earl B. swallowed, still stunned from Mrs. Smiley's appearance. "Where?"

"Over at the church," Mrs. Cartwright continued. "Helping me decorate for a wedding. She was in the side room hanging streamers for the reception. Next thing I knew, there was a loud noise. I ran in there and she was flat on the floor."

"Her leg's broken?" Earl B. asked, looking at the cast.

"That's the least of it," Mrs. Cartwright answered. "Surgeon said it was a mess. Tore up some of the muscles."

"They operated for five hours," Asa added.

A sick feeling rose from Earl B.'s stomach as he remembered his mother's gaping, bloody, chest wound after the bombing. "Were they able to—will she be able to walk again?"

"They hope so." Asa's tone was uneasy. "The doctor said it'll always be weaker than the other leg."

Staring at Mrs. Smiley, Earl B. wondered if his own mother had felt pain or if her death had been instantaneous. He was still trying to swallow the sick feeling when another woman approached the bed, carrying an ice container.

"Aunt Ruby," Asa said, speaking to the new woman, "this is my friend, Earl B. Peterson."

"Good to meet you." She smiled, revealing the same gap between her front teeth that Asa's mother had. She filled a water glass with ice. "You go to Ullman too?"

"Yes, ma'am," Earl B. answered.

"My daughter's a senior there. Shirley Dupree?"

Earl B. realized his mouth was open and shut it quickly. Not wanting other students to know of his tutoring, he hadn't told anybody about it, even Asa.

"She ain't mentioned you, but that's not unusual. She don't tell me nothing." Mrs. Dupree chuckled.

Mrs. Cartwright stopped knitting. "Earl B. Peterson." Her voice was loud enough to make Mrs. Smiley squirm in bed. "Now I know where I've heard your name. Ain't you that big football star? Play quarterback for Ullman?"

"Fullback," he corrected.

"Fullback then." She resumed her knitting.

Earl B. looked at Mrs. Dupree. "They were telling me what happened," he said, steering the conversation back to the bombing.

"Ain't it awful?" Mrs. Dupree shook her head and grunted. "I don't know what this town's coming to."

"Now don't start that, Ruby," Mrs. Cartwright said. "Your sister's already talking about moving. I don't know what I'll do if—"

"Moving?" Earl B. asked.

Asa's mother stirred again, opened her eyes, and cleared her throat. "Oh, hi, Earl B." Her voice was weak.

"Hello, Mrs. Smiley."

Mrs. Dupree helped her sister take a sip of water.

"So what's this about moving?" asked Earl B., glancing at Asa.

"Dad's talking about moving to Ohio where my uncle lives." Asa slumped down in his seat. "They need a preacher. For a long time now, they've been trying to talk him into taking their church."

"Seriously?" asked Earl B. "The bombing was at your church, right? Mount Zion?"

"No," Mrs. Cartwright said. "It was at mine."

"Which one is that?"

"High Praises," Asa said. A meaningful look passed between the two boys.

"High Praises," Earl B. repeated. It was on Thirty-fifth Avenue, the very first street on the Klan note. Of course. He had spoken to Reverend Cartwright, who must be this woman's husband. Glancing at the door, Earl B. half expected the preacher to show up any minute and recognize him.

"I just feel awful about it," said Mrs. Cartwright. "I wish I'd never asked her to help out."

"There's no way you could have known, Loretta," Mrs. Smiley said, her voice now stronger.

Earl B. felt as if he had been slapped. Yes, everyone could have known—if the bombing list had only been decoded. He made a mental note to himself to write *High Praises* next to the first address on the Klan note.

"I still feel terrible," Mrs. Cartwright repeated, her mouth in a grim line.

"Did anybody see who did it?" Earl B. asked, releasing a pent-up breath.

"Klan, most likely," said Mrs. Dupree.

"But did anybody see anything?" Earl B. pressed.

Mrs. Cartwright stopped knitting and cleared her throat. "Well, a neighbor down the street was sitting on his front porch that evening. He saw two white guys get out of a black Pontiac and walk toward the church."

"Did he get a good look at 'em?" Earl B. asked.

"He couldn't remember many details," she answered. "You know how they all look alike. But one of 'em was bald. Completely bald."

Chapter 11

Before dawn on Saturday, Earl B. heard footsteps outside his bedroom. Grammaw was getting ready to leave for work. He rose and dressed, then opened the top desk drawer and pulled out the original Klan note. Two bombings had occurred since the mass meeting, and he still hadn't decoded it. Listed third was 109 Jefferson Avenue SW. Earl B. opened up the Birmingham map and studied it. This road was either on the outskirts of town or in the country. He couldn't tell, but he aimed to find out. Today.

The front door of the house slammed shut. His grandmother was now gone. Earl B. rummaged through his desk drawers, looking for his working copy of the Klan list, but couldn't find it. Glancing at the clock, he decided to find the paper later. Earl B. gathered a pencil, notepad, and the original Klan note, then left the house, slipping his key into his pants pocket.

An uncomfortable feeling came over him. On the day he and Asa had been pelted with eggs, someone might have been watching them. Feeling paranoid, Earl B. glanced behind but saw no signs of anyone following. A lawn mower roared to life in a nearby yard, making him jump. Finally, he reached the bus stop and boarded.

Before taking a seat, Earl B. scanned the vehicle for any suspicious passengers. A handful of people wore work uniforms. A white teenager had his nose stuck in a comic book and seemed lost in his own world. A white woman with two children sat near the front. None of them appeared to be threats. But a white man with salt and pepper hair, dressed in a business suit, rode alone. He rose from his seat about the same time as Earl B. and got off at the same stop. Outside, the man crossed some railroad tracks and headed toward a small corner store. In the parking lot, he disappeared into a phone booth.

Earl B. walked away from town, along Jefferson Avenue, his hands in his coat pockets. Small houses lined the street. White tree blossoms littered the sidewalk. He kept going until a few businesses appeared. Using his notepad, he jotted down some names and addresses of possible targets in black neighborhoods, including a paint and body shop.

The first church he came to was River of Jordan. The parking lot was empty, and there was no answer at the door. It was definitely a black neighborhood. Asking in a nearby gas station, he received directions to the preacher's home, where a hefty, black man answered the door. Earl B. introduced himself.

The man stepped outside and offered his hand. "I'm Reverend Goss." His belt dangled open at the front. The two shook hands and talked on the front porch, with Earl B. pulling out the Klansman's paper and explaining why he had come.

"Son," Reverend Goss said, after he was finished, "I appreciate your concern. I really do. But do you realize we've had dozens of bomb threats during the past five years? I can't just shut down my church for each one. That's what them people want."

"But sir, four places on this sheet—"

"You don't even have a date. If you knew when it was supposed to happen, I'd take it more seriously. I could get people out for one day. But seeing as you don't . . ."

Earl B. swallowed. It was the same old story. With deliberate motions, he folded the Klansman's paper and stuck it back in his jacket pocket. He was wasting his time. Without speaking, Earl B. turned and went down the stairs.

The minister called after him. "Son, I don't mean to be . . ."

If the man finished his sentence, Earl B. didn't hear it. As far as he was concerned, these people didn't want to be helped. "I'm done," he said aloud. Nobody else might have heard the words, but it felt good to say them. He was only in it for himself now. For revenge.

At the corner, Earl B. turned back to the main road and headed in the same direction he had been going earlier. At a building supply place, a man was getting into a black Pontiac—someone who looked like Elmer Fudd. Could there be two in Birmingham?

Putting the uncomfortable thought out of his mind, Earl B. passed the Nabors Branch House of God and added its name to his list. He didn't try the door. Farther out the road changed names, so he turned around and headed back toward town. Tearing out the sheet of paper from his notebook, he folded it and stuffed it in the tiny watch pocket of his pants.

Before long, Earl B. passed the River of Jordan Church again. It reminded him of what Reverend Goss had said, which was almost identical to what Reverend Cartwright had told him. And look what had happened to Cartwright's church.

A thousand what-ifs bounced around inside his head. Last autumn, would he have listened if someone had told him his house was about to be bombed? Maybe, but it was a moot point.

His thoughts returned to that rainy night at his home. Could he have prevented his mother's death? That evening, he had stared out the window into the darkness. Perhaps he had missed something, like a car idling outside or someone crawling under the porch. On the other hand, it could have been a drive-by attack.

Earl B. reached into his pants pocket for the moss agate but came up empty. It was in his desk at home. He didn't know what it was about that stone, but it calmed him. Maybe it was the gem's smoothness, or maybe it was the connection to his mother, strong like the thread of spider's silk.

Up ahead, a car cruised toward him. Glancing around, Earl B. noticed he was in an area with no businesses. A few lonely houses stood far back from the road. The car, a black Pontiac, slowed as it reached him. Earl B.'s heart raced. The car's windows were down. Inside, white men talked and laughed. Keeping his head down, Earl B. avoided eye contact. The Pontiac crept along, now just in front of him. The sun came out from behind a cloud and bore down. Beads of sweat tickled as they ran under his arms. His mouth felt dry and pasty.

"Where're ya going, nigger?" yelled a man from the car, as it came to a complete stop beside him.

Keeping his head down, Earl B. kept going and passed them.

The car moved, the brakes squealed, and the engine was thrown into reverse, then back into drive. Now, it sounded as if it was approaching from behind.

Earl B. increased his pace, his adrenaline kicking into high gear. Up ahead, there was the paint and body shop he had seen earlier. If he could just make it that far . . .

The Pontiac came up beside him, this time going in the same direction as he was walking.

"Hey, nigger boy!" the man yelled again. The car came to a stop. "You didn't answer me. I asked where're ya going?"

Fear clutched Earl B. and he silently pushed onward. The car jerked forward and stopped. He started jogging, then heard someone jump out. Footsteps pummeled the ground. Earl B. sprinted ahead. Someone pursued him.

The driver gunned the motor. Another passenger leaped out, cut in front of Earl B., and tackled him. He lay facedown on the ground. The others gathered around. The man on top of him grabbed his left arm, yanking it backward until it felt like it would snap off. A searing pain shot through his shoulder. His right hand was still tucked underneath his body.

"I said, where're you going, nigger?" one of the other men growled. "Answer me!"

Extending his neck, Earl B. looked into the hostile eyes of an unfamiliar guy in a flattop haircut. "Home," he answered, then added, "sir."

"Stand up, boy."

He struggled and raised himself to his knees. At the same time, the man behind him seized his right hand, and Earl B. saw it—the missing finger. Four Fingers, the guy who looked like Elmer Fudd, now held both of his wrists, pinned behind his back.

"We got you, boy," Four Fingers said, in his raspy voice, right next to Earl B.'s ear. "You might as well quit fighting."

"I said stand up," Flattop bellowed.

Four Fingers jerked him to his feet.

Flattop got in Earl B.'s face. "You live in this neighborhood?" he asked, exuding tobacco-tainted breath.

"No, sir."

"Then why're you here?"

"Just on a walk, sir."

A sharp blow hit Earl B. in the head. "Lying nigger. Let me tell you something, boy. You go home and stay home. 'Cause next time, we'll bring a rope. Understand?" Earl B. felt another sharp blow and everything went black.

Chapter 12

Something wet was on Earl B.'s face. He reached up, tried to wipe it off, then opened one eye. A disgusting, gray, slimy substance, mixed with blood, was smeared on his fingers. His other eye wouldn't open. In front of his face, on top of the weeds, lay a wet paper bag, a beer bottle, some chicken bones, a gum wrapper. This wasn't his bed at home. He groaned, remembering. His bed was a long way from here.

So this is what I get for trying to help people. He tried to raise himself, but his effort was met with a piercing pain in his left shoulder. A car passed by. Then another. The stuff around him smelled like ripe garbage in August. It permeated his nostrils. Again, he tried to get up. The same searing pain ripped through him. Earl B. managed to brace himself up with his right shoulder. A surge of dizziness temporarily blinded him, and he almost fell over. Leaning to his left, he was finally able to sit up. Then a headache punched in, a constant pressure, making his brain feel like it was about to burst. Blood dripped from his face onto the ground. Another car passed by. Using his one eye, he could tell he was in a ditch by the side of the road. A wave of nausea came over him, and he vomited, adding fresh material to the pile of garbage. It was puke green, the color of the paint on his house. What on earth had he eaten?

Earl B. rehashed the events that had landed him here. Four Fingers, who had been so quick to help a white woman on the bus, had savagely attacked him. Maybe he was also the Klansman who had dropped the paper. And the one who'd harassed him over the phone.

Another car passed, and Earl B. heard the sound of squealing tires. He looked up, but no vehicle was visible. Footsteps sounded on the pavement. The breath caught in his chest. He desperately hoped—and even prayed—that the person wouldn't be a redneck. Or a cop.

The footsteps stopped, and Earl B. turned to see if his prayer had been answered. A white man stood by the side of the road.

"Good God Almighty," the man said.

A female voice called out.

"It's just a nigger, Martha," the white man answered, walking away.

The words made Earl B. tighten inside, but at the same time, he breathed a sigh of relief that the guy hadn't bothered him. The man got back into his car and drove away. As more vehicles whipped by, Earl B. thought about his attackers. He must be on the trail of something big or they wouldn't be trying to stop him. But *nobody*— no horde of rednecks, no gang of Nazis, or the Grand Dragon himself—was going to intimidate him.

Another car passed, this one heading away from Birmingham, more slowly than the rest. It stopped. Earl B., aware of his every breath, looked up. About twenty feet away, a red Ford Galaxie had parked on the side of the road. He couldn't see anybody inside.

A white man in a suit and tie walked around from the driver's side. A big guy. "What happened?" He had a southern drawl and kept one hand on the back of his car, as if he were ready to jump back inside at any minute. This man was more timid than the last.

"I . . ." Earl B. couldn't finish. The words were in his mind, but his tongue wouldn't cooperate. It kept sticking to the inside of his mouth.

The stranger glanced around warily, twisting both ways, then looked at him again, with an expression that read, "I hoped you wouldn't still be there."

Earl B. tried again to speak but failed.

Walking closer, the man dodged the trash in the ditch and stopped three feet away. "What happened, son?"

It was only one word—son—but it meant everything. This person wasn't going to throw things at him. He wasn't going to beat him. The man might be too scared to help, but at least he wouldn't make things worse. Earl B.'s throat, his stomach, his every muscle relaxed. "I was beaten, sir," he managed to say.

"How long have you been here?"

"I'm not sure, sir. Maybe a couple of hours or more."

"Where do you live?"

Earl B. told him.

"Can you stand?"

He tried. Pain shot through his body and he wobbled back. The white man reached out to steady him but caught the injured shoulder.

"Aaaah!" Earl B. screamed in pain. The dizziness returned, and he collapsed again, sitting on the ground. More blood dripped from his head.

There was a lull as neither one moved. The man seemed to come to a decision. He leaned toward Earl B. "Try again, son. This time, hang on to my neck."

Earl B. did.

The man picked him up and partly carried, partly dragged him to his car. Earl B. leaned against it while the man opened the back door. "Can you lie down in here?"

Blood and garbage stained the seat as Earl B. collapsed inside. Soon, the car was rolling. He tried to ignore the pain in his head and shoulder. The nausea had subsided. Now, the man seemed to be turning around in a driveway. Once again, he asked Earl B. for his address. He told him. A few more turns, and the nausea came back. Forcing down a swallow, he tried to stave it off. Finally the man stopped, turned off the ignition, and got out. Earl B. waited. Nothing happened. The queasiness eased. The back door opened.

"Do you have a key?" the man asked.

Of course he had a key. Earl B. struggled to reach into his pocket.

"Oh—never mind. Someone answered." The stranger was gone for a moment.

Next, Grammaw's voice came closer.

Earl B. finally got his hand into one pocket. Empty. Then the other. Empty. He checked both jacket pockets. Nothing. The only thing left was the slip of paper he had made notes on during the walk, which was stuffed inside the tiny watch pocket of his pants.

The thugs had taken everything else, including the Klan note and his house key.

* * * * *

The next day, Earl B. lay in bed on his right side, with an ice pack balanced on his left shoulder. He turned the dial of his radio until a song came in.

Earl B. sipped water through a straw. For the hundredth time, he lifted the tissue box on his bedside table, in hopes that his working copy of the Klan note was there. But it wasn't. Just his luck to lose the original. Without his other copy, he might as well forget about decoding it.

The song ended. "You're listening to the Contours on WENN. Shelley the Playboy, 'the Mouth of the South,' here. Stay tuned. We've got the Four Seasons coming up after this message."

Grammaw shuffled into his bedroom. "I'm glad you're awake, child. You been sleeping all morning." Her tone carried more warmth than it had the night before, when she had learned a Klansman had their house key. "Here's your aspirin." She handed him two pills. "Dr. Crutcher said to take these every four hours."

After Earl B. took the medicine, Grammaw pulled up a chair, sat, and turned the volume down on the radio. All the way. He knew what that meant. It was time for an interrogation.

"What day is it?" Earl B. asked, trying to divert her attention.

"Sunday, child." She put her hand on his arm. "Dr. Crutcher said you need to stay home from school tomorrow. If you're feeling okay, you can go back on Tuesday."

Earl B. grunted. He had a study session with Shirley tomorrow. He'd have to call her and reschedule.

"Listen," said Grammaw, patting his arm, "I want to know why you was all the way out on Jefferson Avenue yesterday."

All day Earl B. had anticipated this, but he hadn't come up with a decent story. The truth would get him in trouble. Big trouble.

"Earl B.?" she prompted, when he didn't respond.

"Trying to find a friend's house." It sounded lame and Grammaw didn't believe him. He could tell because she got a certain look in her eye. He had seen it since he was five years old. Earl B. forgot what he had done, but it had something to do with sweet potato pie.

"A friend's house?" she said, her voice rising a little. "Who?"

"Nobody you know." Truth was, he knew no one on Jefferson Avenue.

"Try me." She could be persistent.

"Luther Pennington." The first name that popped into his mind.

Her eyebrows wrinkled together. "Luther Pennington? His family don't live out that way."

Just his luck to choose someone she knew. "Well, I didn't know that."

After taking a slow, purposeful breath, Grammaw put her hand on his forehead. "You was lucky you wasn't killed." He winced as she examined the cut on the side of his face, near the hairline. "Nine stitches. Gonna have a scar." She put her hand back on his arm and squeezed it. "Big Ben's coming sometime today to change the lock on that front door."

"Okay."

"You gonna be able to take care of yourself tonight? I got to work at the hospital."

"I'll be fine."

Grammaw kissed him on the forehead, something he hadn't let her do in years. "Dr. Crutcher said if that Reverend Newton hadn't found you, you might've been . . ."

"Reverend Newton?" Earl B.'s memory of the time after the attack was spotty.

"Yeah. That nice white man that brought you here. Did you hear what he said?" she asked, primping her hair. "He said to me, 'Nice to meet you, ma'am.' Ain't that something? 'Nice to meet you, ma'am.'" She laughed softly.

After Grammaw left, Earl B. fell asleep again. He didn't wake up until he heard a man's voice. And it wasn't Big Ben's.

Chapter 13

"Well, lookee here." It was a familiar, raspy voice. Earl B.'s head jerked sideways. Four Fingers stood, framed by the bedroom doorway, with a smile on his face that would grow mold on a cactus. "Your sweet dreams are over, boy."

Earl B. sat up. The room spun in circles a few times. Something hot and sour rose in his throat, and his heart hammered. He glanced toward his bedside table. A tissue box, a glass of water, his clock, a small lamp. Nothing he could use as a weapon. His algebra book, ordinarily a deadly missile, sat on the other side of the room. "What're you here for?" The question was weak, but Earl B. needed time. Time to think.

Four Fingers laughed. "I'm tired of you sticking your nose where it don't belong, boy."

"You bombed my house, didn't you?" Earl B. swung his legs to the opposite side of the bed and stood. The room spun again, but he grabbed the bedside table for support. Now, he was facing Four Fingers, with the bed between them.

"You know, I lose track, there are so many."

Earl B. felt the wall behind him. He was trapped, with this thug between him and the door. "When's the next bombing?"

"None of your damn business, you nosy nigger."

The words made every cell in Earl B.'s body want to scream.

"Lost that list, didn't you?" Four Fingers forced a sharp laugh.

Ignoring his question, Earl B. glanced at the man's hands and pockets but saw no evidence of a weapon. Had he really come without one?

"I'll take care of you first," Four Fingers said, taking a step toward him "Then I'll help myself to a few things around the house."

Earl B. backed up. His leg hit the bedside table, knocking the lamp over. It smashed and a piece of glass hit his ankle, but he kept his gaze locked on the man.

Creeping toward him, Four Fingers moved around to the foot of the bed.

"My mother died in that bombing, did you know that?" Earl B.'s bare foot brushed against something. With his toes, he felt the object on the floor. A shoe, but which one?

Four Fingers let out a mirthless laugh.

Earl B.'s foot felt something metal. A cleat. One of his baseball cleats.

The man inched closer. A thud came from the front room. Four Fingers jerked his head around. Another sound, like a thousand screws in a big metal can. Earl B. stooped down, grabbed the cleat, and slashed the metal spikes across the man's face.

Four Fingers screamed. Earl B. shoved him backward to the floor, leaped over his body, and headed for the door.

"Earl B.?" a voice boomed from the front room.

"Big Ben!" Earl B. yelled, running down the hall. "It's the Klan!"

"The Klan?" his uncle echoed.

Charging into the living room, Earl B. collided with Big Ben, who stood in the front doorway, with his toolbox open on the floor.

Four Fingers entered the room. Three deep, linear cuts on his face dripped blood.

With a huge adjustable wrench in each hand, Big Ben bellowed, "Get out!" He stood aside to make way for the white man.

"No!" Earl B. said. "That man was going to kill me."

Big Ben didn't take his eyes off Four Fingers, didn't even glance at Earl B. Talking through gritted teeth, he said, "I understand that, boy. But we can't do nothing else."

Earl B.'s hands were balled into fists. "What do you mean we can't—?"

"I mean what I say, boy."

"But he bombed our house!" Earl B. screamed. "And killed my mother!"

"Listen to me, son." Big Ben's tone was softer, but he kept watching the Klansman. "We can't do nothing else. Now you get out of the way and let this white man pass."

Tears welled up in Earl B.'s eyes as he stepped aside.

Walking toward the door, Four Fingers glared at them. He stopped in front of Earl B. and drawled, "You're just like your—"

"Get out!" Big Ben repeated, stomping his foot and shaking the house. "Get the hell out of here before I kick your lily-white Klan ass."

Four Fingers left. Earl B. stood in the doorway, watching him walk away. Tears streamed down his face. Big Ben put his arms around him.

Drawing his hands up, Earl B. pounded his fists on his uncle's chest. "You let him get away!" he wailed.

Big Ben just tightened his hold. "We can't do nothing else. If we did, we'd find ourselves swinging from a tree."

Realizing his uncle was right, Earl B. felt himself collapse into the big man's arms, his body shuddering as he wept.

"It's all right, son," Big Ben said, clutching him firmly. "It's all right."

Chapter 14

Where's your assignment sheet?" Shirley whispered. Her gaze drifted to the side of his face, probably focused on his new scar. Earl B. had just had his stitches removed.

Pulling out a piece of paper from his algebra book, he unfolded it and almost gasped. It was his working copy of the Klan note—that's where it had been. Earl B. surreptitiously slipped it into his folder. Flipping through his book, he found his assignment sheet and handed it to her.

They were in the Smithfield Library, the only one blacks were allowed to visit. For several weeks, Shirley had continued to help him with homework, putting up with his indifference, but he could tell her patience was running out. Motivating himself to study just wasn't happening. The only thing that fired him up was the possibility of getting revenge on the Klan, Four Fingers in particular. Now that he had found the list, Earl B. could get back to decoding it. Shirley's help would be nice, but the problem would most likely bring out the nervous grandmother in her.

"Inequalities." She leaned toward him and thumbed through the book. "So how much have you done?"

He caught the scent of her perfume and immediately regretted not doing the work. It was too late now. "Nothing," he answered.

"Nothing?"

"Nope."

She glared at him. "It's the same story every week. Mr. Ross is going to think I'm a terrible tutor."

"Is that all you're concerned about?"

If possible, her expression hardened. Shirley countered with a question. "How do you expect to improve your grade when you're not doing the work?"

Earl B. didn't look her in the eye, but he felt her hostile stare before she turned back to the book. Why on earth did he keep having these feelings for her? She was a conceited smart-ass. Every time he was in her presence, he'd float off on a cloud, until she brought him in for a rock-hard landing with one of her cold, selfish remarks.

While Shirley scanned the homework instructions, he looked around the library. His mother used to bring him here to check out books. After growing older, Earl B. realized they were usually dog-eared discards from the white libraries. Once again, blacks got the leftovers.

"Okay, let's get started," she said. Shirley walked him through the entire assignment. After they finished, she closed the book. "Why can't you do these problems by yourself? You don't have any trouble when I'm here."

"I don't know." Earl B. rested his elbows on the table and glanced around. Behind the front desk, the librarian worked, her hair puffed up at the crown, reminding him of the lead singer in the Chiffons.

"You've got to learn to do this stuff without me, pull yourself up by your own bootstraps," Shirley said. "I can't be with you all the time to hold your hand and make you work."

She sounds like a typical nagging teacher. "Look," he said, "I hate this stuff. I'll never use it. You won't either."

Her voice rose. "What do you mean, I won't use it?"

"Shh!" came from the librarian.

"You say you want to be a bio whatever."

"Biochemist," she said sharply.

"But you'll just end up cleaning houses like all the other girls," he said, not bothering to keep his voice down. "And you don't need this stuff for that. What're you gonna do? Count the dust particles? Look at mold under a microscope?"

The librarian showed up at their table and glowered at them. "The two of you need to take your argument outside."

Grabbing her sweater, Shirley headed for the door. Earl B. picked up his book and papers and rushed after her.

"This is a waste of my time." She slipped on her sweater and charged along. "You want everything handed to you, don't you?"

"I never said that." He caught up with her at the intersection.

"Then you're being lazy, and I'm supposed to help save your scholarship." She crossed the street and kept going. "You've got it made. Do you know how many people want to go to college and can't pay for it?" Shirley stopped and faced him, seemingly unaware of the people staring. "Me for one. It's not fair. I'm hammering away, getting good grades, doing extra projects, and even tutoring another student, and *I* can't get a scholarship." She started walking again. "You've got one, and you throw it away."

"Do you think I'm doing this on purpose?" Earl B. jogged to keep up with her.

"Look," she said, slowing her pace slightly. "If you don't wanna do this . . ."

"Do what?"

"Learn this stuff." Shirley sped up again. "Graduate. Go to college. Play . . . football."

Did she have to make football *sound as appetizing as a rotting deer carcass on the side of the road?* "In case you haven't noticed, I'd make more money playing football than I would with one of your college degrees."

"But your chances of playing professional football—"

"You don't know what my chances are. You don't know anything about me. Or football. This stuff"—he grabbed his algebra book and waved it around—"is all you know about. Besides, if I don't play football, my chance of working in some factory for the rest of my life is a hundred percent, that's for damn sure!"

Shirley stopped, her mouth hanging open. When she spoke again, her voice was more subdued. "I thought you wanted a football scholarship. That means going to college."

Earl B. didn't answer. He knew she was right. Big Ben was right. Coach Richards was right. He needed that scholarship.

She shook her head and resumed walking. "I don't know what to do. Mr. Ross asked me to—" Her voice cut off and her expression stiffened.

Strolling beside her, Earl B. wondered what else Big Ben had said. Now, they were almost downtown. The overcast sky reflected his mood. "Look, I'm sorry we got into an argument. It's just that lately, I've had a hard time studying."

"I'm sorry, too." Her voice was gentle. "Mr. Ross said you've had some personal problems." Shirley paused, but when he didn't continue, she added, "But he didn't say what."

"My house got bombed," he heard himself say.

She stopped walking. "Bombed?" Her voice was barely above a whisper. "When?"

"November."

Something changed in Shirley's expression. Maybe her eyes opened a little wider, or her usual stubborn look melted away. Whatever it was signaled a U-turn in her attitude.

"Oh my," she said. "I didn't know. I remember hearing about . . . there've been so many." Reaching Kelly Ingram Park, they cut diagonally across the grass. "Anybody hurt?" She sat, spreading her skirt around her.

Normally, Earl B. didn't like talking about it, but after their argument, he was enjoying her reaction. Sitting beside her, he cleared his throat, then told her the whole story. It was difficult keeping his voice steady.

"I'm so sorry," Shirley said afterward, touching him on the arm. He immediately tensed up and drew back. She lifted her hand and held it poised above him. "Did I hurt you?"

"No." Regretting his reaction, Earl B. laid his hand over hers and placed it back on his arm, giving it a gentle squeeze. After a moment, he dropped his hand but left hers. His skin tingled under her touch.

"So what about your father?" she asked.

His stomach clenched. Earl B. didn't want to open up that can of worms or he'd be answering questions for days. "He's gone."

"Gone?" She dropped her hand.

"Yep." An awkward pause followed, before he looked back up at Shirley. "It's just me and my grandmother." The wind picked up and thunder rumbled in the distance. Dark clouds had gathered, moving so fast the sky looked like a scene from *The Ten Commandments*. Out of the corner of his eye, Earl B. noticed she was still looking at him. "Don't you ever feel like things are pointless?" he asked.

"What do you mean?"

He shrugged. "No matter what—no matter how much you learn, what grades you get, you'll still end up doing the same thing in ten years."

"Is that why you can't study?"

Teachers had asked him a thousand times why he couldn't study. Earl B. had given as many smart-aleck replies. But something about her made him let down his guard. "I can't concentrate. All I can think about is getting my hands on the guy that bombed our house."

"That wouldn't help matters. You'd just get locked up—or worse."

Another rumble of thunder sounded. "Maybe. But if I could take that guy out—"

"You'd get lynched. So forget about it. Working in the movement is the only way to defeat those people."

Earl B. didn't answer.

"Go with me to the ARC office on Saturday," she said, her voice soft. "If you saw it firsthand, you'd know what I'm talking about."

"And work with a bunch of white people?"

"Rachel and Larry? And—"

"Who's Larry?"

"Rachel's boyfriend. You'd like him. Not all white people are bad, you know."

Earl B. saw a streak of lightning along the horizon. "What's in it for them, anyway?"

"Do you always have to ask that?"

Her question made him realize she was no longer the one with the selfish point of view.

"Maybe they just want to make the country a better place," she continued.

"You mean the land where all men are created equal?" He snorted. "What a joke. People have been trying to do that for a hundred years. It ain't gonna happen." Thunder boomed in the distance.

"But we can't just give up." Putting her hand on his arm again, she lowered her voice. "So how about it? Will you go with me to the ARC office?"

"Look." Earl B. kept his voice from rising, trying to avoid another argument. "I told you I don't like that stuff."

Shirley hesitated, then spoke gently. "Won't you come once? Just to see what it's about?"

Swallowing hard, Earl B. met her gaze. Her face, with her dark brown eyes and smooth skin, was only a few inches away. She took his hand, and that tingling feeling came back, traveling up his arm. It felt good. "All right," he said.

Her face relaxed. Shirley pulled her hand away, dug a notepad from her purse, and wrote down something on a sheet of paper. "The address," she said, handing it to him. "I usually get there around one o'clock."

He took it. "How about we go out to lunch beforehand?" Might as well get something extra on the deal.

"I'm too busy with school and now the movement. I don't have time."

"It's just lunch. You do take time to eat lunch, don't you?"

Closing her purse, Shirley avoided his gaze. "I've made it my policy not to go out."

Geez, this girl doesn't believe in having any fun.

She must have detected his disgust, because she added, "Of course, if it's a place near the office, I might be able to."

"Loveman's?"

Her face fell. "Loveman's?" A clap of thunder sounded. It was closer now.

"You said someplace near the office. What's wrong with it?"

"I haven't shopped at that store in over a year." She lifted the frayed hem of her dress. "It's on the boycott list. They don't let us eat at the lunch counter. They don't let us try on clothes."

"You got a better place?" Earl B. didn't mean for his question to come out as sharp as it sounded. A drop of rain hit his face. Then another. They both stood and started toward the bus stop.

"Okay," she said. "I'll make an exception this one time."

Her words lifted his spirits. As they walked, Earl B. slipped his hand in his pocket, fingering the moss agate. Pulling it out, he palmed it and held it in his hand. Thunder sounded again, and it continued to sprinkle.

"Should we meet there at noon?" she asked.

"Sure." He heard a noise on the sidewalk and realized the gemstone had fallen out of his hand.

Shirley was quick retrieving it. "What's this?"

Earl B. told her.

"It's beautiful," she said, examining it. "I'm glad you've got something of your mother's to hold onto." Shirley handed it to him. "You should get it repaired, though."

"So I can wear it?" he joked, holding it to his chest. "What would happen if I showed up at school wearing this thing?"

She laughed, but her voice turned serious again. "I mean it. You should get it fixed."

Still holding the pendant to his chest, he flashed a snooty facial expression, which made her chuckle again. Earl B. joined in, and the whole thing escalated until they were reacting to each other's laughter. The rain began beating down and they ran, doubled over, giggling. When was the last time he had laughed like that? He couldn't remember.

Near the bus stop, they ducked under a store awning, out of breath and still laughing. Earl B. looked at Shirley, and she met his gaze. Her soaked hair and the rivers of raindrops streaming down her face made something tighten inside him, and he wanted to stare at her that way forever.

A man rushed under the awning, ruining the moment. Shirley's bus came, and the stranger also boarded, leaving Earl B. alone. The rain slacked off to a steady drizzle and cars whooshed by, their tires sending sheets of water upward.

His bus arrived, and Earl B. paid in front. On a spur-of-the-moment decision to cause trouble, he turned, heading down the aisle.

A forceful hand grabbed his upper arm. "You know the rules, boy. Get off and board at the back."

Earl B. jerked his arm away from the bus driver, turned, and descended the stairs. Glancing up, he stopped in his tracks. On the opposite corner, Four Fingers stood under an umbrella, looking his way. Earl B.'s stomach lurched. The thug's stony gaze made his blood turn cold, but Earl B. continued staring, determined not to back down. The bus jerked as the driver prepared to take off. Breaking eye contact, he rushed toward the back and barely made it inside before the door closed. By the time he found a seat, Four Fingers was gone.

At home that evening, Earl B. pulled out his algebra book and tried to catch up, but his mind kept wandering. Four Fingers might have seen Shirley with him at the bus stop. Earl B. didn't want to think about what might happen if that man discovered he cared for her.

Did he care for her? He had to admit it was nice confiding in someone about his problems. Shirley was relentless when it came to school, but part of her made him feel good in a way he'd never felt before. Earl B. looked forward to lunch on Saturday.

The phone rang, and he ambled down the hall to answer.

"Hello," Earl B. said.

"It's me again." It was the same husky, male voice he had heard once before on the phone.

"Who is this?" Earl B. asked.

"Still got that list?" The caller laughed. "Or did you . . . lose it?"

The question took Earl B. by surprise. It was similar to what Four Fingers had asked when he had entered his house. Would he ask the same question twice? Perhaps this wasn't him. "Who is this?" he repeated, needing to hear more of the man's voice.

"That's what happens when you go meddling in other people's business."

Maybe it was Four Fingers. But there was something about the man's tone that made him unsure.

"I got people watching you," the caller drawled. "Keep it up, boy, and we'll blow your ass up again."

Click.

Earl B. felt his heart pounding up to his throat as he laid the phone back in the cradle. His head was spinning. Still standing, he leaned forward and placed his hands on his knees. Those last words kept bothering him. Would they really bomb his house again?

Heading back to his room, he sat on the bed. A glimmer of hope rose inside him. The caller hadn't mentioned Shirley. Maybe that meant he hadn't seen her at the bus stop. The last thing Earl B.

wanted to do was drag her into this mess. Maybe he shouldn't have agreed to help at the ARC office this weekend, but he didn't want to give up spending a few hours with Shirley—time that didn't involve studying.

Earl B. pulled out the slip of paper she had given him. The ARC office was on Seventh Avenue North. Something about it seemed familiar. Opening his folder, he pulled out his copy of the Klan paper and glanced at the addresses. There it was, plain as day, fifth on the list.

Chapter 15

The next afternoon, Earl B. made a show at doing homework. The books were out on the table, but he hadn't made any real progress.

For the third time, he got up and dialed Shirley's number. No answer. Earl B. hadn't seen her at school all day. Why hadn't he called last night as soon as he'd learned the ARC office might be a bombing site?

Heading into the kitchen, Earl B. poured a glass of water. The incident at the bus stop came back to him, with Four Fingers's steely glare. Two things were certain—Earl B. needed to have a long talk with Shirley about the Klansman and he'd have to explain about the bombing list. It would set her off, but she'd eventually calm down. He could definitely use her help decoding it.

The doorbell rang. In the living room, Earl B. moved the front curtain aside to peek out. It was Asa. He opened the door. "Hey, come on in."

His friend shuffled by, with his thumbs hooked in his pockets. No baseball glove.

"Something wrong?" Earl B. asked.

"Came to say goodbye."

"You mean you guys are really moving?"

"Yep."

"Today? Like right now?"

"Yep."

Earl B.'s chest suddenly felt very empty. "You said you might move, but I didn't think it would be this soon."

Asa responded with a shrug.

"You aren't happy about it, are you?"

"Nope." Asa sighed and plunged his hands into his pockets.

"Where're you moving?"

"Cleveland."

"Seriously?" Earl B.'s voice rose. "Man, that's raw. You know how cold it gets up there? It's like Siberia."

"Thanks for that. Listen, I can't stay long. They're waiting on me."

"Okay."

The kitchen clock ticked as each waited for the other to speak. Earl B. thought of all the time he and his friend had spent together growing up. He couldn't remember ever not having Asa as a friend. During childhood, they'd played everything from hide-and-seek to cops and robbers. In junior high, they'd played on team sports together. Asa had been someone he could talk to—a friend who could keep a secret. After the bombing, he had been a huge help. This whole thing was happening too fast.

Earl B. swallowed. "Maybe we can keep in touch. You got my address." But in the back of his mind, he knew full well that neither of them would actually write a letter.

"Yeah, I'll let you know once we're settled in." Asa's voice sounded strained.

They walked to the front door and awkwardly shook hands. Then Asa left.

Staring out the kitchen window, Earl B. sipped his water. So this was what a seventeen-year friendship came to. A handshake and a goodbye.

Outside, it was springtime and sunny, mocking his dark mood. Draining his glass, he put it in the sink and went out the front door. Surely, he could find something to do besides homework. Walking down the street, Earl B. saw kids playing outside. A group of girls were jumping rope, singing rhymes. Young boys played marbles. He used to play marbles with Asa. His throat tightened and he pushed the memory away.

Earl B. wound his way through the neighborhood. Once he sensed someone was behind him, but when he looked, no one was there. Four Fingers had made him jumpy.

At High Point, three kids were playing basketball. Walking closer, Earl B. realized they looked familiar. He'd seen them in the halls at school.

One of them grabbed the rebound and stopped playing. He was dark-skinned and had an angular face, with high cheekbones and a sharp chin. "Well, look who's here," the boy said. "Mr. Football Superstar hisself. Ain't you too good to play with us?"

"Earl B. Peterson." Offering his hand, he tried to keep all emotion out of his face. This guy was trying to get under his skin.

"Woo-eeh! The man has manners. Won't you look at that!" He shook Earl B.'s hand a little too enthusiastically. "I'm proud to meet you, Mr. Earl B. Peterson." The guy had to crane his neck to look up at him. Not exactly the tallest dude on the planet.

"What's your name?" Earl B. asked, ignoring his sarcasm.

"Ray Cunningham. Or excuse me. Mr. Ray E. Cunningham." He glanced at the two other guys, who laughed at his joke.

What a jackass, Earl B. thought, then looked at the other two.

One was scrawny and had a cross-eyed gaze. "I'm Huey," he said.

"Rex," said the other, who was so bulked out he could have played defensive tackle. Then he glanced at Ray. "Rex P. Johnson."

"Well, now we got an even number," Ray said. "How about"—he looked at Earl B.—"me and Rex against you and Huey." It wasn't a question.

For several minutes, the boys played at a steady pace. Earl B.'s blood raced; he always got a charge from playing sports. After grabbing a rebound, he dribbled the ball, faked to the right, then turned left and put up the shot. *Swish.* Right through the middle, didn't even touch the rim.

That's when things turned serious. Ray got the rebound, took the ball back to the mid-court line, then advanced. Earl B. planted himself in his path. Ray stopped, anchoring his foot, trying to pass. Earl B. blocked his attempts.

"Come on, Rex!" Ray shouted.

Rex darted to one side, then the other, trying to get clear for a pass, but Huey blocked him.

"Idiot," Ray mumbled, aiming for the basket. He shot the ball, but Earl B. jumped at the same time and knocked it to the side.

"Foul," Ray shouted, as all four boys scrambled to recover the ball.

"Was not," Earl B. muttered.

Ray got the ball and sauntered toward the grass. "Let's stop for a while. I'm tired of playing."

Earl B.'s energy plummeted. It seemed convenient that Ray got tired of playing when he was falling behind.

Huey waved and walked away. "Gotta go."

Leaning over, with his hands on his thighs, Earl B. tried to catch his breath. A car passed on the street behind the goal.

Ray still had a frown on his face. He picked up the ball, paced back and forth, then mumbled, "I should've gotten two free throws."

"That was a clean block, and you know it." Earl B. rose from his stooped position, and it occurred to him that Ray probably resented his height advantage.

"It was a foul, you stinking moron!" Ray shouted, slamming the ball down.

Another car came by—a big blue Cadillac. It came to a halt next to the basketball goal, and the driver, a white man in a suit and silk tie, rolled down the window. A woman in a dress sat next to him, nervously adjusting her fur shawl. "Boys, can you tell me where Eighth Avenue is?" the man asked.

"Couldn't tell ya," Ray said, laughing.

The stranger stared at Rex. "What about you?"

Rex looked back and forth between Ray and the white man. "No idea," he finally said.

The man appeared irritated. He turned his gaze to Earl B. "And you, boy? Are you as dumb as these other two?"

"Stanley!" the woman beside him exclaimed, fidgeting uncomfortably in her seat.

Any sympathy Earl B. had felt for the lost traveler vanished. "Ain't it next to Seventh Avenue?"

"Stupid niggers," the man muttered, stepping on the gas.

As he drove away, Ray yelled, "At least we ain't the ones lost, whitey!" Then he turned to Rex, laughing. "You know, the more I see of this world, the more I think Malcolm's ideas are right. Not only are white people devils, but they're damn idiots, man."

"Malcolm who?" Rex asked.

"Malcolm X," Ray said, picking up the ball and dribbling it.

Earl B. had heard the name. "Isn't he up north?" he asked.

"Ain't you guys heard of Malcolm X?" Ray shot the ball, missed, then continued. "Where you been? He's the guy that's gonna really give us our freedom. None of this namby-pamby stuff the Reverend Doctor Chickenwing talks about. Malcolm tells the truth, man."

"Like what?" Earl B. asked.

"Like the black man was here first—way before the white man. We're descended from black kings and queens. Africans were living in palaces when Europeans were still living in caves. Malcolm tells what whitey don't want us to hear. We're actually superior to them." Ray tried a jump shot and missed again.

Earl B. got the rebound and did a hook shot, putting the ball home. *Some of us might be superior to the whites.* But he kept that thought to himself. "What else?"

"And the fact that we should be able to defend ourselves. None of this turn-the-other-cheek shit."

That caught Earl B.'s attention.

During the rest of the day, as he went home and waited for Grammaw, Earl B. was preoccupied with the things Ray had said. *None of this turn-the-other-cheek shit.* That kind of thinking made sense. He'd have to look into this Malcolm X guy. People should be allowed to defend themselves. For the first time in a long time, Earl B. felt as if something had clicked into place.

Chapter 16

Loveman's was a Birmingham icon, a huge, magnificent building, featuring a clock on the street corner that had become a city landmark. Inside, Shirley and Earl B. entered the lunch counter on the mezzanine. A sign on the wall shouted at them with big, bold letters: "Seating for Whites Only." They ordered sandwiches and paid. The waitress, who had her red hair bunched up in a net, put their drinks in paper cups. While waiting, they sipped their Cokes. On a nearby stool, a little boy stared at them, as if he'd never seen anybody who wasn't white before.

"Here you are," the waitress said, handing a bag to Earl B.

Outside, he and Shirley put their drinks on the sidewalk and stood next to the building. As they ate, Earl B. recalled their last study session. It had started off with a major argument, then ended with them laughing in the rain. Today, he had meant to recapture some of those good feelings. Maybe Loveman's hadn't been such a hot idea. It wasn't exactly fun, standing outside in the March wind. Besides, when the time was right, he had to give her some unpleasant news: *Did I mention the ARC office is about to be bombed? Oh, and by the way, there's a crazy Klansman who'll probably chase after you.* Earl B. could already hear her grilling him with questions. Was there even a way to tell her these things without setting off another round of bickering?

"I'm gonna sit down at one of these lunch counters someday," Shirley said. A gust of wind whipped her dress around as she ate.

"Wouldn't do any good," Earl B. said, before he could stop himself.

"It might if enough folks did it."

"This ain't Greensboro," he muttered. Why did he always get sucked into a fight?

Shirley bent over and sipped from her paper cup. "You expecting somebody? You keep looking around."

Jerking his gaze back to her, he realized he had been watching for Four Fingers. "No." His thoughts returned to the bombing list. "Tell me something."

"What?"

"Has the ARC office ever been bombed?"

Shirley stopped chewing. "Bombed?" She finished and swallowed. "No. Why do you ask?"

He sipped his drink. "What if I told you it might?"

"How do you know?"

Earl B. carefully chose his words. "A friend of mine got hold of something he thinks is a list of Klan bombing sites."

"Who?"

He took a deep breath. "I can't say who it is."

Her hand was poised in midair, holding her sandwich. "What kind of people are you hanging out with anyway?"

Earl B. didn't answer. Instead, he took another bite.

"So when's this bombing going to happen?" Shirley asked.

"Sometime soon. He doesn't know the exact date."

She raised her eyebrows. "There's no date? What are we supposed to do? Quit our work? That's exactly what they want, you know."

It was the same thing Earl B. had heard from the preachers. "Look, I just thought you might want to know. You don't have to do anything."

"And it's definitely the ARC office?"

"It's a list of addresses."

"But it gives the address of the ARC office?"

"It gives the street name."

She stared at him, holding her cup in her hand, ready to take a drink. "You do realize there are plenty of other possible targets on that street, right?"

"But it's a place the Klan would love to hit."

"Of course. But do you know how often we get bomb threats there? All the time. We don't even pay attention to them anymore." She took the last bite of her sandwich.

Earl B. stopped pressing the issue. He was angry with himself for—once again—warning people who didn't give a damn. He sure as hell wasn't going to warn her about Four Fingers. She was on her own. Eating his last mouthful, he picked up his drink and gestured for Shirley to follow.

As they walked, Earl B. saw white women in their bouffants and flared skirts entering Kress's, another department store with policies that invited boycotts and demonstrations. A bald man in a business suit who emerged from the store made him stop in his tracks. After realizing it wasn't Four Fingers, Earl B. shuffled ahead to catch up with Shirley. At the intersection, he turned on Fourth Avenue.

Shirley called after him. "Let's go this way." She pointed down Nineteenth Street.

Earl B. backtracked and caught up to her at the light. Before they crossed, he glanced behind and saw another bald man rushing into the alley behind them. "How much farther?"

She threw him a quizzical look but didn't answer.

At this point, Earl B. was measuring distance not by the number of blocks walked, but by the number of bald white men they passed. Turning left at the Greyhound Station, they entered the black section of town and walked by a church.

Shirley gestured toward the building. "Here's one possible target on Seventh Avenue."

"They have mass meetings?"

"I'm not sure," she admitted, continuing down the sidewalk. "But that doesn't mean it won't get bombed."

"That could even be a target," she said, as they strolled past the Poole Funeral Chapel.

"A funeral home?" he said. "Really?"

"Why not?" Shirley said.

He walked alongside her. So that's why she had led him on this route. It gave her a chance to show him all the potential bombing targets on Seventh Avenue, where the ARC office was.

They came to another church. "And this place," she said, pointing.

"Okay, you've made your point." Earl B. glanced at the church, then did a double take. A bald, white man darted behind the building. This time, he was certain it was Four Fingers. "How much farther?"

She stopped walking. "What is wrong with you?"

He whirled around and faced her. "Nothing!" From this angle, Earl B. could see if Four Fingers emerged. "I was just wondering."

"Just one more block," she said, walking again.

Earl B. followed as they went past a few small houses. Perhaps Four Fingers was planting a bomb now, he thought uneasily. "So you work here every Saturday?"

"Yeah, in the afternoon. Sometimes, I also go out in the morning to help Rachel deliver the newsletter. But I can't demonstrate."

"Why?"

"My parents won't let me."

"So you can't do anything that runs the risk of changing things?"

Shirley ignored his sarcasm. "My father works at UPCO."

Was he supposed to know what that meant?

She must have seen the confusion on his face. "You haven't heard of it? It stands for United Pipe Company or something like that."

"I've heard of the place," he said. "But I don't understand what that has to do with anything."

"My father doesn't want them seeing our name in the paper. They fire people who demonstrate."

Okay, now he understood.

Shirley paused on the sidewalk in front of a small yellow house with peeling paint and a broken downspout.

"This it?" Earl B. asked. The place looked like it would crumble in a split second in a bombing. He looked behind them. Four Fingers wasn't there.

"Yes." She climbed the stairs, one of which was rotten.

Overgrown weeds shrouded the area underneath the porch like a leafy quilt. A good place to hide a bomb. Earl B. climbed up, avoiding the bad step.

Shirley opened the door and a rumble of noise assaulted their ears—the clattering of typewriters and the wet slapping of a mimeograph machine. Two people were folding flyers, and someone else talked on the phone. Normal things you'd expect in an office. But aside from all that, something seemed wrong. Earl B. couldn't place it, but there was an uncomfortable feeling in the room, a tension too thick for a jigsaw to slice through.

"Welcome!" A man appeared out of nowhere, with a smile engraved on his face. "I'm Larry McKee," he said in a tenor voice, offering his hand. "I've heard a lot about you."

Earl B. locked eyes with Shirley. What had she told him?

Shirley misinterpreted his expression. "Rachel's boyfriend," she muttered.

Larry was a tall, gangly fellow with a sandy blonde crew cut, browline glasses, and a receding hairline. He was also one of those whites who tried a little too hard to be friendly. His expression reminded Earl B. of the sleazy scumbag who had once sold a used car with a bad carburetor to his father.

"Come over and meet Cas Howard," Larry said, walking toward a table along one side of the room. "He's our logistical guru."

Following behind, Earl B. swept the room with his gaze, still convinced a bomb might be ticking in the shadows.

Cas, a white man in horn-rimmed glasses, shook hands with Earl B., then continued drawing with a yellow marker on a street map. He had a pocket-protector stuffed with pens and mechanical pencils. For the hundredth time, Earl B. wondered how he had been talked into spending his day with a bunch of crackpots.

"And here's Gwen," Larry continued, leading them toward a young black woman who stood behind another table, holding a big stack of five-by-seven cards. "We're going door to door today doing voter registration. You two want to join us?"

"Sure," Earl B. said, before Shirley could argue. An afternoon with Larry would be like doing jail time, but it was better than staying here. Anything to get them away from a possible bombing site.

Rachel came through a back door carrying a small trash can. She saw Shirley and Earl B. "Far out! You're both here!"

Near her was Cornell, who had a serious-as-a-stroke expression on his face as he typed.

"Want me to show you how to run the mimeograph machine?" Rachel asked.

"They're going with us to do voter registration," said Larry.

Rachel stared at him. "Oh . . . okay."

Cornell stopped typing, rose, picked up a stack of papers on his desk and slammed it down next to the mimeograph machine. "Yeah," he said loudly, pretending to talk to Rachel. "Larry pounced on 'em as soon as they walked in."

"Now, be fair, Cornell," Larry said, putting his arm around Shirley. "She's worked with you for the past two weeks. And besides, this way, we each have five people. Even steven." He glanced around. "You guys ready?"

"Yep." Cas, who seemed oblivious to the friction in the room, folded up the map.

Larry drove, with Cas beside him as navigator. They pulled away from the curb, zigzagged through the neighborhood, and turned onto the main road. In the back seat, the others chatted.

"Do you two go to the same school?" Gwen asked, looking at Earl B.

"Shirley and I? Yeah," he answered. "Ullman. How about you?"

"Miles College."

"Gwen's our jack-of-all-trades," Shirley said. "Whatever needs to be done, she does it—the newsletter, boycotts, voter registration, demonstrations."

After a while, Earl B. lost track of the streets, and they were in an unfamiliar part of town.

Larry turned onto a residential street and pulled over to the curb. "We'll start here."

The five of them split up. Earl B. suggested he take one side of the street and Shirley take the other.

He knocked on the first door. A black woman in a flowered housedress answered. "What do you want?"

"Ma'am, we're trying to get folks to vote on Election Day. Are you already registered?"

"I ain't getting involved in that mess." She started to close the door.

"But ma'am," Earl B. said, thrusting his arm through the open doorway, "we're trying to change some of the unfair laws in—"

"My husband tried to vote once. Uh uh. Almost lost his job. Never again."

She closed the door, with Earl B. yanking his arm out just in time. It was the same story at the next house and the next. He was met with resistance and suspicion, adults so scared of losing their houses or cars or jobs that they wouldn't consider trying to vote. There was an occasional exception, when someone would fill out a card. Between houses, Earl B. kept watch over Shirley but saw no sign of Four Fingers.

The afternoon crawled by, but finally Earl B. and Shirley headed back toward the car. She held up a small stack of filled-out cards. "Pitiful, ain't it?"

Earl B.'s stack was just as small. He mumbled his agreement.

They rode back to the ARC office, which had not been bombed after all. Walking to the door, Larry collected the cards, apparently happy with the results of their work. Inside, Rachel was running the mimeograph machine and Cornell was typing. Three other people were folding, stacking, and binding newsletters. Cas was the first to leave.

"Okay, people!" Cornell yelled, holding his hand up. "We got a demonstration this Wednesday afternoon at three o'clock at Kress's. We need you to show up this time, okay?"

There were a few halfhearted grunts.

The late afternoon sun beamed through a window onto the side of Cornell's face, emphasizing the thick, ridged scar that ran from his earlobe to his nose. He approached Earl B. "How about you? Can you make it?"

"No," Earl B. said, without smiling.

"Are you sure? It's after school."

"Lay off of him," Larry said, his eyes boring a hole through Cornell. "He already said he couldn't." He shifted his gaze to Earl B. "Sorry. I've tried to tell him those kinds of things don't work anyway."

"Direct action is the only thing that does work," Cornell shot back. "We've tried talking, we've tried voting drives, and that stuff never works."

"But you're not giving it a chance." Larry flashed an embarrassed smile at Earl B.

"Look at the negotiations last spring," Cornell retorted. "A few Jim Crow signs were taken down, but they went right up again. So we're back where we started."

Larry softened his voice. "It's gonna take time. Once we get enough people to vote, we can get some of these politicians out of office and make some legal changes."

"This city ain't like other cities. You could do those things until doomsday and it won't change this place."

"Look, we ought to be able to talk these things out. There's really no need for demonstrations and boycotts. You're wasting time with that stuff." He put his hand on Cornell's shoulder.

Cornell grabbed Larry's hand and threw it off. "Wasting time?" he shouted. "You're telling me about wasting time, after the hours and hours you've spent on voter registration, taking all them cards up to the courthouse? You know what they do with them things? Throw 'em in the trash! Then you run around here bossing us around." He made a sweeping gesture with his hand. "Like we're your darkies or something."

"Okay, you two," said Gwen, in a tone that meant business. She placed her hands on her hips.

The purple vein on Larry's temple was clearly visible beneath his Georgia-clay complexion. "I've *never* treated anybody like that, and you know it."

"Stop it!" yelled Gwen, pointing her finger at them. "Both of you. It all works—direct action and voter registration. Now, can't we just all get along and work together? Don't you two see that this is exactly what the other side wants? Divide and conquer."

The phone rang. Nobody moved. Finally, Gwen went to the table and picked it up. "Hello?"

The mimeograph machine hummed and the conversation resumed.

Cornell moved toward Gwen, who had hung up the phone. "Who was it?" he asked.

She rolled her eyes. "Another bomb threat."

Chapter 17

Earl B. made a C on the next algebra test. A good, solid C. Mr. Miller couldn't argue with that. But instead of his math teacher, it was Coach Richards who called him in for a conference. Since his grade was on the rise, Earl B. figured it wouldn't be a problem. He was wrong.

"What's up with algebra, Peterson?" Coach asked, sitting behind his desk.

"I made a C on my last test."

"And a C-minus before that. You're cutting this thing awfully close, Peterson."

Earl B. opened his mouth to speak, but stopped just in time. *Don't argue, don't argue, don't argue,* he kept telling himself.

"You've got a tutor?"

"Yes, sir."

"Are you two really studying?" Coach stood up behind his desk. "I've heard rumors."

Now Earl B. was being accused of something that wasn't true. Resisting the urge to yell, he fought to keep his voice steady but strong. "Yes, sir. We're studying. And *nothing else.*"

"Make sure you keep it that way. Mr. Miller says the next test counts for a lot. Understand?"

Earl B. took another breath, still fighting for control. "Yes, sir."

"Suck it up, Peterson. Deal with it." He waved his hand. "Okay, you're dismissed." It was obvious he wanted Earl B. out of his office, out of his sight.

The bell rang, and students poured out of classrooms. Earl B. joined them. In the past ten minutes, the tension in his body had skyrocketed. Approaching his locker, he stopped in his tracks. Herds of students were going by, but on the opposite side of the hallway, Carl Washington faced Shirley, who stood against the wall. He smiled, his face only a few inches from hers, and his arm rested on her shoulder.

Dialing in the combination to his padlock, Earl B. told himself he didn't care. He was forced to get along with Carl since they played on the same football team, but there had always been an underlying rivalry. Lately, with Earl B.'s failing grades, the quarterback seemed to be looming over him, ready to scoop up his college scholarship. And now their tug-of-war was escalating, with Carl threatening to take Shirley. The coach's words replayed in his mind: *Are you two really studying? I've heard rumors.* If gossip had reached the coach, it must have already reached Carl. Was he doing this to prove a point?

Earl B. messed up his combination and started over. He couldn't keep his eyes off Shirley and Carl. She shook her head and spoke, with that familiar no-nonsense expression on her face. He obviously wanted something from her, and she wasn't caving in. Earl B. could imagine him asking her out and Shirley telling him she'd made it her policy not to date. With a smug feeling, Earl B. finally opened his locker, switched out books, and slammed it shut.

Now, Carl was talking again, and Shirley's face had softened into a demure look that Earl B. had never seen. She started to say something, but stopped when he kept talking, his face now closer to hers. She spoke, then Carl walked away. Shirley watched him, with an uncertain smile on her face. The crowd was thinning out. She glanced at her watch and left.

Again, Earl B. told himself it didn't matter. For all he cared, she could go out with Sam Cooke or Wilt Chamberlain. It wasn't any of his business. But the smug feeling he had felt only moments ago had evaporated.

* * * * *

Earl B. hadn't really wanted to go to the school dance. And Carolyn Owens hadn't outright asked him, although she had dropped plenty of hints. He didn't even remember inviting her. She had trapped him by his locker, in much the same way Carl had cornered Shirley. They'd had a long conversation, mostly one-sided, and afterward, somehow, it had been arranged. So when Friday evening came, Earl B. stood on the side of the dance floor, shifting his weight from side to side, while Carolyn chatted with one person after another.

"Hello, people!" a voice shouted. "I'm Shelley the Playboy, 'the Mouth of the South!'" The deejay—in real life—stood across the gym, holding a microphone and spinning records.

Cheers erupted and echoed in the gymnasium.

"How many of you remember how to do the twist?"

The noise level got even louder, making Earl B.'s ears ring.

"I thought so," yelled Shelley the Playboy. "And I'm getting ready to play the magnificent Sam Cooke, singing his hit, 'Twisting the Night Away.'" He slipped a record onto the turntable and yelled, "Timber! Let it fall!" The music blared out.

Earl B. and Carolyn danced to "Mashed Potato Time" and "The Loco-Motion." He had never been a confident dancer, so he tried to copy what others were doing. Afterward, they went to the punch table to get drinks. Scanning the floor, Earl B. told himself he wasn't looking for anyone in particular. He did see Jackie Edwards, Asa's old girlfriend, dancing with one of the linebackers on his team. After her yearlong relationship with Asa, she hadn't wasted any time finding someone new. Earl B. shook his head. Girls were so fickle.

With the next song, the tempo slowed, and he and Carolyn danced to "You've Really Got a Hold on Me." She had her arms around his neck for most of the song. Pivoting slightly, Earl B. glanced up and saw Shirley, dancing with Carl Washington. Yes, Miss Shirley Dupree, who had previously told him it was her *policy* not to go out. So that's what they had been whispering about in the school hallway. Her hair was in a high bun, with curls framing her face. As they came closer, Carl turned so he was facing Earl B. and smirked. Carolyn put her hand on the back of Earl B.'s head and ran her fingers through his hair. Carl rotated, so Shirley faced Earl B., and their eyes locked. Shirley pressed her lips together like a child who didn't want to take nasty medicine. Carl swung her in another direction, and the whole incident was over.

After the dance, a few teachers carted students over to Green Acres, a local greasy-spoon eatery. As Earl B. helped Carolyn climb out of the car, a black Pontiac cruised by. Doing a double take, he saw Four Fingers in the driver's seat.

"Ain't you gonna shut the door?" Carolyn asked.

Earl B. pushed it closed, and they followed Big Ben down the street toward a green awning. The place had no tables or chairs, just a bar along one side of the restaurant. Some of the students, including Earl B. and Carolyn, spilled outside, chatting and munching on their food. Earl B. ate a pork chop sandwich, his fingers leaving an imprint, soaking through the bread. He was about to take another bite when the sound of an explosion reverberated through the neighborhood. Everyone froze, staring at one another, and a pall of silence came over the crowd.

"What on earth was that?" Big Ben asked. He wandered down the block and disappeared.

The conversation was subdued as Earl B. and Carolyn finished eating. People milled about on the street. Twenty minutes went by, and Big Ben hadn't returned. As Carolyn talked to another girl, Earl B.'s eyes were drawn to Shirley, who stood next to Carl. Her legs looked longer than he remembered, perhaps because of her dress shoes.

Carolyn eased up next to Earl B. "I don't know what Carl sees in that girl," she said, following his gaze. "People say those two are an item now. And she's always wearing them funny-looking, raggedy-old dresses. She's had that one forever."

Earl B. answered with an exasperated tone. "Look, maybe her family can't afford—"

"Oh, that's a bunch of baloney. Her father works at the same place mine does. If my dad can afford to dress us right, her family can also. Some people just don't have any taste, that's all."

"She also boycotts some of the stores." Earl B. didn't know why he was defending Shirley, especially since she had made an exception to her dating policy to go out with someone else.

"That's just an excuse for not buying decent clothes." Carolyn threw a sideways glance at him. "Since when has she been so gung-ho about boycotts, anyway?"

Earl B. felt the muscles in his jaw constrict. "Long enough. She spends almost all her free time on the movement."

Carolyn's expression changed slightly—maybe her lips tightened or her eyes got wider. "Well, I just hate that girl," she continued. "One time, she had the nerve to call me a snob."

About that time, Big Ben returned, his expression grave. "Another bombing," he said.

"Where?" a student asked.

"Not sure," he replied. "Somebody said it was over near the AME church."

Chapter 18

The phone rang. Earl B. woke up out of the fog of a dream. He listened for his grandmother's footsteps, rushing to answer, but the house was silent. It rang again. Saturday morning. Grammaw was probably cleaning the church, getting it ready for tomorrow's service. Rolling out of bed, he ran down the hall and picked it up after the sixth ring.

"Hello?"

"Earl B.?" It was a female voice. A young female voice. "This is Shirley."

He waited, but she didn't continue. He grunted.

"Did I wake you up?"

"Kinda." Earl B. tried to always tell the truth—when it was convenient.

"Sorry. Listen, I've got bad news."

He knew what it was before she continued.

"The ARC office was bombed."

"Last night?"

"Yeah. The explosion everybody heard at Green Acres. Can you come over this morning and help out? Nobody seems to know how to deal with it. I thought since you had rebuilt the front of your house—"

"It was mainly the porch. And I had Big Ben's help."

"But you'll know more than they do. Please?"

Why don't you ask Carl Washington to do it? Earl B. bit his tongue to stop himself from actually speaking.

"Do you have something else going on this morning?"

Sleep, he immediately thought, but he didn't say it. Pitch with Asa—oops, couldn't do that anymore. Shoot some hoops with the guys at High Point. None of those would impress Shirley. If he lied and said homework, she would see right through him.

"Please?" she asked again. He saw her face in his mind, with her silky complexion and deep, dark eyes.

"Okay," he heard himself say.

"So I can tell them you'll be over here in a few minutes?"

Then Earl B. remembered something he really did need to do. But he couldn't tell her about that either. "I need to go somewhere first," he said.

"When can you come?"

"An hour. Two at the most."

She thanked him and hung up.

He threw on some clothes, caught the bus, and got off downtown. Half a block later, Earl B. entered a jewelry store, where a white-haired man sat at a desk, wearing a magnifier on his head.

"May I help you?" the jeweler asked, rising from his chair.

Earl B. placed a slip of paper on the counter.

A look of recognition came over the man's face. "Oh, yes." He picked up the slip, then turned around and opened a drawer. "You had the moss agate, didn't you?"

"Yes, sir."

Back at the counter, the jeweler pulled the pendant from an envelope. "Nice piece. The frame of the setting was cracked. I replaced it and added a new clasp and chain."

Earl B. examined the new setting, which looked even better than the old one. He wished his mother could have worn it.

After paying, Earl B. headed toward the ARC office, thinking back to the time when Shirley suggested repairing the pendant. A few days later, he had taken it to the jewelry store. Meanwhile, Earl B. envisioned different scenarios of how he would give it to her and how she would react. It might just melt her enough to make her forget about her no-dating policy. But last night's dance had changed everything.

Yes, Earl B. had paid a pretty penny to have it repaired, all because of her throwaway suggestion. He had let it go to his head. "Damn," he said aloud, angry with himself for being so gullible.

Arriving at the ARC office, Earl B. walked in without knocking and took inventory of the damage. A hole had been blasted in one side of the building, with the windows on either side blown out. Plaster had fallen from the ceiling. Cas was on the phone, and Shirley stood in the middle of the floor, holding a broom and dustpan. Seeing Earl B., she brushed some hair away from her face, leaned the broom against the wall, and walked toward him.

"Thanks for coming," she said. Dust covered her blouse and skirt, and something white was stuck in her hair, probably a piece of plaster, but somehow it made her look even more appealing. The anger he had felt toward her a few moments ago vanished. She lowered her voice. "Gwen was here when it happened."

"Was she hurt?" he asked.

Shirley nodded. "She was near the window. A lot of cuts. But worse, some of the glass got into her eyes."

He chewed his lower lip. Earl B. hadn't really known Gwen that well, but still.

"They're not sure she's going to be able to see," Shirley continued, her voice cracking. "Cornell saw her this morning, but for the most part, they're just letting family in."

Earl B. was still digesting this information when Larry and Cornell, who were on opposite sides of the room, approached him.

"I hear you have experience with this kind of thing," Larry said jovially. He held a hammer and chisel in his hand.

Before Earl B. could respond, Cornell spoke. "You know anything about this type of repair?" His tone was brusque, almost accusatory.

"Some," Earl B. said, walking to get a closer look at the windows. "You'll need some tools and equipment."

Cas approached Cornell and handed him a notepad. "The windows."

"What's this?" Cornell asked.

"I just got off the phone with the window place. That's the cost."

"To replace both of them?"

"Just one. Multiply it by two."

Cornell's eyes widened. "They must think we're made of money." He shoved the notepad back at Cas, then turned toward Earl B. "Can you go to the hardware store with me?"

Earl B. shrugged. Not his idea of a fun Saturday. "Sure." Shirley had started sweeping again.

During the next hour, Earl B. and Cornell figured out what supplies they needed to buy and what they could borrow. Then they climbed in the car.

Cornell backed out of the driveway and made a couple of turns until he was on the main road. "I was surprised when you showed up at the ARC office with Shirley last week." His voice was tentative. "She hadn't mentioned a boyfriend."

"We're just friends," Earl B. answered. An honest mistake, but the remark made him view Cornell in a different light.

"I asked her out once," Cornell continued. "She told me her mother wouldn't let her date a college guy." Approaching the store, he braked and turned into the parking lot. "So I'm waiting for graduation."

Earl B. caught the translation: She's mine, leave her alone. What Cornell didn't know was that he might have to fight the Ullman High School quarterback for her.

* * * * *

Six hours later, the ARC workers called it a day. Earl B., itching to get away from Cornell, left with Shirley and they boarded the same bus. Her stop came first, and he watched out the window as she walked away. Then someone else caught Earl B.'s eye. Four Fingers stood on the corner, watching Shirley, and took off after her.

Shooting up from his seat, Earl B. hollered, "Sir! Can I—may I get off here, sir?"

The bus driver ignored him.

"Sir—"

"Not till the next stop," the driver barked.

Earl B. stayed on his feet, looking backward, although he could no longer see the corner. The bus driver finally stopped. When the doors opened, he dashed out, jaywalked, and ran back the way the bus had come. Reaching the corner, he turned and hurried in the direction Four Fingers had gone. A man emerged from between two buildings, and Earl B. darted away from him, only to collide with a white lady carrying an armload of boxes. As the packages went flying, someone shouted insults at him, but he kept racing along, weaving between people.

Pausing at a big intersection, he glanced both ways. Pedestrians kept wandering into his line of vision at critical times. On his right, far in the distance, he might have caught a glimpse of a bald head, but he wasn't sure. Decision time. Earl B. turned in that direction and sprinted. Before long, the man came into view again—definitely Four Fingers. Farther ahead was a girl in a blue sweater—Shirley.

Earl B. slowed his pace, trying to catch his breath. He followed as they passed through a residential section, where there were fewer cars. Four Fingers gained on her. Turning at an intersection, they entered a rundown area with an out-of-business auto repair shop and boarded-up houses. The road ended in a cul-de-sac, with a footpath taking off through a patch of woods where the street left off. The sun was going down. A sick, helpless feeling came over Earl B. There were no easy exits here. He glanced around, looking for something he could use as a weapon. Nothing.

Shirley neared a narrow alleyway that ran behind a long-gone, mom-and-pop store. Earl B.'s heart stopped. *Don't go into that alley*, he wanted to scream. Four Fingers said something and Shirley swung around, clutching her books in her arms, obviously taken by surprise. Earl B. froze, partially hidden behind a pole. If he was going to help, he needed the element of surprise. Shirley said something. Four Fingers spoke again, taking another step. She answered and backed away. *Throw the books at him and run, Shirley*, Earl B. thought. But he knew she'd never think of books as weapons. Four Fingers kept advancing, and she backed away, until they both disappeared behind the far wall of the store.

Spotting a pile of rocks, gravel, and torn-up concrete, Earl B. rushed over and grabbed a stone, a large one that fit into his palm. He crept past the alley to the store and heard their voices nearby. Standing with his back against the wall, he peered around the edge of the building. The two had rotated. If only they would turn the other way, Earl B. could have better aim. Now, he could hear their conversation.

"Come on, baby," Four Fingers said.

"No!" Shirley said.

Throw the books, Shirley.

Four Fingers laughed. "Gimme a little brown sugar."

The blood pulsed through Earl B.'s head, a repetitious, never-ending snare drum. He peeked around the corner again. They were still in the same position, except closer together. Earl B. carefully backed away in front of the store and turned, heading down the alley. The two high walls on either side made it dark. He scampered along, his foot hitting something metal that clanged. A car horn mercifully sounded at the same time. Earl B. froze. It seemed impossible that Four Fingers hadn't heard it. Earl B. ran toward the alley's end, crossed to the opposite corner, and eased to the edge. He heard their voices again.

"Come on. Just a little brown sugar," Four Fingers said.

"Shut up!" Shirley yelled.

Every fiber inside Earl B. stiffened as he gazed around the corner and took inventory. Four Fingers was in perfect position now and couldn't see him. There was no risk of hitting Shirley. Earl B. turned the rock over in his hand.

"We're just gonna have a little fun," Four Fingers said.

Earl B. made himself take some deep breaths. The rage inside him wouldn't help his aim. This was just like baseball. He was on the mound, pitching. Accuracy first, then speed. Whirling around and executing the fastest windup in baseball history, Earl B. hurled the rock straight at Four Fingers's skull.

It hit the mark. The man collapsed on the ground, but Earl B. didn't wait to see if he had knocked him out. He sprang forward, grabbed Shirley's hand, and pulled her along, heading to—he didn't know where. By now, she was running alongside him, clutching her books, so he dropped her hand. Earl B. jogged, looking back every now and then.

"Is he there?" she asked, breathing heavily.

"Not yet. But it's too soon to slow down."

"This way," Shirley said, hanging a left.

They crossed the railroad tracks and entered a residential section with people on the stoops and an occasional car passing by.

"I've got to let up for a minute," she said, gasping.

Earl B. slowed down. They were likely out of harm's way. He followed as she made a couple of dogleg turns and stopped in front of a white clapboard house with a small porch.

"Is this your place?" he asked.

She nodded, her sides still heaving. A strange expression was on her face, one that was hard to read.

He gazed around. "I wouldn't mind making sure you get inside."

Hiding her face with her hand, she made an odd sound.

"Shirley? You okay?" Earl B. came closer, reached out, and touched her arm.

She lowered her hand, pulled a handkerchief out, and dabbed at the tears streaming down her face. "Oh, Earl B." She lay her head on his chest. "I don't know what I would have done if you hadn't been there."

He wrapped his arms around her and ran his fingers over her shoulder blades. The fragile softness of her body made him realize how vulnerable she had been only moments before. Earl B. glanced about, still keeping watch. They stayed that way for a minute or two, with his face buried in her hair. He breathed in her sweet scent as her weeping subsided and she relaxed in his arms.

Lifting her head, she forced a smile, and muttered, "I'm sorry."

"For what?" He gazed at her face, drinking her in, not wanting the moment of closeness to end.

"Crying." She lowered her eyes.

Sensing she was about to pull away, Earl B. brushed aside a tear from her cheek. "Who said you shouldn't cry?"

Shirley looked into his eyes again and smiled. Another tear ran down her cheek. Her face reminded Earl B. of the way she had looked during the rainstorm in the park.

Do it. Now. Kiss her.

"I guess I better go inside." She pulled away.

Reluctantly, Earl B. dropped his arms. The moment had passed. "Thanks." She smiled again. "You throw a mean fastball."

Plunging his hand into his pocket, Earl B. fingered the moss agate. Maybe he could bring back that moment if he gave it to her . . .

Before Earl B. could pull it out, she turned and walked toward her house. "What an absolute creep that guy is," she called over her shoulder.

He said nothing. She didn't know the half of it.

* * * * *

Earl B. was getting used to unwanted phone calls. Almost.

That evening, he lay on his bed, wondering what he had done to Four Fingers. The whole Klan would be after him now. That's when the phone rang. He rolled out of bed and ran down the hall.

"Hello," Earl B. said.

No answer.

He started to lower the phone to the cradle, without giving the caller a chance. But he heard the familiar husky voice coming from the receiver. "You remember me?"

Earl B.'s hand froze in mid-air, then he put the phone back to his ear. What would the guy say this time?

"See what happens when you hang around places like the ARC office?" After Earl B. didn't answer, the man continued in his lazy, southern drawl. "It's so easy. Just stay away from mass meetings, the ARC office, and don't go sticking your little nigger nose where it don't belong."

Anger rose in Earl B. like hot water and steam from a geyser. "You can't tell me what I can and can't do," he said through gritted teeth.

"Oh, you'll be sorry you said that."

Click.

Afterward, Earl B. realized that the man had only mentioned his work at the ARC office. He hadn't said a word about him beaning Four Fingers.

Chapter 19

Earl B. sat with Shirley in the basement waiting room of the hospital. How had he let her talk him into this?

"You don't care if I get a little homework done, do you?" she asked, opening her literature book.

He shrugged. Nobody in the world brought along schoolwork when visiting someone in the hospital. Nobody except Shirley.

This whole thing had been her idea, visiting Gwen. Earl B. had agreed to do it, thinking it might give them some extra time together, time that didn't involve school. No chance of that. Her nose was already buried in a book.

Across the waiting room, a man held a sleeping boy. Earl B. remembered the times he had settled in his own father's lap—the smell of his dad's aftershave, the pattern of the hair on his arm, the slight scratchiness as he rubbed his finger against his dad's cheek.

After his father disappeared, there had been the initial shock and flurry of activity as friends and family searched. But after a while, people seemed to forget him. Even Earl B.'s mother. He had bickered with her a few times about it. One time especially stood out, when his mother was humming a church tune while washing a casserole dish at the sink. It bothered him. Six months ago, her husband had disappeared, and yet she acted as though everything was A-OK. Laying the dish on the drying rack, she returned to the kitchen table, humming even louder.

"Will you hush?" Earl B. hissed. His elbows rested on the kitchen table, and he clenched a balled-up napkin in his fist.

Mama gave him a hard stare. He knew she was deciding how to react. When she spoke, her voice was low. "What's wrong, child?"

Earl B. dropped the napkin on his plate. "What's wrong? You're asking me what's wrong?"

"Yes, what's wrong? That's what I asked." She picked up the breadbasket. "You done with the cornbread?"

"Will you quit?" Earl B. barked, his voice rising even more.

"Quit what?"

"How can you go on like this? You act like nothing happened."

Mama laid the breadbasket back on the table and sat in the chair next to him. "Is this about your father again?" she asked, putting her hand on his arm.

He pulled away from her.

"I know it's hard, child." Her voice was gentle as she leaned toward him. "I miss him very much, just like you do. But I've done what I can do. Now, I got to leave it to the good Lord. If it's His will for him to come back, then—"

"So you've quit looking."

"Honey, you know yourself how they scoured the land."

Yes, Earl B. knew. The police hadn't been helpful, of course, but Big Ben had organized a search, along with some men from church. They had come up dry. His father seemed to have vanished into thin air.

"You may come in now," a nurse said, holding the door open. Her words brought Earl B. back to the present.

He and Shirley entered the ward. Hospital beds were lined up against the wall. The nurse led them toward one near the back, where a patient lay with bandages over both eyes—Gwen. Drawing closer, Earl B. could see three rows of stitches on her face, with dried blood marking each one. He hung back as Shirley approached the bed.

"Gwen," she said, grabbing her bandaged hand.

"Shirley." Gwen almost smiled, then grimaced in pain. Her entire face was swollen. "I'd know your beautiful voice anywhere."

"Aw, thanks, but you're the one with the Nina Simone voice," Shirley said. "Earl B.'s here, too."

He came closer and spoke.

"Thanks for coming," she said. "My mama's here some, but she's got to work. You know how it is."

"So they operated on your eyes?" Shirley asked.

"Yeah," Gwen said. "The doctor still doesn't know whether I'll be able to see or not. He took pieces of glass out of both of them, but he couldn't get it all. There was a lot in my face, too. I must look pretty ugly."

"Naw," Shirley said. "You'd never look ugly."

"Ain't the English language funny? Pretty ugly—and you knew what I meant, too."

Earl B. couldn't believe it. Some redneck had blinded her, and she was cracking jokes.

"So fill me in," Gwen said. "My mama don't know nothing. What's happened since I been in here?"

"Did you hear Boutwell was elected city mayor?" Shirley asked.

"No!" said Gwen. "So Bull Connor's gone?"

"Not so fast. He's staying in office, fighting the new government."

"Oh." Gwen's voice was full of disappointment. "I should've known. People like him don't go away. He'll be stirring up trouble the rest of his life. When Bull Connor finally dies, he's gonna ornery away."

Shirley laughed. "So now we got two mayors and two city governments."

"Mm, mm," Gwen grunted. "Did they finally start the demonstrations?"

"Yep. The day after the election." Shirley counted them off with her fingers. "Britling Cafeteria, Woolworth's, Loveman's, Pizitz, and Kress's."

Earl B. leaned against the bed railing, feeling like a fifth wheel as they discussed Birmingham politics.

"So lots of people went to jail?" Gwen asked.

"Not enough."

"I was afraid of that. People are worried about being fired, aren't they? Losing their mortgages and car notes?"

"That's what I've heard. They can't get volunteers."

"If they can't fill the jails, the whole campaign'll fail."

Shirley squeezed her hand. "You need to hurry up and get well, girl. We need you on the front lines."

"Earl B., you'll have to fill in for me," Gwen said.

"I just want to get hold of the man who bombed the place," Earl B. fumed.

Shirley opened her mouth to speak but stopped. His statement floated in the air, like the seed head of a dandelion.

"Well, Mr. Earl B., tell me this," Gwen finally said. "What would you do with that man once you got him in your clutches?"

"Same thing he did to you," he fired back.

"An eye for an eye only makes the whole world blind."

"But they shouldn't be allowed to get away with this stuff."

"I'm not saying they should get away with it," Gwen said. "But if you do it back to them, it just gives the other side ammunition."

"Two minute warning," someone said behind them. Earl B. looked back and saw a nurse heading down the line of beds.

"Earl B.," Gwen said.

"Hmm?" he answered.

"I don't want to give you the impression I'm happy about this. Lord knows, I ain't. But it don't do no good to let 'em get under your skin, 'cause it'll just fester and eat you up, make you rot from the inside out. Crush your spirit." She reached out a bandaged hand toward him and he took it. "We just gotta keep on keepin' on, okay?"

"Okay." His throat was tight, and his voice barely made any sound.

"Time's up," a nurse said.

Shirley bent down and kissed Gwen on her forehead. "Thanks."

Earl B. said goodbye, and they left.

Outside, it had started sprinkling. Shirley opened her umbrella. "Wanna share?"

"Naw," he said. "I don't care if I get a little wet." The sprinkles turned into serious rain. "Okay, I care." He ducked under her umbrella as they walked. "You set this up on purpose, didn't you?"

"On purpose?" Shirley asked. "What do you mean?"

"Listen at you, trying to sound like you don't know what I'm talking about."

"Okay. I admit, I was hoping some of her attitude might rub off. She's certainly made me rethink a few things." Shirley gave a tentative smile, making him wonder what those things had been. "Gwen's always had a great outlook on life, even after all the bad things that have happened to her."

"There's more?"

"A couple of years ago, her older brother was badly beaten by four Klansmen. He was traveling down in Florida, somewhere in the panhandle, I think. He hasn't been the same since. Went crazy. Lots of psychological problems."

Earl B. shook his head. "And she just lets that roll off her back?"

"Nothing's gonna make her brother normal again and she knows that. But that's what prompted her to join the movement. She wanted to change things."

A line of white businessmen approached them. Shirley automatically stepped off the curb into the street. Earl B. followed without thinking, then hated himself for it. His whole life was filled with these petty reminders that he was supposed to be inferior to white people.

"Think you can help out at the ARC office on Saturday?"

"I'm done with the ARC office," he said. "All that stuff is a waste of time—boycotts, demonstrating, voter registration."

Shirley answered with an aggravated stare. Reaching the bus stop, they stood huddled under the umbrella.

"Ready for your test?" she asked.

Earl B. sighed. Another bad topic. The algebra test was coming up in three days. As in *the* algebra test. Mr. Miller said it could cost him his life. Or at least a college scholarship.

Shirley continued without waiting for an answer. "I think you'll do fine. During our study sessions, you know the material."

"Problem is, I can't seem to concentrate unless you're there to make me work."

She gave him a friendly nudge with her elbow. "Just pretend I'm there standing over you."

Earl B. wished it were only that simple.

* * * * *

It was Wednesday, the day before the algebra test. All week, Earl B. had focused on math. Earlier that day, he had spent study hall reviewing homework problems.

He was in the hallway between classes when he felt two powerful hands slap his shoulders from behind.

"Peterson!" It was Carl Washington's voice. "We gotta talk."

"What's up?" Earl B. asked, turning to face him.

Carl leaned close and grumbled, "I been hearing things about you and my girl."

Earl B. backed away. "I—" He stopped himself just in time. The last thing he wanted was for Carl to find out Shirley was tutoring him.

"Better keep your hands off her," the quarterback said. "Understood?"

Staring into his eyes, Earl B. felt his jaw tightening. Surely Carl knew he was the underdog here. "I ain't afraid of your threats."

The quarterback dropped his hand, exhaled unevenly, then backed away. His expression changed, with creases forming between his eyes and his chin lifting slightly as they resumed walking. "Ready for tomorrow's test?"

Earl B. relaxed and shrugged. "Guess so." He reached his locker and dialed the combination.

"I actually studied for this one, man," Carl said, stopping beside him. "I think I got it in the bag, 'cause,"—he paused for effect—"only one of us gonna get that A&M scholarship." Then he disappeared down the hall, laughing.

* * * * *

The next morning, Earl B. stood at the bus stop, rehashing countless algebra formulas, equations, and rules. He might just eek this one out. In about an hour and a half, it would all be over.

He glanced at his watch. Five minutes, and the bus should be here. Earl B. was the only one waiting. In the corner of his eye, he saw some movement. At the same time, a car stopped at the curb and two robed Klansmen jumped out. They grabbed his arms and pulled them behind his body. His books and papers went flying. Pain shot through his injured shoulder. Struggling to fend them off, he caught a glimpse of a four-fingered hand. He kicked and squirmed and stomped, but the men's robes kept him from aiming his blows well. They tied his hands, threw him into the back seat of the car, and took off. The two robed Klansmen sat in the back, with Earl B. between them, still fighting against them.

The driver asked something, but through the scuffling, Earl B. couldn't understand it.

One of the men in the back muttered, "No, the boss said not to lynch him."

"What do you want?" Earl B. yelled, craning his neck, trying to see the driver's face.

"Just teaching you a little lesson," one of the robed men said.

Someone wrapped a tight blindfold around his head. After several minutes, the car stopped. Yanking Earl B. out of the back seat, the men launched him forward a few feet, then dragged him, stumbling, up several steps. Now, he seemed to be inside a building. They forced him down a flight of stairs and flung him down. He screamed as his shoulder hit the cold, hard floor. A door slammed shut, a key turned in a lock, then it was silent. Earl B. was alone.

Chapter 20

Earl B. managed to stand, then investigated his surroundings. It wasn't easy, considering he was blindfolded and his hands were tied behind his back. The room was small, with hard walls of concrete or cinder block. He tried to push the blindfold off by rubbing it against the wall. It was too tight. This was how Gwen now lived—with bandages over both eyes. Would the rest of her life be like this?

He sat on the cold, hard floor. *Do something.* Earl B. stood again. The first priority was the blindfold. He walked around the room, systematically feeling the walls with his bare arm. The first two seemed smooth throughout. The third wall had something up high, a rougher surface that he bumped up against with his shoulder. Standing on his tiptoes, he rubbed the blindfold against the coarse material, moving it up slightly. Out of one corner, Earl B. could see he was pushing against a high window ledge. He pushed against the ledge again, and the blindfold moved more. Of course, there was no way of getting to the window with his hands tied. Earl B. pushed again until the blindfold was on his forehead.

Now able to see out of both eyes, he surveyed the room. The fourth wall was covered by a pegboard with empty hooks. At one time, the place had probably been a basement workroom, but it was now empty. Could he use the hooks on the pegboard to pull the rope off his wrists? Backing up to the wall, Earl B. forced his hands upward. It didn't catch. He did it again and again, but it was no use. He jumped and it almost caught. Feeling a hook in the small of his back, Earl B. positioned himself, then tried another jump. It caught, and when it did, the searing pain in his shoulder returned.

Ignoring his self-inflicted agony, he yanked downward, trying to loosen the rope. It wouldn't budge. If Earl B. could get one end of the rope loose, perhaps he could pull a hand out. He tried again, but it didn't move. Each effort worsened the soreness in his shoulder. The uncomfortable thought crossed his mind that he might be tightening it, making the situation worse. *Just keep trying.* Earl B. jumped and tugged again. Something happened, but he wasn't sure what. Arching his back, he drew away from the pegboard. The rope came off the hook, but it was now loose, and he pulled his wrists apart. Wriggling his right hand out, Earl B. untied the rope from his other hand and took his blindfold off.

The door was locked. He'd have to use the window, which had a crank opener, but it looked barely large enough for him to squeeze through. A stepladder would be nice right now. So would a tommy gun for that matter, but he didn't have either. Running his fingers over the window ledge, Earl B. felt a ridge on the far side that might give him something to hold onto so he could climb. Not much choice. He'd have to try.

Grasping the ledge, Earl B. pulled himself up. Pain immediately shot through his shoulder, causing him to lose his grip and fall to the floor. He stood up and examined the window again, gathering his nerve. *Come on, it's just a chin-up.* Gripping the ledge again, he braced himself for another bout of agony and pulled up. Turning loose with his right hand, Earl B. grasped the crank opener, which gave him more leverage. He pulled himself up farther. With any luck, the crank would support his body weight. He threw one knee up on the ledge, then the other. Balancing himself, he turned the crank. The window was barely above ground.

First order of business—make sure no one was guarding the window. Scanning his surroundings, Earl B. saw a backyard with a swing set and several trees. No people. He got one leg through, then the second, and finally squeezed his body through. Straight ahead was another backyard, probably on another street. That's the direction he went, stopping every few feet to make sure no one was watching.

Earl B. didn't recognize the street names. Definitely a white neighborhood. He needed to get out. Soon. Winding his way through the streets, he came to a main thoroughfare. Now, there were plenty of pedestrians and heavy traffic.

Up ahead was a bus stop. Earl B. stood there and waited, wondering where on earth he was. After about twenty minutes, a black man in overalls approached him. *My lucky day.*

The next moment, the man was giving him directions to his high school. But by the time Earl B. got there, he had missed his algebra test.

* * * * *

The following morning, Earl B. headed to study hall, with a note in his hand requesting to be excused to meet with Mr. Miller. Down the hallway, Carl Washington sauntered, as if he didn't have a care in the world, walking hand in hand with Shirley. Earl B. slowed his pace as he approached his classroom and watched them. Carl leaned close to her, whispering something in her ear. She looked up at him and smiled. Inside, Earl B. felt empty and hollow. Was it too much to ask, just to have one person around who cared? He didn't even have a best friend anymore, now that Asa had moved away.

After being excused from study hall, Earl B. headed toward Mr. Miller's room with his insides fluttering, anticipating his algebra teacher's reaction. Pausing at the doorway, he heard two male voices in quiet conversation. Earl B. hesitated, wondering if he shouldn't interrupt, but finally knocked since Mr. Miller was expecting him.

"Come in," a voice said.

Earl B. stepped inside. Two men stared at him, the ones who had the power to give him a second chance—Mr. Miller and Coach Richards.

"Have a seat." His algebra teacher, who sounded tired, gestured to an empty wooden chair. Settled behind his desk, he removed his glasses and wiped his face with his hand.

Coach Richards paced back and forth, along the side of the office, as Earl B. sat down and waited.

"Now," Mr. Miller began, laying his reading glasses aside. "Could you please tell both of us why you missed the test."

With his insides still quivering, Earl B. told them how he had been kidnapped. Coach Richards quit pacing. Both men listened to the entire story without interrupting. Afterward, a thick silence blanketed the air. Mr. Miller put his reading glasses back on. Coach Richards paced again. Earl B.'s eyes wandered and noticed the picture was still on Mr. Miller's desk, the one showing his intact family.

Finally, the algebra teacher spoke. "That," he said, looking at Earl B. over the top of his glasses, "is one of the most inane, fantastic stories I've ever heard in my sixteen years of teaching."

"What?" Earl B.'s voice cracked. He noticed Coach Richards had quit pacing again. "You don't believe me? Every word is true, I'm telling you."

"You could have saved time by just saying the dog ate your homework."

"I don't have a dog." A warning went off inside Earl B.'s head that either his volume or tone had reached a level where it could hurt his case, but he ignored it.

"That kind of mouthing off will get you nowhere."

"I'm telling the truth!"

"Earl B.," Mr. Miller said, emphatically, "how have you managed—consistently, over and over again—to be in the wrong place at the wrong time? I was willing to give you the benefit of the doubt when you missed school because of that last saga, how somebody beat you and left you on the side of the road—"

"You can ask my doctor about that," Earl B. interrupted. "He said I'm lucky to be alive." Actually his grandmother had said that.

Mr. Miller glanced toward Coach Richards but came short of making eye contact. "Did you notify the police of this latest incident?"

Earl B. couldn't believe what he was hearing. "No."

"We're supposed to accept an absurd excuse like that when you didn't even report it?"

"Excuse me, *sir*. But are you talking about the Birmingham police?" He snorted. "Yeah, they were a lot of help when my house was bombed."

Mr. Miller's eyes told Earl B. that he caught the sarcasm. But the teacher shook his head. "I'm sorry. You're out of luck. It's not fair to the other students. You weren't here for the test. The grade stands as a zero."

"This is unfair," Earl B. said, his voice rising.

Mr. Miller raised his eyebrows, then turned his head. "What do you think, Coach? Am I being unfair?"

"Absolutely not," Coach said. "You've given this boy every opportunity. He's squandered it. From what you've told me, he was still turning in his homework late half the time."

"I was making Fs at the beginning of the semester. I've tried—"

"Trying doesn't get you anywhere in life, Peterson," the coach replied. "You got to win the game." His gaze shifted to Mr. Miller. "To tell you the truth, Hubert, I don't think he's college material. A&M knows about his trouble. They've already said they're willing to give it to Washington since he's doing much better in classes right now. That boy knows not to fool around when grades are on the line."

Steam rose up inside Earl B. "This is what you had in mind all along. You wanted him to get the scholarship. You lied to me!" he shouted, springing from his chair. Not wanting to hear more, Earl B. grabbed Mr. Miller's family picture and flung it across the room, where it shattered with a crash, then he stomped out of the office.

"Get back in here!" Coach Richards bellowed.

But Earl B. didn't stop. He dashed down the hall, out the door of the school, then turned at the corner and crossed the intersection. Two pedestrians stepped aside as they saw him barreling down the street with his hands balled into fists. At Sixth Avenue, he turned west. Earl B. forced himself to calm down and slow his pace. He entered Titusville but didn't turn to go back home. Instead, he continued on the main drag, passing the meat and fish market and Zenith Cleaners. His thoughts drifted back to Carl Washington. Until this year, Earl B. had been making better grades than the quarterback. Everyone knew Carl was just skating through school and didn't deserve that scholarship. The images of him with Shirley replayed in Earl B.'s mind—at the dance last month and in the hallway earlier today holding hands. It occurred to him that

Shirley could be tutoring him as well. More resentment bubbled up inside.

Approaching High Point, Earl B. slowed even more. Playing ball was often his refuge, something he used to work off steam. Ray's guys were the only ones who saw things as they really were. The high ideals of Shirley's crowd weren't useful when the rubber hit the road.

But the place was deserted. It was a school day, after all. Sitting on the curb, Earl B. rested his elbows on his knees. He stayed there for a long time, reviewing what had happened, mulling it over until it made his head reel. Heavy fatigue hit him. Making himself get up, Earl B. shuffled home, with his hands in his pockets. Grammaw wasn't there—probably at work.

Out of habit, he picked up the phone to call Asa, then remembered his friend was gone. As soon as he hung up, it rang. Earl B. hesitated, wondering if it was the Klansman calling to harass him again. But what if it was his grandmother, needing to talk to him? Earl B. picked it up but didn't say hello.

"Esther?" a voice said. It was a man, asking for Grammaw. "Esther? Earl B.?"

Now he recognized the voice—Big Ben.

"Anybody there?"

Not in the mood to talk to him, Earl B. gently pushed down on the button to hang up the phone. His uncle was probably calling about what had happened at school earlier—news like that traveled fast among teachers. Earl B. replaced the receiver and went to his room. He collapsed on his bed, with his shoes still on, and rubbed his sore shoulder.

Now, Earl B. had lost football, which was bad enough. But after losing his father, his mother, and his best friend, it made it a thousand times worse. It was as if someone had it in for him.

* * * * *

Lying in bed that night, Earl B. had the radio on. "Little Eva, doing her 'Loco-motion' thang!" the deejay shouted. "Shelley the

Playboy, the mouth of the South, on WENN! Keep it right here, 'cause next up is Esther Phillips!" It went to a commercial.

Shelley the Playboy was way too peppy and happy for Earl B. right now. He played with the radio dial, turning it slowly. Lots of talking. No music. Easing the dial back and forth, he searched for his favorite—the Chicago station. But all he heard was something that sounded like a speech. Earl B. kept it there. Not that he was interested in speeches, but just in case it was the Chicago station and they would go to music soon. The man sounded black, and his words caught Earl B.'s attention. He was talking about the race problem in the country.

The station didn't switch to music, but Earl B. kept listening. It wasn't just the fervor in the man's voice that made him sit up, it was also what the man said. The speaker believed there were two types of Negroes, the house Negro and the field Negro. The house Negro was an Uncle Tom, ashamed of being black, and he wanted to be white. He wanted to work with the white man and eat in his restaurants. But the field Negro didn't want that. He wanted to own land. He wanted to own the restaurant.

Earl B. was entranced. Nobody had made him feel proud to be black before. The man's words struck a chord deep inside him. This guy's ideas made sense. The new Negro didn't feel inferior. He should be respected as a human being, no matter what color he was. The new Negro didn't believe in turning the other cheek. If attacked, he retaliated.

After the speech ended, Earl B. learned the man had been Malcolm X.

* * * * *

The next day was Saturday and Earl B. planned to spend his time at High Point, shooting some hoops. But first, he had to call off tomorrow's study session with Shirley. Picking up the phone, he dialed her number and waited as it rang. How was he going to word this? A woman answered.

"Can I speak with Shirley, please?"

"Just a minute—she's getting ready to walk out the door." Then a shout: "Shirley!" A muffled whisper: "I think it's Carl."

"Hello?"

"Shirley? This is Earl B."

"Oh, hi." Was there disappointment in her voice? He couldn't tell.

"Listen. About our meeting tomorrow. I won't be able to make it."

"Oh? When do you want to meet?"

He ran his fingers up and down the telephone cord. "I don't need . . . there's no use in us meeting anymore."

"What do you mean? Did something happen?"

Earl B. opened his mouth to talk but nothing came out.

"You still there?"

He forced the words out. "I'm not going to college."

"Does this have to do with the test?"

"It's a long story."

"I'm listening."

He leaned against the wall and heaved a sigh. "I'm not in a talking mood."

"You're still in algebra class, right?"

"Yeah."

"How about we still meet after school on Monday? We can just talk if you don't want to study."

"I don't know."

"How about the school bleachers?"

"I really don't—"

"No homework, I promise." He heard a smile in her voice.

"Okay."

* * * * *

"Wonder what whitey's doing in this neighborhood," Ray mumbled, dribbling the basketball.

Earl B. followed his gaze. A white man in a fedora left Brother Jack's Barbeque and climbed into a car.

"Probably lost," Rex said, grabbing the ball and heading toward the basket.

"Might be Klan," Earl B. muttered, as the white man drove away. "Sizing up the place." He saw Klan everywhere now.

Huey got the rebound and passed the ball to Earl B.

"Ooh, fellows," Ray said. "Do you see what I see?"

They all looked. At Brother Jack's, a girl had just gotten out of a Chevy Nomad. A girl Earl B. recognized—Shirley Dupree.

Ray took a few steps closer to Brother Jack's. "That is one hot mama."

"There's a white girl driving the car," Rex said. "She ain't bad looking either."

Cradling the ball, Earl B. came up behind Ray and Rex. The driver was Rachel, the white woman who worked at the ARC office. "Don't bother her, man," he said. "She's a friend of mine."

"Friends of yours?" Ray said, as Shirley went inside the restaurant. "The white girl too?"

Earl B. worked out possible answers in his mind. Any response could make the situation worse.

Ray walked closer to Brother Jack's and gestured for Earl B. to follow. "Come on, man. Introduce me to them girls. It ain't fair, keeping all the good ones to yourself."

Shirley came out of the restaurant and got in the car.

"Look at that chick move," Ray said, watching her.

The Nomad pulled away, and the boys returned to the goal. Earl B. shot the ball and missed. Rex got the rebound.

"So Mr. Football Superstar is friends with a white girl," Ray said, whistling. "Tell me what she's doing anyway, driving around with that good-looking sista."

Earl B. felt his muscles tighten. "Working in the movement," he said, before he could stop himself.

"The movement," Ray said mockingly. He glanced at Rex and Huey and chuckled. "Listen to the man here. The movement, huh? The only movement them people know about is a bowel movement."

Rex and Huey took his cue and laughed.

"So you really know them girls, do ya?" Ray said, staring at Earl B. "Is that why you don't want me messing with 'em?"

Earl B. ignored him.

Rex passed the ball to Ray, who held it against his chest, then spoke again. "Well, tell me this. What're they doing riding around together, going to places like Brother Jack's?"

"Ain't none of my business." Earl B. swiped at the ball but missed.

Ray made a pass to Rex. "Well, lemme tell ya, that sista, she's real fine. What's her name, anyway?"

Earl B. felt his face getting warm. He didn't like the way Ray was talking about Shirley.

"Is she your girlfriend?" Ray asked with a mocking tone.

Still not answering, Earl B. stole the ball from Rex and did a layup.

After snatching the rebound, Ray absent-mindedly dribbled the ball. "Hey, man, wasn't your house bombed last fall?"

"Yep," Earl B. answered, wondering where this was leading.

Ray stopped and secured the ball in his arms. "Don't you ever wanna get revenge on them crackers, man?"

"Never thought about it," Earl B. said sarcastically.

Rex and Huey gathered around them.

"You ought to bomb some whitey's house." Ray shifted the ball to his side, holding it against one hip.

Earl B. swallowed.

"Or better yet," Ray continued, "we could break in and steal a few of their prized possessions. Then we'd get something out of it besides revenge."

"Like a TV," Huey added.

Rex laughed. "How about Bull Connor's place?"

Huey guffawed. "Bull Connor. Sure, we'll run over there right now."

Ray dribbled the ball. "Come on, I'm serious. We need some ideas."

"I know where some rich white people live," Rex offered. "My mama works for 'em. Over near that big fancy country club."

"See how this man operates?" Ray asked, looking at Earl B. and Huey. "Y'all could learn a thing or two."

"Actually, I got something better." Rex was now on a roll, trying to toady up to Ray. "The other day, my mama overheard them rich white folk talking about a neighbor of theirs who's in the Klan."

Ray's eyes narrowed. "What's his name?"

"Don't know," said Rex. "But I'll ask. She'll remember. I can find out where he lives."

"All right," Ray said, passing the ball to Rex. "You're my man."

Rex made a jump shot and Ray got the rebound.

"We could even have a go at one of their daughters," Ray added, smirking.

"Count me in for that." Rex laughed.

"You guys are asking to be lynched." Earl B. remembered the murdered and mutilated body of Emmett Till, the fourteen-year-old boy who had supposedly flirted with a white woman in Mississippi. Every black person in America had seen it since the picture of the open casket had been in *Jet* magazine.

Ray dribbled the ball a few times, then stopped. "Listen to Mr. Superstar here. They tell me you're going to college on a football scholarship," he said with a mocking tone. "You think you're better than everybody else, don't you? Are you too good to help us get a little revenge? Or maybe you're afraid?"

Earl B. met his gaze. "I'm not afraid," he said, reaching for the ball.

"That's what I want to hear." Ray twisted around, holding the ball away from him. "We'll help you. Won't we?" He looked around at the others.

"Sure," Rex said.

Huey reluctantly nodded.

Ray put his arm on Earl B.'s shoulder. "Won't it make you feel good, getting revenge?"

Earl B. turned away from him. "What'll make me feel good is getting back at the person that did it."

"Don't matter who did it, man," Ray said. "Any whitey'll do."

"And if they ain't done nothing wrong, you can bet their ancestors did." Rex grabbed the ball and charged toward the basket.

Earl B. went in for the rebound, then headed toward mid-court.

Ray approached him, reaching for the ball. Earl B. stopped dribbling and held the ball above his head.

"Come on, Earl B.," Ray said. "Or don't you hold with the idea they're all blue-eyed devils, like Malcolm X says?"

"He doesn't say it's okay to attack any white person," Earl B. countered.

"Oh, so now you're an expert on Malcolm X," Ray said. "A month ago, you hadn't even heard of him." He made an unsuccessful swipe at the ball. "And he does say it's okay to retaliate."

"*If* you're attacked."

"Oh, so a bombing isn't an attack? I think you're chicken."

"I'm not chicken," Earl B. said, slipping past Ray and going in for a layup.

"Then let's do it," Ray said, grabbing the rebound. He stopped and held the ball, facing Earl B. "Okay?"

"You find the guy that blew up my house, and I'm in on it." Earl B. didn't say he might have already found him.

Chapter 21

Monday after school, Shirley was waiting for Earl B. on the bleachers, while the band practiced on the field. He sat down next to her and avoided eye contact.

"So what happened?" she asked, when he didn't speak.

Earl B. told her about being kidnapped and about his meeting with Mr. Miller and Coach Richards. Sometime during the lengthy explanation, he became aware of how the abduction sounded like a tall tale.

To her credit, Shirley didn't interrupt, and afterward, she took her time responding. "These white guys who kidnapped you. Had you—or your friends—done something to them?"

"What do you mean by that?"

"Did it have anything to do with that Cunningham gang you've been hanging out with?"

Earl B. was left with his mouth open. So she had seen them at High Point. "No," he said, shaking his head in disbelief. "It didn't have anything to do with them."

"No wonder you've had trouble with your grades. You're too busy hanging out with thugs."

"Too busy? You're the one who talks about that." He mocked her voice. "*I'm busy. I've made it my policy not to go out.* I noticed you weren't too busy when Carl Washington asked you."

"Don't change the subject."

"You're the one—"

"Hanging out with those hoodlums'll get you in big trouble."

"I said this has nothing to do with them."

Shirley's face still showed disbelief. "So you're telling me . . ." She drew out the words and paused for effect. "These Klansmen came and kidnapped you for no reason at all. And it happened to be on the day of your most important math test."

"You don't have to believe me," he said, with resignation. "I don't care anymore."

"Did you ever care?"

"Care if I got a football scholarship?" He gave her a stony gaze. "Yes. For your information, I *did* care."

"You have to admit it's a pretty fantastic tale."

"I'm telling you, it happened."

"And you've never seen them before."

Earl B. studied his hands, suddenly concerned about some dirt underneath a fingernail. "I've seen one before." He looked at her. "*You've* seen one before."

"Me?"

"The guy that followed you."

"I get the feeling you're not telling me everything."

On the field, band members practiced drill formations. "Okay," he finally said. "I warned you, it's a long story." Pulling out his handwritten copy of the bombing addresses, Earl B. explained about finding the paper at the mass meeting.

"Wait a minute," she interrupted. "Is this the list you told me a friend of yours found?"

"Yeah. Except I found it," he admitted.

She gave him a look of disapproval but listened as he continued.

"On the first of March, a church in the north part of town, High Praises Community Church, was bombed." Earl B. pointed to the first listing. "It's on this street, but not at that number."

Shirley's eyes widened. "My aunt almost got her leg blown off in that bombing."

"Mrs. Smiley."

Her brow furrowed into a question. "How did you know that?"

"Asa was my best friend." His words sounded hollow.

"Oh."

Earl B. pointed to the second address. "My house is on this street, but not at that number." He showed her the fourth listing. "There was a bombing on that street, near Miles College, but not at that number." His finger moved to another address. "The ARC office is on this street but not at that number. And Bethel Baptist," he pointed to the next one. "It was bombed in December. It's on this street—"

"But not at that number," they both said in unison.

"Oh, my," she said. Her combative attitude had vanished.

"Right."

"It's a list of bombing sites."

"Right."

"And it's encoded."

"Exactly."

"And this one?" She pointed to Jefferson Avenue Southwest.

"Yeah, that one." Earl B. gathered his thoughts and told her the rest of the story, about the time he was egged near Bethel Baptist. About Four Fingers and the black Pontiac. He told her how the preachers wouldn't listen and how some rednecks assaulted him in the country, putting a gash on the side of his face. He showed her his handwritten list of possible bombing sites on Jefferson Avenue.

"So that one's still to happen," she said.

"I think so."

"And this one? Fourth Court North?"

"I don't know. I haven't had a chance to look on that street."

"So it's either already happened and we don't know about it, or it's still to happen."

He nodded. "It's not too far from my neighborhood. I should be able to go there soon."

"Are you crazy? You've been incredibly lucky so far. These guys are Klan. You could get lynched."

"But five of the seven places on this list have already been bombed," Earl B. said, his voice rising. "I've got to get my hands on this guy."

"No." Shirley's tone was emphatic. "This thing has gotten out of hand. Gwen was right. It's eating at you. You've got to quit."

"So you're willing to sit by and watch while people get injured. Or killed."

"I didn't say that. We should focus on decoding it so we can warn people."

"Well, that's worked real well so far, hasn't it? I've told preachers about it, and they don't care. Meanwhile, people are getting hurt. Going blind."

She flinched at his words, then pulled out a pencil and sheet of paper. "Let me work on it. If I can figure out how it's encoded, maybe they'll listen."

Earl B. rubbed his temples while she copied the list. The endless drumming of the band was giving him a headache.

Shirley finished and stared at the paper, chewing on the end of her pencil. "We're missing the bombing dates and address numbers. Those are what we need. What's your address?"

He told her, and she jotted it down. But he didn't have the information for the others.

She handed the original sheet back to him. "You know any dates? Like this Miles College thing?"

Earl B. shook his head. "No, I saw it in the newspaper but didn't write it down."

"And your house?"

"November 17. I know that one by heart."

"I know the ARC office date," she said, writing. "They aren't listed in chronological order."

"No."

"We need the date for Bethel Baptist."

"I don't know that one. I guess we could go to the church and ask."

"We could. Our library won't have all this information. Or I could go to the *World* office," she said, referring to the town's black newspaper. "They might have all the dates." Shirley studied the list, then tried out one mathematical equation after another, filling up the page with algebra. Then she seemed to come to a roadblock and a visible shiver ran through her. Earl B. wasn't sure if it was the chill in the air or the bombing list.

"Well," she said, looking at her watch. "If I'm catching the bus, I better go."

They packed up, walked to the bus stop, and sat on the bench. While waiting, Shirley pulled out her copy of the list and studied it again. Then she handed it to Earl B. "Take this for a minute."

He did.

"See if I'm right," she said, closing her eyes, "59, 341, 109, 30, 81, 130, and 384."

"You missed two," Earl B. said, handing her the paper.

"Darn!" she said, studying the list again.

"Shirley . . ."

Still focusing on the paper, she seemed to be ignoring him. Finally, his voice registered, and she looked up. "What?"

"This isn't a game."

Chapter 22

After his meeting on the bleachers with Shirley, Earl B. had ridden the bus and gotten off at his usual stop. Evening was approaching—the between time, neither daylight nor dark. He went past Franklin's on the corner, where Big Booty Judy fried the best chicken wings in Birmingham. She used to throw in an extra wing at no charge for his mother, just because they were friends. Earl B. hadn't been there since Mama had died.

Heading into his neighborhood, his mind shifted to his last conversation with Shirley. No matter what she thought, he was still going to search on Fourth Court North, the last bombing site on the list.

Up ahead was Dixson's Grocery, a little mom-and-pop store. Passing by, he glanced in the window and saw something that made him stop—the reflection of a man on the opposite side of the street. A bald man, who immediately ducked behind a car. Earl B. was being followed.

He increased his pace, keeping his eye on the window. After passing the store, Earl B. turned his head to one side, using his peripheral vision to watch. His body was revved up, as if he'd drunk too much caffeine. Home was still two blocks away. If he could make it, the new deadbolt would give him some protection.

Not paying attention to the sidewalk, Earl B. accidentally plunged his foot into a deep puddle. Water seeped through the soles of his shoes. One more block. His heart made some weird thump-a-dump drum beat that he felt all the way up to his throat, making him cough. Turning his head slightly, he saw some motion on the opposite sidewalk. Earl B. spun around and stopped. Nobody. He continued to walk, increasing his pace, with his key in hand, at the ready.

Finally arriving at his house, he took the stairs two at a time, then whipped around but saw no one. Earl B. unlocked the door, ducked inside, and turned the deadbolt. Without turning on the light, he gazed out the front window, using the curtain as a shield. All was quiet under the feeble, yellow glow of the streetlight. Nothing unusual. His hand almost hit the light switch when Four Fingers appeared out of nowhere and headed away from his house. Earl B. watched him leave, wondering where he was going, then decided to find out.

Slipping outside again, Earl B. locked the door and followed the man, keeping a safe distance between them. Excitement built inside him. Four Fingers might be leading him to his home or meeting place. How did he make a living, this man who spent so much time pursuing people? An occasional car passed by, but the neighborhood sidewalks were devoid of other people at this hour. A strange feeling of satisfaction settled in Earl B.'s chest as he realized that, for a change, Four Fingers was the one being shadowed.

Before long, they were going down a main thoroughfare, with plenty of businesses, cars, and other pedestrians. The man never turned to look behind. Not once.

Four Fingers made several doglegs, winding through the streets near downtown. Climbing a hill, he turned onto a residential street, then slowed his pace. A woman came out of a small apartment building just ahead of him. And not just any woman—Rachel Cohen. Earl B. eased sideways, hiding between two apartment buildings on the opposite side of the street, and watched. Four Fingers stopped and said something to her. She answered, gesturing forward with her hand. After another exchange, she got into a Chevy Nomad and drove off.

Crossing the street, Four Fingers opened the door of a black Pontiac. *The* black Pontiac. As the Klansman pulled out and drove up the street, Earl B. emerged and took off running, trying to keep Four Fingers in sight. Finally, he lost track of the Pontiac and headed back home, mulling over everything that had just happened. But try as he might, Earl B. couldn't think of a justifiable reason for Rachel to be talking to a Klansman.

Chapter 23

Earl B. shoved his tray toward the lunchroom worker, then headed back toward his seat. Soon, the bell would ring, and there would be a chaotic mass exodus of students from the cafeteria.

"Hey there," a deep voice said. Earl B. turned and saw Big Ben. "How're you holding up?"

A guy at a nearby table, known for being the class clown, said something in a phony British accent and a chorus of laughter erupted. Staring at his uncle, Earl B. felt his throat tighten, making it difficult to answer.

Big Ben put an arm around him and guided him toward the side of the cafeteria, away from other students. The look on his face made it clear—he knew all about the scholarship. "I do think you should keep up the tutoring. You need as good a grade as you can get in that class. I've already talked to Shirley, and she's willing to continue."

Didn't bother asking me, Earl B. thought. But he didn't say anything.

"Look, I talked to both teachers," Big Ben said. "I tried to intercede. But quite frankly, I've run out of political clout. Especially after the way you behaved."

Earl B. stared at his uncle's shoes, a pair of ancient, two-toned wingtips, probably from the 1930s.

Big Ben continued. "They were willing to give you a second chance after some tutoring. And a third chance after that odyssey out on Jefferson Avenue. But after—"

"That really happened." Earl B. glared at him.

The bell rang and chairs grated against the floor as students rose to leave.

His uncle shrugged. "Maybe it did."

Earl B.'s voice rose. "I'm telling you—"

"Tell me something," Big Ben said crisply. "Why were you out on Jefferson Avenue in the first place?"

The other kids chattered as they formed a bottleneck at the lunchroom door. Earl B.'s mouth became rigid. He couldn't exactly tell him the reason, and Big Ben seemed to know when he wasn't telling the truth.

"The Klan bombs your house." Big Ben was counting off with his fingers. "The Klan attacks you out on Jefferson Avenue. The Klan kidnaps you at the bus stop. Are you going to tell me what's going on here?"

"Are you saying it's my fault they bombed my house?"

"Not at all. But something's been happening ever since. Somebody's keeping this thing going. Are you going to tell me about it?" Big Ben raised his hands to his upper chest with both thumbs extended. It was a gesture familiar to Earl B., one he'd seen many times before—when his uncle would hook his thumbs into the straps of his overalls. Except he was at school and not wearing them, so his thumbs came up empty. "You aren't doing something foolish like chasing after them, are you?"

Earl B.'s lips were clenched tightly together. He wasn't going to answer that. The commotion in the lunchroom had subsided, and only a few stragglers remained.

His uncle sighed. "Listen, son. There are people in this world with so much venom inside, they go around destroying things and hurting other folk. One of these days, you'll learn that them people—they ain't worth so much as the leftover scraps in a hog pen."

To his embarrassment, Earl B.'s eyes welled up, either from anger or from sadness, he wasn't sure. Leaning against the wall, he covered his face with his hand.

"They ain't worth it, son." Big Ben's voice was soft, barely above a whisper. "Just let 'em go."

* * * * *

Earl B. hardly ever got any mail—maybe one thing a year. Okay, well, he'd gotten more during the past few months because of colleges. But it wasn't enough to make him go through the stack he carried inside from the mailbox. He always left it on the kitchen table for his grandmother to deal with.

But this particular afternoon was different. He brought the stack of mail inside as always, and after throwing it on the table, he noticed his name on the top envelope and tore it open. Inside was a single sheet of paper with glued letters, spelling the message: *Search again and hang under the iron man.*

The envelope had no return address, and it was postmarked, *Birmingham.* A lot of help that was. Taking off his jacket, Earl B. hurled it into a chair and paced back and forth a few times in the kitchen. He lifted the towel off the breadbasket. No biscuits.

"Nobody's gonna tell me what I can and can't do," Earl B. muttered. Then he remembered saying almost the same thing to the mysterious phone caller. *You'll be sorry you said that,* the man had said. Afterward, Earl B. had been kidnapped on test day.

Hearing a key in the front door, he refolded the paper and slipped it into the envelope.

The door opened and Grammaw came in. "Hey, baby."

Earl B. slipped the envelope into his pocket folder, then opened his algebra book to a random page. "Hey."

She closed the door and shuffled through the front room. "Can't wait to get these shoes off. I tell you, them church people are some of the dirtiest folks. They leave such a mess." Grammaw went past him, into her bedroom.

Getting up, Earl B. sifted through the drawer of the buffet, pulled out the Birmingham map, and slipped it into his pocket folder. He needed it to figure out how to get to Fourth Court North.

Grammaw returned with her house shoes on and sorted through the mail. "Bills." Throwing the envelopes aside, she picked up the first section of the newspaper, which Earl B. had ignored, and leafed through it. "Here it is. Page four."

"Here what is?" he asked, pretending to look at his algebra book.

"There was another bombing yesterday. I heard the minister talking on the phone about it." She was reading the article.

"Another bombing?" Earl B. closed his math book and looked up.

"Yeah, a place out on Jefferson Avenue." Grammaw eyeballed him before continuing. "River of Jordan Church. Never heard of it." She closed the paper.

Earl B. didn't have to look that one up. He had gone out of his way to find the minister's home. *Serves him right,* he thought bitterly. The preacher had completely ignored him. "Anybody hurt?"

Grammaw was at the kitchen sink, washing dishes. "Two children," she said. "They were taken to Hillman. These bombings are enough to keep that hospital in business."

Chapter 24

"How did you get so far behind?" Shirley grumbled, turning a page in the algebra book.

Instead of answering, Earl B. sipped his drink. Why was she in such a bad mood?

They were sitting at a table at Brother Jack's, with their dirty dishes pushed to one side. Earl B. had just finished his pig burger and cowboy beans. The study session had been her idea. Brother Jack's had been his.

He did the next problem. And the next. Shirley only spoke when absolutely necessary. A couple of times, she snapped at him for silly mistakes.

After they finished, she pulled out her copy of the list of bombing sites and showed it to him. "I found the details." Next to five items, Shirley had written the name, date, and complete address of the location. Studying each one, Earl B. couldn't find any relationship between the numbers the Klansman had assigned and the information she had found. "I haven't figured it out yet," she said, answering his unasked question.

Pulling out a clean sheet of paper, Earl B. copied down the facts. He'd look at it again later. But if Shirley, the math whiz, couldn't figure it out, he didn't hold out much hope.

"In any other city," she said, "you'd go to the cops with this."

"Any decent city, you mean," he retorted. "Here, they're probably the ones doing it. What I'd really like to do is catch the guy that bombed my house."

"And what would you do then?"

163

"The same thing he did to my mother."

"So you'd kill him," she whispered. "Are you willing to pay the price for murdering a Klansman in Alabama? That's like taking out a Mafia guy in New Jersey. They'll come after you."

"I'll cross that bridge when I come to it."

"You'll get yourself killed."

"Maybe it's worth it."

Shirley's mouth hung open for a moment. "You're crazy."

"Maybe I don't need that list. Four Fingers all but admitted he had done some bombings. If I could get my hands on him—"

"Will you quit saying that? You're gonna get yourself lynched."

"And will you quit saying that?" A few heads turned in the restaurant. He lowered his voice. "I'm tired of these guys running around, killing people."

"Don't you understand? You're doing it for the wrong reason."

"What do you mean, the wrong reason?"

"For revenge," she said. "It's eating at you. Look at you! Either work on this thing to save the next victims or don't do it at all."

"Thanks, but I've tried that. It doesn't work. Nobody listens."

"But they might if we decode it. Then, we'd have specific dates to give them."

"So in the meantime," he said sarcastically, "we let them keep killing people."

"We don't have much choice, do we?"

"Somebody needs to do something. Now."

"Well, what do you propose, Mr. Malcolm X?" she spat, using a forced whisper. "Violence certainly doesn't work."

His mouth gaped open. She knew about Malcolm X? Then he recovered his voice. "Ain't nothing wrong with a black man defending himself. It's better than that nonviolence crap those preachers preach. All that church trash, it's just opium for the masses. Turn the other cheek. I've told you before, that doesn't work."

"But if you go out there and do tit-for-tat, you'll just alienate the decent white people and make things worse for all of us."

Earl B. forced a laugh. "Decent white people. There ain't no such thing. They're a race of devils."

"Oh, yeah?" The veins in her neck were protruding. "Just in case you haven't noticed, the people you call devils are in the majority. If we want to make a difference, we have to change how those people think. You've got to let the decent white people—and there are a few out there—see what's happening to *nonviolent* blacks."

He put his head in his hands.

"Besides," Shirley continued, "there are good people and bad people of all races. Just look at that bunch of no-good hoodlums you hang out with."

"Oh, God," muttered Earl B. "Here we go again."

"Well, it's true," she said.

"Speaking of bad white people," he said, "I followed Four Fingers back to his car the other day."

"You didn't! Sure enough, you're asking to get—"

"Shut up and listen!" he said, louder than he meant.

Shirley didn't respond, but her mouth was set in a hard line.

"I'm sorry I yelled," Earl B. continued. "But will you please just listen for a minute? Four Fingers was parked in the neighborhood where Rachel lives. She came out of an apartment building as he passed by on the sidewalk. They stopped and talked."

Shirley's eyes widened.

"Yeah," he said. "It was like they knew each other."

"Are you sure it was Four Fingers?" she whispered.

"I've had enough dealings with that man. I think I know him by now."

"And you're absolutely sure it was Rachel?"

"Yeah, I'm sure. Besides, she got into that Nomad of hers. The same one I saw you riding in."

Shirley's face had a dead-serious expression on it now. "Well, I'm sure there's a perfectly reasonable explanation."

"What? I can't believe you're saying that!"

"She can't be dealing with the Klan."

Earl B. was getting nowhere, so he let it drop and told her about the warning he had received in the mail.

"The iron man?" she asked. "I don't know what it means, but it doesn't sound like an empty threat."

"I don't care. I'm still going to search on Fourth Court North."

"No!"

"I have to do this, Shirley."

"Please don't."

"How many people are gonna be murdered before we do something about it?"

"You'll be the one who gets killed," she said, her voice cracking.

He answered in a softer tone. "Look, we're just going round and round, saying the same thing over and over. I don't wanna argue."

Her mouth drew into a frown and her eyes welled up.

Earl B. put his hand on her arm. "Shirley," he said, tentatively, "the whole time we were working, it seemed like you were upset. Is something wrong? I mean, something besides me being shiftless and stupid?"

She responded with a laugh, which quickly turned to crying.

"What?" he asked.

Pulling a handkerchief from her purse, she wiped her eyes and blew her nose. "My daddy was fired."

"Fired?" Earl B. didn't know what he had expected to hear, but it wasn't that. "Why?"

"His company found out I was working in the movement."

"How?"

"I don't know."

"I'm sorry."

She dabbed at her eyes. They sat for a few more minutes, then got up and left the restaurant. Approaching the bus stop, Earl B. placed his hand on Shirley's back. "Listen, I've not really said this before, but thanks for all your help."

"You're welcome." She turned her face away and started crying again.

Earl B. leaned over, trying to look her in the eye. "Did I say something wrong?"

She shook her head and wiped her tears. "No, I'm sorry. It's just that I can't figure you out."

"What do you mean?"

"One minute I'm furious with you. But then the next . . ." Her voice trailed off as she gazed at him.

The scent of her perfume filled the air as she stood near. Even with her bloodshot eyes and red nose, he was drawn toward her. Earl B. leaned over, even closer. The urge to kiss her was overwhelming. But he straightened, and with a breath, let the feeling pass.

Chapter 25

School was over, and the halls were crowded with excited teenagers, weaving their way toward the exits. Earl B. took the stairs two at a time, down to the main floor, then turned, heading toward his locker. But what he saw up ahead made him pause—Carl Washington was walking hand in hand with a girl, and it wasn't Shirley. It was one of the cheerleaders. She rested her chin on his shoulder, beaming and talking to him as they strolled along.

Earl B. would have smiled if he hadn't been worried whether Carl was doing it behind Shirley's back. Maybe they had broken up. Stopping at his locker, he threw a couple of books inside, then turned to leave. Coming toward him was Shirley. Had she seen Carl?

Drawing closer, she asked, "Can I talk to you?"

"Sure." He moved toward a corner, away from the hall traffic. "Did you decode the list?"

"No." She took a deep breath. "When are you going to search on Fourth Court North?"

"Friday afternoon, after I get home from school. Why?"

"I wish you'd reconsider this thing. I think it's too—"

"Forget it. I'm not talking about it anymore," he said, walking away.

"Wait!" Shirley ran after him and grabbed his arm. "If you're absolutely determined, you should go directly from here. Ride the bus there. It might throw him off, at least for a little while."

Earl B. turned to face her. "Good idea. By the time he finds out, I'll be done."

She frowned. "But it would be better if you didn't go at all."

"I'm done talking about it." He marched away again.

"Please!" she hollered.

It was hard to ignore her, but he did. And that time, she didn't follow him.

* * * * *

After school on Friday, Earl B. took Shirley's advice. That is, he rode the bus directly from school to Smithfield, where Fourth Court was. The vehicle was crowded. He stood at first, but later found an empty space on the back seat. Taking shallow breaths of the stale, stuffy air, Earl B. braced himself while the bus lurched back and forth. As the blundering buggy approached his stop, its screeching brakes brought the vehicle to a halt.

The fresh, outdoor air was a welcome change. At first, Earl B. wandered through a residential neighborhood. The sun made his neck hot as a frying pan. At the intersection with Fourth Court North, there was nothing but a small corner store. He looked around, uncertain which way to go. A bead of sweat ran down his back as Earl B. stood there, trying to decide.

A cop car approached. Not wanting to look like a vagrant, he walked closer to the store. The grocery window was painted with advertisements—pork roast for thirty-nine cents a pound and cake mixes four for a dollar. After the policeman passed, Earl B. returned to the sidewalk and took a right. A pick-up whirred by, blowing a gust of wind.

Two blocks ahead, a steeple came into view. He picked up his pace and drew closer. Earl B. pulled out his pencil and notebook, ready to write down the name and address. The church was a simple, white clapboard building, with an empty parking lot adjacent to it. There was no evidence it had been bombed. Yet. No gaping holes, no barriers. For a moment, intense memories of his own ravaged home flashed before him—scorching flames, thick dust and smoke, his mother's limp body draped over his arm.

Wrapped up in his thoughts, Earl B. was taken by surprise as a car sped into the church parking lot and skidded to a halt right in front of him. The black Pontiac. His heart lunged into his throat as two men jumped out, each grabbing one of his arms. Earl B. yelled out and pulled against them, trying to wriggle free. He kicked and thrashed about, but it didn't matter. Something rock-hard struck his head, as if he had collided with a freight train. A rush of sparks blazed across his field of vision before fading to complete darkness.

* * * * *

Earl B. had no idea how much time passed before he woke up. At first, sounds seemed to come from far away. The rumbling of a car's engine appeared to come from the other end of a long tunnel. Then he became aware of snippets of conversation, and words like "Red Mountain" and "lynching" caught his attention.

"Take a right here," a nearby raspy voice said.

A familiar voice. Earl B. felt his neck tighten. He was in real trouble. Keeping his eyes closed, he made a conscious effort not to move while taking inventory. Earl B. was lying on his belly in the back seat of a moving car. No broken bones, but his body felt banged up, worse than any Friday night football game. A torn place in the upholstery rubbed against his cheek. His face felt twice its usual size, and the warm stickiness around his mouth told him his lip was bleeding.

"You sure the boss said this was okay?" the voice in the front seat asked.

"Will you quit worrying about that?" Four Fingers responded.

"But he told us not to lynch him."

"Shut up!" After a weighty pause, Four Fingers muttered, "I don't care. I've had enough of this nigger."

Something gripped Earl B. deep inside. They were taking him to hang. His only hope was pretending to be unconscious until he found a way to escape. But what if he never got that chance?

The car hit a pothole, and Earl B. almost rolled off the seat. Keeping his body limp, he let a hand fall to the floor. After two more turns, the car seemed to be creeping uphill.

"Stop right here," Four Fingers ordered.

The driver pulled over and both men got out.

In the moments that followed, Earl B. took some deep breaths and willed the brisk thumping of his heart to slow. The door near his head opened, and one of the men yanked him out of the car.

"Roy," Four Fingers barked. "Get the rope." He dragged Earl B. by the arms across the blacktop and into the grass, scraping his knees and shins across the rough ground.

The trunk of the car slammed shut, and rapid footsteps sounded.

"Still out?" Roy asked as he caught up.

"Out like a light." Four Fingers grunted as he pulled Earl B. along.

Wind rustled through the leaves, birds and squirrels chattered. They were in the woods. Earl B.'s mind raced through the possibilities. He could maybe manage to deal with one of the men. Maybe. But two of them?

"How about this one?" Roy asked.

"The limb ain't high enough," Four Fingers argued.

They trudged along farther through the leaves, with Earl B.'s legs dragging on the ground.

"Is he even alive?" Roy asked.

Four Fingers dumped Earl B. face down onto the damp leaves. "Course he's alive," he snapped, his voice laced with irritation. "He's breathing, ain't he?"

Earl B. let his chest rise and fall with regular, shallow breaths.

"I hit him good and hard, that's all," Four Fingers said with an air of satisfaction.

"Just seems like he'd have woken up by now."

"Probably in a coma."

The wind picked up and something rustled in the leaves close by.

"What was that?" Roy asked.

"Just a squirrel," Four Fingers said. "Give me that rope."

"I gotta piss," Roy said. "I'll be back in a minute."

"You ain't going nowhere," Four Fingers said. "We ain't on no picnic here."

"But I need to piss." Roy's voice was insistent.

"Do it here."

"What?"

"Right here." Four Fingers's voice was booming right over him.

Earl B. heard the sound of a zipper, then felt the warm stream of fluid run over his body, seeping into his clothes. As the pungent smell of urine assaulted his nose, anger swelled inside him. If it was the last thing he did, he was determined to make life miserable for these two animals.

After Roy finished, Earl B. took a chance and opened his eyes slightly. What he saw unnerved him. Four Fingers was fashioning a loop for a noose, his hands surprisingly nimble even with his missing finger. When it was done, he pitched it to Roy. "Now, make yourself useful and stay with him so I can look for a good tree." His footsteps faded away.

While waiting, Roy, who was whistling an unrecognizable tune, tried throwing the rope over a limb. Could Earl B. overtake this guy? It might be his only chance. In his weakened condition, Earl B. had only one thing going for him—the element of surprise. A tremor coursed through him. However, Roy didn't see it because he was too busy making one unsuccessful attempt after another with the rope. More precious seconds ticked by. It was now or never. The next time Roy threw the rope, Earl B. shot up, ignoring the painful protests of his sore body, and lunged at the man.

Roy shouted, as Earl B. tackled him to the ground and drew back to deliver a blow. But the man caught his hand in midair and threw him off balance. The two rolled over, and Earl B. was now underneath Roy with his hands pinned to the dirt.

In the distance, Four Fingers hollered, aware something had gone wrong. Earl B.'s time was running out. Mustering all his power, he shoved his knee up into Roy's crotch. It didn't completely disable him, but the maneuver bought enough time to free Earl B.'s hands from the man's grip. With a heavy grunt, he grabbed Roy's shoulder and pushed, propelling them into a somersault. Earl B. landed on top, hopped up, and took a swing while Roy tried to stand. It hit the mark, landing squarely on the man's jaw. Roy's face went blank, and he collapsed like a rag doll. Four Fingers came running into the clearing.

Earl B. whirled around and bolted away. With the momentum of a train engine, Four Fingers caught up, grabbing his body and right arm from behind. The two strained against each other, neither one able to gain control. Four Fingers turned loose, drew his right arm back, and swung. The same instant, Earl B. rammed his palm into the man's right shoulder, sending the punch wide. Stepping forward, he locked one hand under Four Fingers's arm and the other hand on the back of his neck. Earl B. shifted to the side and yanked downward on his head, throwing him off balance, then with a bellow, smashed his knee upward into the man's face.

Four Fingers shrieked in pain and fell to the ground. The ruckus had awakened Roy, who was raising himself up on his elbow. Earl B. made a break for it, running through the woods, with no sense of direction, going downhill, scampering over logs and rocks. Shouts rang out behind him. As Earl B. swerved to avoid a tree, he glanced around and saw the two men pursuing him. Fresh adrenaline surged through his body. A crow took off from a nearby limb, its caws adding to the commotion. Twigs slapped against his face. He splashed through a creek bed and barreled diagonally up the next hill. A squirrel zigzagged in front of him, then scampered up a tree trunk. The racket and footfall behind told him the two weren't far away. Gasping for breath, Earl B. reached the pinnacle and started downhill again. The men were still hot on his trail, as he careened off a tree and veered off in another direction. Aiming for another stream, Earl B. reached the bottom at breakneck pace, vaulted over to the other side, and charged up again. One of the men let out a yelp. Glancing back, he saw Four Fingers sprawled out in the water, with Roy hovering over him.

Earl B. kept going, his sides heaving, but knowing he needed more distance between him and the two men. He reached another ridge and started downhill, now at a jog. Something out of the corner of his eye caught his attention. It appeared to be a collection of concrete rubble. He walked closer and examined it. Amidst the chunks of concrete was a hole in the ground. It was almost covered completely, but the opening was still there, and it might be big enough for him to fit through. People always talked about the old iron ore mines around Birmingham, but he'd never seen one before. The voices of

Four Fingers and Roy came from the other side of the ridge. Earl B. stuck one leg inside the hole. His foot hit solid earth. He stuck the other leg in and squeezed through the opening. The ground slanted downward, but Earl B. was able to stoop near the door of the abandoned mine shaft.

What he saw was utter darkness. What he smelled was the stench of Roy's urine, still damp on his clothes. The humiliation of what had happened descended upon him. His jaw tightened. He rammed one fist into the other palm.

Voices sounded outside, then leaves rustled. Earl B.'s mouth went dry. Surely, they could hear his heart hammering. But the men passed by without stopping. For a while, they seemed to be gone, then they returned.

"I know I saw him up here." It was Four Fingers's raspy voice, perhaps twenty yards away.

The men's voices faded, and the birds and squirrels started their chitchat. Earl B. gave it more time. Twenty minutes. Thirty even. The foul odor of urine overwhelmed him, choked him. Still no sign of them.

He stuck his head out of the hole to make sure, but saw nobody. Quietly, Earl B. eased himself outside into the dappled sunlight, and after a quick glance around, he trudged through the woods, continuing in the same direction he had been going previously. At the bottom of the hill was yet another creek. After splashing water on his face, he followed it downstream, wading through the underbrush. The tiny, young leaves provided a canopy of every shade of green. Up ahead, the creek meandered through a field before it dived back into the woods again. When Earl B. reached the clearing, he turned and looked around. In the distance was a mountain with a statue perched on top—the Vulcan statue, made out of cast iron and named after the Roman god of fire. It was a major landmark, watching over the city like a sentinel.

Search again and hang under the iron man. The words of the note Earl B. had received in the mail came back to him. Of course. Now it all made sense. He let out a long, slow breath. If things hadn't gone his way, he'd be hanging from a tree by now. Earl B. took another look at the Vulcan statue. The front of it faced the city. Now, he had his bearings.

Hiking beside the creek, he kept going. Finally, a road came into view. Earl B. knew better than to walk on the blacktop, choosing instead to tromp alongside it in the woods, hopping over logs and rocks.

Up ahead, a car approached. Without thinking, Earl B. hit the ground and froze. The vehicle drew near, and his heart tumbled as he saw it—the black Pontiac. It was barely moving, maybe actually slowing down. Had they seen him? He swallowed, then wondered if they could perhaps see the tiny movement of his throat muscles. A tree trunk partially blocked his view. He heard their voices but couldn't tell what they were saying. The car almost came to a full stop, then crept along a little farther. Finally, it accelerated uphill.

Earl B. let out a breath he didn't know he was holding. With his heart already racing, he shot up and ran through the woods, prodded by the knowledge they were scouting the area for him. The Vulcan man was no longer visible, but the road was now his guide, leading down Red Mountain into town.

From behind, another car approached. He hit the ground again and hid beside a fallen log. By the vehicle's slow speed, Earl B. suspected it was the Pontiac again, still searching. After it passed, his suspicions were confirmed when he saw it heading downhill.

Standing again, Earl B. scampered onward. The woods ended, and the road led to a residential neighborhood with winding streets. The Vulcan statue was nowhere in sight. Earl B. was hopelessly lost. He jogged along, turning left, then right, then left, then right again. Up ahead was a sign: Dead End. Was that a bad omen?

Turning around, Earl B. wandered on and finally came to a numbered street, which gave him a better sense of direction. He cut through people's yards, avoiding sidewalks, still afraid that every passing car would be the Pontiac. It was now dusk, with only a fingernail moon on the horizon, which made hiding easier. He grew especially wary entering his own neighborhood. The men might be waiting for him. Taking the long way around, Earl B. passed through someone else's property to the back door of his house. By now it was dark. His key at the ready, he slipped inside, closed the door, and secured the lock.

Grammaw was probably working and wouldn't be back until late. Without turning on any lights, Earl B. made his way to the front room window. Barely moving the curtain aside, he peered through the tiny slit. Across the street, the Pontiac was parked next to the curb. Two figures sat in the front seat. An involuntary shudder traveled through his body.

In the darkness, Earl B. made his way to the bathroom, stripped off his clothes, and took a shower. It took two good lathers with strong lye soap before his skin felt clean again. The warm water eased the aching in his muscles, but it didn't do much for the jittery nerves caused by that car parked outside his house. After putting on some clean clothes, he returned to the front room and peeked outside again. Tension oozed out of his body. The Pontiac was gone.

Chapter 26

"Look what the cat dragged in," Ray said, as Earl B. approached High Top the next day. "What in the hell happened to you?"

"Nothing," Earl B. muttered. He didn't feel like talking to Ray about it. Or anybody, for that matter. It was Saturday. Grammaw had gotten home late from the hospital last night, then left for work at the church that morning, so he'd managed to avoid her so far.

"Nothing, my ass," Ray said. "You look like you got trapped in a hornet's nest."

Rex stood nearby, dribbling the ball.

"Just a fight." Earl B.'s split lip hurt every time he talked, and every fiber in his body was sore.

"With who?" Ray asked, stealing the ball from Rex. He took a jump shot, then looked at Earl B. out of the corner of his eye. "The Klan?"

Earl B. clenched his jaw. Kicking at the edge of the concrete, he avoided eye contact, while Rex chased after the ball.

"I thought so." Ray let out a mirthless laugh. "Ready to get revenge on 'em yet?"

"Maybe the Right Reverend Martin Chickenwing'll take care of it," Rex said, dribbling.

Ray snorted. "He don't stand a chance in Birmingham. They'll chew him up and spit him out."

Rex shot an air ball, and Earl B. got the rebound. "Ain't he in jail now?" he asked, glad the subject had changed. He had heard Dr. King had marched and been arrested in a last-ditch effort to get more volunteers.

"Yep," said Ray. "The whole thing's collapsing. They'll run him out before long."

Huey arrived, stole the ball away from Earl B., and went in for a layup. The boys scrimmaged for a minute or two. The motion actually felt good—it chased away the stiffness in Earl B.'s joints and helped him get more limber.

After grabbing a rebound, Ray paused. "Well, look who's here." He dropped the ball and headed toward Brother Jack's.

Earl B. looked. Rachel's Nomad was back, and Shirley was getting out of the passenger side. Ray was already halfway there. Rex and Huey followed, then stopped and gawked.

Ray let out a piercing catcall. Shirley glanced toward him and quickened her pace.

"Hey, girl," hollered Ray, "come here for a minute!"

Shirley made a beeline for Brother Jack's.

"Looking good in your bright red dress today," Ray said.

She walked fast, reached the door, and opened it.

"Aw, girl, come on," he pressed. "I just wanna talk."

Shirley disappeared, and Ray turned toward the Nomad.

"Leave them girls alone!" Earl B. yelled, walking closer.

Ray waved his hand, dismissing his comment, then leaned on the driver's side of the Nomad, talking to Rachel. He reached inside the window, and she pushed him away.

Earl B. hollered at him again.

Yanking Rachel's door open, Ray reached inside. Earl B. ran toward the car. By the time he got there, Ray had his arms wrapped under Rachel's, dragging her out of the vehicle. She kicked and screamed.

"Let her go!" Earl B. shouted, approaching the Nomad.

Ray smiled but held onto her as she struggled. "You ain't gonna spoil a little fun, are you, bruh?"

Rex, who stood nearby, laughed and said, "Now myself, I don't mind a little brown sugar." He moved toward Shirley, who was now back outside, with a look of horror on her face.

Earl B.'s fight-or-flight instincts kicked in as he glanced back and forth between Ray and Rex, uncertain what to do first.

Shirley tried to run, but Rex was too fast and grabbed her arm. She shrieked and fought against him.

"You're a feisty one, ain't you?" he said, laughing and grabbing her other arm from behind.

Making a quick decision, Earl B. charged toward the ringleader and loomed over him. He stood half a head taller than Ray. "You wanna be lynched?" he barked through gritted teeth. "Let her go."

Ray quit smiling and looked at the others. Huey backed away, but Rex maintained his hold on Shirley. Both girls continued to struggle.

Releasing Rachel's arm, Ray swung at Earl B., who caught his wrist in midair. Rachel tried to break free, but she was no match for her captor, who held on tightly.

"Let her go!" Earl B. bellowed, hitting Ray in the face.

Ray collided with the asphalt, blood gushing from his nose. Rachel lay next to him.

Earl B. then headed toward Shirley, who did a double take when she saw his swollen face up close. "Let her go, Rex," he growled, his arm muscles still taut.

"Hey, man," Rex answered, turning loose of Shirley and holding up his hands. "Don't get all bent out of shape. I was just having a little fun."

Shirley started to run toward Rachel, but Earl B. blocked her. "Get in the car," he said.

Earl B. leaned over Rachel and held his hand out. She hesitated, then grabbed it, and he helped her into the Nomad. However, Shirley was still outside, waiting next to the passenger door. "Get in the car," he repeated, then looked at Rachel. "Get outta here quick."

After Shirley jumped in, Rachel blasted out of the parking lot, spewing gravel as she skidded onto the street.

A black man rushed out of Brother Jack's. "You boys," he bellowed, "get off my property and stay off!"

Blood seeped out of Ray's nose as he lay on the pavement.

"Troublemakers," the man muttered, turning to go back inside.

Standing up, Ray held his hand to his bloody face. "What'd you do that for, Peterson?"

Without answering, Earl B. shuffled back toward the basketball goal, with the other boys trailing behind.

"I think my nose is broke," Ray said, still holding his hand to his face.

Earl B. pulled Ray's hand away. "It ain't broken." Then he took a handkerchief out of his pocket and threw it at him. "What were you thinking, doing that to a white woman? Now we're as good as lynched!"

"I thought you knew her," said Ray. "Or was that just a lie?" The handkerchief was already soaked with blood.

"I know her, but that doesn't mean anything. We could still get lynched." Earl B. kept walking, without saying goodbye. Heading home, he wondered what the two girls were saying right now. Would Rachel tell anyone? Most likely, Shirley wasn't singing his praises for rescuing them. She had complained more than once about his hanging out with hoodlums, as she called them.

The late afternoon sun baked his neck and shoulders, but that didn't stop a shudder from rippling through his body. He had no choice but to wait and see what would happen. Even if Rachel didn't tell, Shirley was probably mad enough to kill Earl B. herself.

Chapter 27

Earl B. needed to find Shirley and apologize. Also, maybe she would tell him if Rachel was going to talk. Ray could be a jerk, but Earl B. never dreamed he was low enough to threaten the two girls.

Monday morning brought the expected stares from other students when they saw his banged-up appearance. During Grammaw's earlier cross-examination, Earl B. had blamed it on a fight with another kid. Now he had to deflect questions at school.

Shirley seemed to have disappeared into thin air. All day, Earl B. kept his eye out for her, but she wasn't in the hallways or the cafeteria. That wasn't exactly unusual; they had no classes together, and their paths didn't always cross.

After school, he searched again. Ahead, a female student stood in the middle of the hall with a stack of flyers in her arm. Earl B. tried to avoid her, but she stuck one in front of his face saying, "Spread the word." He grabbed the paper, tucked it in his English book, and continued, dodging around students.

Earl B. headed toward Shirley's locker. He had to talk to her.

Now, all the students seemed to have the flyers, some waving them in their hands and shouting. Something bigger was happening than the routine end-of-day excitement. Earl B. would check it out later, after finding Shirley.

Rounding the last turn, he saw her and called her name. She didn't respond.

"Shirley!" Earl B. repeated, coming up beside her. She shot him a look that could freeze magma. "Listen, I'm sorry about what happened." He rushed to keep up with her.

She wove through students in the hallway without speaking.

"Did you hear me?" Earl B. followed her into the foyer.

Exiting the building, she let the door slam in his face. He kept going, calling after her, vaguely aware of a few snickers from nearby students.

Outside, he grabbed her arm. "Shirley!"

She whirled around, shaking his hand off. "What?"

A crowd of students had gathered to watch. "I'm sorry about what happened."

Her voice rose in pitch. "*Sorry?* I've been trying to tell you about that sorry bunch of fools for how long? And you just say you're sorry?"

"What do you want me to say?" Too late, he realized it was a poor choice of words. A student walked between them. Someone else bumped into Earl B. and knocked him sideways.

Shirley got in his face, lowered her voice, and spoke through gritted teeth. "I hope you're satisfied. I almost got raped and killed by those no-good thugs that you call friends."

Now Earl B. was exasperated. "And this is the thanks I get! You should be glad I was there. I stopped them guys from hurting both of you, and you know it."

"You're begging to be lynched, hanging out with that miserable bunch of fools." She turned and charged toward the bus stop.

"Shirley, please." He caught up, walking beside her.

"I'm done with you," she snapped, rounding on him. "I've been wasting my time, trying to help you."

"If you felt that way about it, why'd you agree to do it in the first place?"

"Mr. Ross asked me to." Tears welled up in her eyes.

Something snapped in Earl B. "This was all about you, wasn't it? I should have known. You said it yourself. I was just something that would look good on your college applications."

She opened her mouth to speak, then closed it. Her lower lip trembled. "I didn't mean . . . but I was willing to help, even after you lost your scholarship."

"It wasn't my idea to continue."

"Then it's settled. If you don't want to do it, I don't see the point in meeting again." She stomped away.

"Fine!" If she was going to be like that, he didn't care anymore. "I guess you're happy your boyfriend got the scholarship."

She turned on her heel and faced him. "What?"

"Carl Washington. He got the scholarship."

Her voice rose. "He's not my—Earl B., that's not fair!"

"But you're still glad!" he yelled. "What've you been doing? Helping him on the side?"

Shirley balled her hands into fists. "How can you say that? I've spent so much time trying to help you, meeting with you. When sometimes I didn't think you even wanted that scholarship."

"Right," he said, sarcastically. "If I hadn't wanted it, you think I would've been meeting with you all those times?"

Pressing her lips together, she turned and marched away.

He took a deep breath and let it out slowly, trying to calm down, as he headed toward the bus stop.

Riding home that afternoon, all Earl B. could think about was the argument with Shirley. He fingered the moss agate in his pocket, but it didn't calm him like it usually did. His list of losses was growing. First, his father. Then his mother. Asa. After that, football. And yes, now Shirley. It made him think of something his daddy used to say: *You never miss the water till the well runs dry.*

Chapter 28

Electrical crackling noises signaled that the loudspeaker in Earl B.'s classroom was coming on. "This is Dr. Bell," the principal said. "It has come to my attention some of the students have plans for this afternoon that do not involve school. The gates of the schoolyard have been locked. No students will be allowed to leave the school property unless given special permission. I repeat, nobody will be allowed to leave without special permission."

"Okay, people," Big Ben said. "Settle down and pay attention."

Nobody heard him. Kids were talking, yelling, running around the room, and looking out the window.

It was Thursday, the second of May. D-Day, according to Shelley the Playboy. Earl B. had heard the deejay yesterday telling his listeners to "bring your toothbrushes." In other words, come prepared to march and go to jail.

One of the flyers that had been circulating since Monday lay on the floor. Earl B. picked it up. The breakup with Shirley, if you could call it that, had put him in a funk all week, and he'd never bothered to look at his. At the top, it said, "Fight for freedom first, then go to school." Underneath, it urged kids to be at the Sixteenth Street Baptist Church by noon on Thursday. It closed with, "It's up to you to free our teachers, our parents, yourself, and our country."

In spite of his melancholy, Earl B. laughed out loud. The leaders were so desperate for marchers they had resorted to using kids. This was the strategy they thought was going to change Birmingham?

Students gathered at the window, and Earl B. stood up to see. Just outside was a wall marking the boundary of the school property.

Someone on the other side held up a handwritten sign that read, "It's time!" A young man was shouting into a megaphone.

Writing on the chalkboard, Big Ben turned around to see kids crawling out the window, and a faint smile crossed his face. More students left, then climbed over the wall, leaving the classroom almost deserted. Outside, a steady stream of teenagers headed away from the building. Earl B. perked up as he caught a momentary glimpse of someone who looked like Shirley among them. Now, he couldn't get outside fast enough. Getting in line with the others, he slipped out the window and scaled the wall.

Earl B. wove his way among the kids, coursing toward town, all the time keeping his eye out for Shirley. Ever since their falling out, he'd been in survival mode, sleeping most of the time, waking up when he had to, and eating very little. Grammaw had threatened to call the doctor. In a way, this blow had hit him worse than losing the scholarship. After having second and third and fourth thoughts about their argument, he wanted to try another apology.

Half an hour later, the orange brick arches of Sixteenth Street Baptist came into view. Earl B. still hadn't seen any trace of Shirley. Some of his classmates ran toward the building, then a hoard of kids poured inside, going through the front, back, and basement doors.

Wandering around outside the church, Earl B. scanned the crowd. He had rehearsed what to say to Shirley over and over. If he could just talk to her, perhaps she would listen.

Sometime before one o'clock, the massive oak double doors of the church opened, and the first group of children emerged, with much fanfare. After kneeling and praying, they marched. The crowd cheered them on. Earl B. wound his way through the people, trying to get a closer look at the marchers. Another group came out of the church.

"Sing, children, sing!" a woman cried.

Someone started "We Shall Overcome," and soon the song reverberated throughout the city streets.

Earl B. watched group after group, as they descended the steps of the church, pouring out like a waterfall. Most were teenagers, but a few were younger. He didn't see Shirley. With people laughing and happily heading into the paddy wagons and buses, the atmosphere was more like a party than a demonstration. Finally, no more children were released.

Nearby, someone announced that a mass meeting was being held at Sixth Avenue Baptist that evening. Maybe Earl B. could find Shirley there.

* * * * *

The church was like an anthill, swarming with bodies, packed with a thousand people, maybe even two thousand. Earl B. wove his way through them. The likelihood of finding Shirley here would be low. He suddenly felt exhausted from the long day of standing.

People clapped and stomped to the music, and speaker after speaker took the pulpit. "'A little child shall lead them,' the Bible says," one preacher shouted. "Well, our children are doing what us grownups wouldn't—fill the jails and tighten the screws on the bigwigs in town!"

Easing along the side aisle, Earl B. examined the pews one by one, still hoping to find Shirley. Now, Rev. James Bevel was in the pulpit, punctuating his speech by repeated shouts of, "You ain't seen nothing yet!"

Earl B. finally reached the front pew, only to get trapped against the wall by a sweaty man in work clothes. Wriggling around the guy, he headed back the other way, still scouring the crowd for Shirley, then wound his way around the edge of the sanctuary to the opposite side.

Now, Rev. Ralph Abernathy was speaking. "The problem with us is we're too afraid of dying. When you go home tonight you better stand up in the corner and not go to bed, because more folk have died in the bed than anyplace I know."

Returning to the back of the church, Earl B. zigzagged his way through the frenzied throng as Dr. Martin Luther King Jr. was introduced. He stood on his toes and craned his neck, eager to see the man he had heard so much about. His line of sight was partially blocked by a woman in her Sunday best—a violet beaded jacket over a lavender dress and an ivory cloche hat with purple feathers. King told how the children had inspired and moved him that day, then went on to explain nonviolence in a way Earl B. had never heard. Though the preacher cloaked his ideas in the churchly language of love, he essentially asserted that nonviolent protesters were not yellow-bellied, kowtowing stooges. Instead, they were fearless resisters. When people were under the thumb of cold-blooded tyrants, nonviolence was a powerful tactic, a persuasive way of playing hardball and getting real results. Earl B. was mesmerized. For a while, he forgot where he was. As the man's words captivated him, all else faded away, as if this imposing orator were speaking only to him.

Gaining momentum, King drew the audience into a poetic call and response, then closed by saying, "I call upon you to be as Amos, who in the midst of the injustices of his day cried out in words that echo across the generation, 'Let judgment run down like waters and righteousness like a mighty stream!'"

As strains of "We Shall Overcome" rang through the sanctuary, people on either side of Earl B. grabbed his hands and swayed back and forth. A heavy feeling came over him, and he sensed that he'd been missing out on something momentous. Maybe these folks did have a chance at changing the city. Shirley had tried to tell him, but he hadn't realized the scope of what had been going on in his own hometown.

Chapter 29

A rat scampered away from a dumpster as Earl B. walked past. Up ahead at High Point, Ray paced back and forth dribbling the basketball. Rex was sitting on the curb. A typical Saturday morning.

Ray glanced at Earl B. as he approached. "Well, look who's here." He stopped pacing and cradled the ball. "Mr. Football Superstar hisself finally shows up."

"Probably too busy getting him some," Rex said, laughing.

"Shut up," snapped Earl B.

"Or too scared to show his face again," Ray said. "You knocked my tooth out, man." He opened his mouth and showed a gap. Then he put his index finger to Earl B.'s chest. "And kept me from getting some."

"Me too," said Rex. "That girl of yours, man, she's one fine looking sista."

"Yeah," said Ray. "She's a fine piece of meat. But Earl B. don't wanna share his pussy."

Seizing the front of his shirt, Earl B. almost lifted him off the ground. "Shut your punk-ass mouth or I'll knock a few more of your teeth out."

Ray's smile slowly disappeared and turned into an ugly grimace. The seconds seemed to stretch into minutes as the two glared at each other. Then Earl B. shoved him away, knocking him off balance. Ray caught himself, gave a nervous laugh, and dribbled the ball again. "Ooh, he's all upset, now."

It had been a week since the attack on the girls. Earl B. was so over it, tired of thinking of it. Because of these guys, his friendship with Shirley was over, done, finished. Why had he even come here? He turned to leave.

"You heard about Huey, didn't you?" Ray asked.

Earl B. kept walking.

"So you don't care what happened to Huey?"

This time, his words stopped Earl B. in his tracks. He turned around. "What are you talking about?"

Ray shot a basket, got his own rebound, then threw his shoulders back. "You ain't heard?"

A sick feeling came over Earl B. "No. You gonna tell me what happened?" Coming closer, he looked back and forth between Ray and Rex.

"They found him dead, man," Ray said. "Last night."

Earl B. had already guessed, but the certainty of it sank heavy in his chest. "Who did it?" An image entered his mind—Rachel's face as she had pulled out of the parking lot.

"Nobody's admitting to it," Ray said. "But you know it had to be the Klan. And we gotta get back at 'em. Right, Rex? For a while, you was all riled up about it."

Rex looked at Earl B. "I got the address of a Klan member."

"So we're gonna break into his house." Ray's voice took on the tone of a kindergarten teacher. "Take a few things." He switched his gaze to Rex. "Right? You ain't weaseling out on me now, are ya?"

"No."

Ray narrowed his eyes at Earl B. "Last month, you were in on it. How about it? Are you getting all lily-livered on me now?"

"I said if you found the guy that bombed my house, I was in on it," he corrected.

"Come on. Klan's Klan. They killed Huey. We need to do this for him."

King's words about nonviolence came back to Earl B., then other thoughts ping-ponged back and forth. Didn't people have a right to defend themselves? But that didn't mean going on the offensive. This plan had the potential to backfire. "This guy's Klan?" he asked Rex, stalling for time.

"Yep," he answered. "My mother works for them white people. She hears things."

"He's Klan, all right," Ray said. "So're you in now?"

"Maybe," muttered Earl B.

"Maybe?" Ray's voice rose. "Is that the kind of loyalty you show? I thought you and Huey were friends."

"I'd be more excited if I knew it was the person who killed him," Earl B. said, shrugging. "Or the guy who bombed my house. *That's* who I'd like to get my hands on."

Ray snorted. "So you're the holdout, huh?" He got in Earl B.'s face. "Come on, man. We gotta do it this week. We gotta prove a point. Hit them whiteys when they least expect it."

Earl B. thought about the incident at Brother Jack's. So this was how it happened. No publicity. No ugly newspaper articles about how a white girl had been nearly raped. It all took place in the quiet, with nightriders coming out under cover of darkness and getting even. Just like with Emmett Till.

Maybe a Klansman had witnessed the whole thing, a man who only cared because a white girl had been involved. A man who wouldn't have given a rat's ass if Rachel hadn't been there—if it had only happened to Shirley. Then he killed Huey, who had barely been involved. The blood drained from Earl B.'s face, then surged back in with such fury he couldn't speak.

"Come on, man," Ray pressed. "Or are you one o' these religious-Uncle-Tom-traitor-Reverend-Doctor-Chickenwing followers? Huh?"

Revenge would feel good, Earl B. thought, *and Klan is Klan*. "I'll be there," he finally said.

"All right." Ray smirked. "We're all in. We'll meet here on Friday morning at nine o'clock. When everyone's supposed to be out of the house."

Chapter 30

"Hey there, Peterson!"

The shout came from behind, but Earl B. recognized the voice—Carl Washington.

The big jerk caught up with him in the school hallway. "Too bad about your scholarship, huh?" Carl grinned, then forced a laugh. "But your loss is my gain, ain't it?"

Earl B. frowned. "How'd you pass? Did you get help from your girlfriend?"

The quarterback looked confused. "Who're you talking about, man?"

"Shirley."

Carl glared at Earl B. "No. Besides, I ain't even with her no more. That girl's an egghead. Too uptight," he said, walking away.

"She's worth ten of you," Earl B. muttered, dumping an armload of books into his locker. Second period had just ended, but he had no intention of staying at school. Now was his chance to find out about the one remaining address—Fourth Court North. On the last search, he had almost ended up swinging from a tree. But Four Fingers wouldn't expect him to go now, during school hours.

A few minutes later, Earl B. stood in the aisle of the bus, holding on to a pole. Unable to shake the feeling of being watched, he shifted his gaze from one passenger to the next. He got off in Smithfield, but at a different stop than before. A black woman with two children also got off. Earl B. glanced around. Nobody was watching.

But that didn't stop him from feeling jittery. He passed one yard after another. A man was perched on a ladder, painting the trim of his house. After a few blocks, Earl B. came to the beginning of Fourth Court North. He'd start here, and, if nothing went wrong, make his way to the other end.

The first part was residential. A man dressed in overalls mowed his lawn. There was very little traffic, only an occasional car. He passed a church and jotted down its name—Grace Redemption— along with the address. The parking lot was empty.

Earl B. continued walking. The neighborhood gradually changed, but he couldn't put his finger on what the difference was. Another large building loomed in the distance, the cross on top clearly visible against the sky. He kept walking, then crossed the street. Yes, definitely a church, right at the intersection of two streets. In front was a big sign—Creekside Full Gospel Church. A white man came out of the building and locked the door. Earl B. didn't bother writing down the name.

Feeling pressure to finish, he covered the rest of the street quickly, at a moderate jog. There were no more churches. At the end of the road, he turned right, heading past more houses, and eventually came to a bus stop at the main road. A crowd had already gathered. Pulling his pencil and paper out, Earl B. circled *Grace Redemption Church*. He knew the target. Now, he needed a date.

* * * * *

Back home, Earl B. sat at his desk, again staring at his copy of the Klan paper. He had filled in all the known information, including the correct numbers of the addresses, the names of the bombing sites, and the dates:

59	2410 35th Ave. N.	*High Praises Community Church*	*Feb 28*
321	358 2nd St. S.	*My house*	*Nov 17*
109	3712 Jefferson Ave. SW	*River of Jordan Church*	*April 19*
30	198 Court G Alley	*near Miles College*	*Jan 30*
81	1319 7th Ave. N.	*ARC office*	*Mar 22*
130	224(?) 4th Ct. N.	*?? Grace Redemption Church ??*	*??*
348	3233 29th Ave. N.	*Bethel Baptist*	*Dec 14*

There seemed to be no mathematical relationship between the numbers on the sheet and the numbers in the addresses. They didn't appear to be dates either. Earl B. stared at the list till his eyes crossed. Most likely, Grace Redemption Church was the next target, and the bombing would happen soon. But to figure out the exact date, he needed a hotshot math genius to help crack the code. Someone like Shirley.

* * * * *

The bell rang, and Earl B. rose to leave class.

Big Ben approached and put a hand on his arm. "Stay for a second. I been meaning to talk to you."

The other student walked out the door. And yes, only one other student was in class. Everyone else was in jail from the daily marches, making the school seem like a ghost town.

"How are things?" asked Big Ben.

Earl B. shrugged. "Okay." *If you don't press for details.*

"How's algebra going?"

"About the same."

"Not marching, huh?"

"Sir?" Was his uncle expecting him to protest?

Big Ben let out a frustrated sigh. "Well, you'll have a substitute tomorrow. I'm taking off to help a friend with a big plumbing problem."

Earl B. didn't respond. *Why is he telling me this?*

"You know, son," Big Ben said, softening his voice, "you can talk to me about anything, anytime."

Dropping his gaze, Earl B. drew his mouth together. His eyes began to sting.

"I know you're still wrestling with that bombing. I can tell it's fresh, like it happened yesterday."

Earl B. shifted his weight but tried his best not to squirm. He wanted out of this situation.

"You don't have to talk." His uncle's voice was gentle. "Just remember what I said about people who go around hurting other folk. Leave 'em be. If that's all they live for, then let 'em dig their own grave."

* * * * *

Carolyn Owens hadn't marched, of course. After algebra class, she caught up with Earl B. in the hall. "Susan Hayward's playing at the Carver Theatre."

He got the hint but ignored it. Earl B. had better things to do than watch rich, white people in a second-run movie.

"It's called *Back Street*," she persisted. "You haven't seen it yet, have you?"

"No, but I'm busy this weekend," he lied. Or maybe it wasn't a lie. Right now, he had no way of knowing.

"Oh," she said, her tone slightly dejected. They walked downstairs together. "Did you hear what happened to the kids on Friday?"

Earl B. grunted. Grammaw had told him all about them being attacked by police dogs and high-pressure fire hoses. After the story had been splashed across the front page of the *New York Times*, it had created a national uproar. The *Birmingham News* had bumped it to page two.

"Yeah." Carolyn smirked. "Serves 'em right for getting involved in that mess." She stopped at the landing. "Heard Shirley Dupree got arrested."

Coming to a standstill, Earl B. stared at Carolyn. Was she trying to bait him?

"Someone said the cops sicced a dog on her."

Earl B. swallowed, waiting for her to continue. She didn't. "Was she hurt?"

"I don't know." Carolyn looked satisfied as she walked downstairs, leaving him alone on the landing.

Chapter 31

Grammaw wiped her mouth on her napkin. "Why you eating supper so fast?"

"I'm late." Earl B. took a bite from a chicken leg.

"Late for what?"

"Meeting somebody." He wasn't about to tell her the whole truth.

"Don't chew with your mouth open," she said. "Is it that girlfriend of yours?"

Earl B. put the chicken back on his plate and sighed. "No, Grammaw."

She took a bite of her biscuit. "Who you meeting with?"

"Just some friends." He scooped up the last of his mashed potatoes.

"Sometimes I wonder 'bout your friends."

"There's nothing wrong with my friends." Earl B. ate the last bite of chicken, picked up his plate, and took it into the kitchen.

"You ain't getting involved in that mess downtown, are you?" she hollered after him.

"Grammaw, I've been going to school every day." He dropped the chicken bone and dirty napkin into the trash.

She stood up. "I just don't want you getting arrested like the rest of them kids. They'll have a record for the rest of their lives."

Earl B. headed toward the door.

"Don't stay out too late," Grammaw added.

"I won't." She was delaying him with all her questions. At this rate, he'd be lucky to get there by the time it was over.

"I'm turning in early tonight. I gotta work at the church tomorrow morning, so I won't be here when you leave for school."

His hand was on the doorknob. "I know."

Twenty minutes later, Earl B. was on the bus. Raindrops shuddered down the window. Ever since that afternoon, when Carolyn had told him about Shirley, he had been in panic mode. He needed to find her. Surely, someone at tonight's mass meeting would have some information.

Earl B. glanced at his watch. The meeting had started long ago. The brakes squealed in protest as the bus slowed to a stop. He got off and walked down the sidewalk in the light rain. Up ahead, a crowd of people stood outside the church. Picking up his pace, Earl B. approached a woman with an umbrella in one hand and two blankets in her other arm. "Is this where the mass meeting is?" he asked.

"Was," she corrected him. "It just ended."

"Do you know who Shirley Dupree is?"

"No," she answered. "Why?"

"I heard she was arrested."

"Honey, over two thousand kids are in jail."

Earl B. started to ask another question, but someone else had gotten her attention. He threaded his way through the folks milling outside, then got caught in the crowd streaming out of the church. A woman walked beside him with an armful of blankets.

"What are those for?" he asked.

"We're taking them to the fairgrounds for the kids," she answered.

"The fairgrounds?"

"Haven't you heard? The jails are full, so they put a lot of kids there in the stockyards."

Earl B. had a vague idea where the fairgrounds were, maybe a few miles out of town. The buses might not even go out that far, especially this time of night. He was about to ask the woman for a ride, when he heard someone calling his name.

Turning, he saw Mrs. DuBose, his next-door neighbor, in a bright yellow dress and a white hat trimmed with lace. Her husband stood next to her in a coat and tie. Earl B. wanted to disappear.

"I thought that was you," she said.

"Hey," he mumbled.

"Don't suppose your grandmama's here, is she?" asked Mr. DuBose, walking out the front door into the rain with his wife. Earl B. followed, as the couple opened their umbrellas.

"No, sir." A raindrop hit him in the eye.

"Guess you haven't marched yet?" Mrs. DuBose asked, as they walked down the steps.

"No, ma'am," he said impatiently. His neighbors were holding him up. He scanned the crowd for someone he knew, anyone who could give him a ride to the fairgrounds.

They came to a standstill at the foot of the stairs. "Well, there's still time." She shifted her purse to the other arm. "We can give you a ride home."

Earl B. hesitated. An awkward situation was becoming even more so. "I'm not going home right now," he said.

"No? Where you going?"

Mr. DuBose put his hand on his wife's arm. "Bessie," he murmured.

Earl B. stammered, unsure of what to say. She was as nosy as his grandmother. "I'm getting a ride out to the fairgrounds," he finally said. "A friend of mine got arrested."

"Who's taking you?"

He looked around. The crowd had thinned out because of the rain. "I'll find a ride," he said, trying to sound convincing.

"We can take you," Mr. DuBose offered.

"I been worried about 'em anyway," his wife said, as if the matter had been decided. "There're a couple of kids we know out there. I can't imagine—them outside in the rain and everything. Come on, child, we'll take you there."

Not having much choice, Earl B. followed.

Mrs. DuBose insisted on swinging by their house first to get candy bars and blankets for the children. Waiting in the car, Earl B. noticed his own house was already dark.

After backing out of the driveway, Mr. DuBose wound through Titusville toward the main road. "Your grandmother home tonight?" he asked.

"Yes, sir. She's probably already in bed."

"Did she know you was coming to a meeting?"

Earl B. swallowed. *The interrogation continues.* "No, sir."

The man chuckled. "Don't surprise me none. I've tried to get her to come to one, but she won't have nothing to do with it." He turned onto the highway. The rain picked up, and the windshield wipers slapped back and forth. Mr. DuBose looked into the rearview mirror at him. "Don't worry, son. We won't say nothing to your grandmama."

Earl B. relaxed against the back seat—until the next question.

Twisting around, Mrs. DuBose pinned him with her stare. "Who're you going to see?"

"Maybe we're asking too many questions," Mr. DuBose said, glancing at his wife.

"Somebody from school," Earl B. mumbled.

"Girlfriend?" she pressed.

"Bessie," said Mr. DuBose, throwing a sharp look at his wife.

"Well, I was just wondering, that's all."

"She's not my girlfriend," Earl B. said, knowing they would find out soon anyway.

"What's her name?" she asked.

Mr. DuBose opened his mouth to speak, but Earl B. answered first. "Shirley."

She wrinkled her forehead. "Shirley Dupree?"

"Yes, ma'am."

"The Duprees go to our church," Mr. DuBose said.

"Poor Shirley," his wife said. "J. D. and Ruby probably don't know some of the kids have been moved to the fairgrounds."

"Well, if the rumors are correct," Mr. DuBose said, "there's a chance this whole thing might end any day now."

Earl B. stared out the window as they pulled into the fairgrounds. The rain had turned into drizzle. Mr. DuBose parked, and they got out. Earl B. felt his heartbeat quicken as he approached a tall fence, where parents tossed blankets and other items over to their children. Trying his best to see, he peered over and around the adults.

Mr. DuBose came up beside Earl B. "These are the boys. Someone said the girls are over there." He pointed to their left.

With water dripping down his face and into his eyes, Earl B. trudged through the mire toward the other enclosure. The back of his shirt stuck to his skin. Another group of parents stood at the second fence, tossing over supplies. Earl B. stood on his toes but didn't see anybody he recognized. He walked around to the side and stood in the mud. There were fewer parents in this area, so he could get closer to the fence. The stockyard was packed with people. Earl B. caught a whiff of something like the mixture of rotten meat and manure. Behind the crowd of kids near the fence stood a small girl, maybe seven years old, alone and crying. The others, too busy grabbing blankets and food, were ignoring her. Another girl, slightly older, was squatting and holding her dress up off the ground. Earl B. scanned the children. Their hair and clothes were soaked and dripping. For a brief moment, he caught a glimpse of someone who looked like Shirley, but another person moved, blocking his view. Shifting sideways, he finally saw her.

Earl B. cupped his hands around his mouth and called out her name. At the same time, girls cheered as parents threw items over the fence. When she didn't respond, he bellowed louder. "Shirley!"

She looked, and he waved his hands. Shirley wound her way through the other girls toward the fence, plodding through the muck, with drenched hair, a soaked, stained dress, and dirt smeared on her cheek. Reaching the fence, she self-consciously folded her arms across the front of her body. "Hey," she said.

He swallowed but his throat was dry. The moment had arrived, and Earl B. had forgotten what to say. "We got some blankets," he managed. "Candy bars too."

"Thanks," Shirley said, glancing at his empty hands.

"Mr. and Mrs. DuBose have them. They drove me here." Earl B. pointed at Shirley's torn sleeve. "What happened?"

"One of the dogs."

Earl B. nodded. "You marched on Friday?"

"Yes."

He took a breath to start talking, to tell her he was going to get the blankets, but she started at the same time. They both stopped. Earl B. waited.

"Don't leave yet," she said. Water dripped down both sides of her face.

"I was just going to get the blankets."

"But I need to tell you something." Her mud-streaked hair was plastered to her head. She appeared to be collecting her thoughts. "You know the paper? The one the Klansman dropped?"

"Yeah. I need to talk to you about—"

"I think I figured it out." Shirley rubbed the side of her face with her hand, smearing more slimy clay.

"You did?"

"The last one is on May 10. I've lost track of the days. Is that tomorrow?"

A jolt coursed through him. "Yes, it's tomorrow. Are you sure?" If she was right, he could warn people. Prevent injuries. Prevent deaths.

She nodded. "It was pretty simple, actually. The numbers *are* the date. Each one is the number day of the year." Shirley paused, and raindrops splattered in the surrounding puddles. "Check my math to make sure. I had to do it from memory. My copy disintegrated a long time ago."

Earl B. didn't respond.

"But I don't know the location. The target."

"I figured that out," he said, his voice hoarse. "Grace Redemption Church in Smithfield."

Her eyes widened. "Is tomorrow Friday?"

He nodded.

Shirley's voice went up an octave. "Grace Redemption? Are you sure?"

"Unless they've changed their plans. There are only two churches on that street, and the other one's white." He wiped raindrops away from his eyes. "Why?"

"Oh, my God, Earl B." Her voice trembled. "My father works there now." Beads of water ran down her face. "He took on a job as a janitor at that church, and he works all day on Friday."

Earl B. took a few deep breaths. His mind was racing.

"I knew it was in Smithfield," she muttered. "But I didn't know . . . oh, my God."

He wasn't sure what to say.

"You've got to do something, Earl B.," she said, with urgency.

"I guess we don't know for certain, right?" he said, trying to reassure her. "It could be somebody's home instead of a church."

His words had the opposite effect. "But we can't take that chance. The preacher there—he's real active in the movement," she said, her voice now panic-stricken. *"Please.* You've *got* to stop my daddy from going to that church tomorrow."

In spite of his efforts to remain calm, Earl B.'s voice rose. "How? I don't even know your dad! What if he doesn't believe me? What if—"

"There you are!" Mrs. DuBose came up behind Earl B. with an armload of blankets and food. Then her gaze traveled to Shirley. "Poor thing! You look miserable." She looked back at Earl B. "Child, where's your manners? Don't let her stand there all cold and wet. Give her this stuff and then do your visiting." Earl B. took the supplies out of her hands and pitched them over the fence to Shirley. "Lord, child," the woman continued. "I'm glad your mother ain't here to see you in this mess."

The DuBoses talked to Shirley for a couple of minutes and then said goodbye. As Earl B. turned to leave with them, Shirley stood at the fence, a blanket draped over her shoulders and a candy bar clutched in her fist. Her pleading eyes stared into his, as droplets of rain streamed down her face. Or maybe they were tears.

Chapter 32

Early next morning, Earl B. dressed, tiptoed out of his bedroom, and crept down the hall. Grammaw wasn't up yet, and he wanted to keep it that way. After looking up Shirley's address in the phone book, he slipped out the front door and closed it without a sound. In one direction was the church. The other, Shirley's house. He glanced at his watch. Six thirty. There were so many unanswered questions, all because Mr. and Mrs. DuBose had interrupted his conversation with Shirley, the most important being what time her father left for work.

Earl B. made a quick decision and turned, heading toward her house. Reaching the main road, he bypassed the bus stop and kept going. Etched in his memory was the image of Shirley standing at the fence, staring at him, with the blanket draped around her soaked dress. He shook his head, trying to erase it. Her eyes were burning a hole in his brain.

Turning down Center Street, Earl B. slowed his pace and wandered into South Titusville. Shirley's community had the occasional road that curved around and veered in an odd direction. One time, while walking home from her house, he had taken a wrong turn and gotten thoroughly lost. Now, feeling his way, he zigzagged through the neighborhood, made a mistake, and backtracked. A drunk clown had designed this place. Earl B. pulled the slip of paper out of his pocket and glanced at her address. He kept going and got turned around in a puzzle of street names. Nothing made sense. He looked at his watch. Seven fifteen.

Finally figuring out which way to go, Earl B. increased his pace, jogged toward an intersection, and turned the corner. He was now on her street. Sweat ran into his eyes. Up ahead, a light-skinned, tall man in work clothes emerged from Shirley's home, lunch box in hand.

"Mr. Dupree?" Earl B. asked, stopping at the bottom of the porch.

"Yes?" The man's brow was furrowed.

Relax. He's still at home. Making a conscious effort to slow his breathing, Earl B. introduced himself. Mrs. Dupree showed up in the doorway, and he remembered meeting her during his visit with Asa's mother in the hospital.

"Sir, I'm a friend of Shirley's," Earl B. said.

"I remember you," said Mrs. Dupree. "We met a couple of months ago."

"Is something wrong?" her husband asked, approaching Earl B.

"Did something happen to Shirley?" Mrs. Dupree came down the steps. Worry was written all over her face.

"No, ma'am. She's fine."

"You've seen her?" Mr. Dupree asked. "Where is she? We know she's in jail, but we haven't been able to locate her."

"When did you see her?" Shirley's mother asked.

"Last night, ma'am," Earl B. said.

"At the jail?" she pressed.

"No, ma'am. Well, yes. She's in the stockyards at the fairgrounds."

Her voice rose. "The stockyards?"

"Yes, ma'am. They ran out of room in the—"

"The open stockyards?" she exclaimed. "In that thunderstorm?"

"But she's okay, ma'am," Earl B. said. "In fact, she wanted me to give you a message."

"What's that?" Mr. Dupree asked.

"Sir, do you work at Grace Redemption Church?"

"Yes."

"It might get bombed today."

"You see, J. D.?" Shirley's mother said. "I was afraid of this. That's why I didn't want you working there."

"What makes you say that?" Mr. Dupree asked, ignoring his wife's comment.

"I found this note—a note written by the Klan." Earl B. pulled out the list. "It's written in code, and it gives a listing of places they planned to bomb.

"Oh, my Lord!" Shirley's mother gasped.

"And it had Grace Redemption on there?" Mr. Dupree asked.

"Not the name, only the street."

Mr. Dupree pointed to the number beside the street name. "But that's not the right address."

"None of the numbers match the addresses, sir. Each one stands for a date. The number day of the year. Shirley figured that out."

"But the location—that could be anywhere on that street," Mr. Dupree reasoned.

"I know. But the minister there—Shirley said he's—"

"And you found this out last night?" Mr. Dupree asked, cutting him off.

"Yes, sir. She wanted me to tell you to stay away from the church today."

Shirley's mother put a hand on her husband's arm. "Oh, J. D."

A charged silence passed as Mr. Dupree sighed, looked back and forth between his wife and Earl B., then cleared his throat and shook his head back and forth. "I appreciate it, son, but that's the only job I got."

"Don't worry, child, he ain't going," Mrs. Dupree said. "I'll see to it." The look on her face was the same one Grammaw sometimes got. It meant the argument was over.

Unfortunately, her husband didn't see it that way. "Now, Ruby, I have to go. I got to raise bail money to get Shirley out of jail. And the people at church won't understand if that plumbing problem's not fixed."

Mrs. Dupree snorted. "Them people won't care about a plumbing problem if the place blows up."

"But if it doesn't, they won't understand, and I'll lose my job. Ruby, this whole thing is probably just hearsay."

"Hearsay?" Mrs. Dupree exploded. "Once upon a time, it was hearsay that High Praises would get bombed."

They were ignoring Earl B. He shifted his weight, feeling as if he were eavesdropping on a private argument.

Mr. Dupree looked at his watch. "I'm going to be late." He brushed past Earl B. and charged down the walkway.

Tears formed in Mrs. Dupree's eyes. "J. D.," she screamed, with her hands on her hips, "if you do this, I'll never—so help me, if you die because of this, next time I see you, I'll—" She let out a mixture of a shriek and a sob.

Her husband turned his head slightly, yelling, "I'll be fine!" then broke into a run, heading northward.

It was as if a big weight had dropped deep inside Earl B.'s body. He felt rooted to the ground, unable to respond. *No! This isn't happening.*

Mrs. Dupree watched, then turned her head, trying to hide the tears streaming down her face. She hurried inside and slammed the door.

Finally able to move, Earl B. backed away from the house and watched Mr. Dupree turn the corner at an intersection. He shuffled a few steps along the sidewalk, stuck his hand in his pocket, and fingered the moss agate. Shirley's dark eyes were boring through his brain like a drill. He quickened his pace.

Agonizing visions shot through Earl B.'s head, one after another. A cloud of smoke suffocated him as he carried his grandmother out of the burning house. Mama lay on the ground, with a gaping, bloody wound. He wandered among the rubble in his front yard, feeling more lost than he'd ever been before. Grammaw sobbed against his chest.

The memories lit a fire under him. "Mr. Dupree!" Earl B. hollered, racing after Shirley's father. He sprinted down the street and turned the corner. Shirley's dad was in the distance, way ahead of him. Earl B. called his name again. Mr. Dupree gestured with his hand, dismissing him, and kept going. However, his momentum had slowed, and the young fullback was gaining on him.

By the time they reached Sixth Avenue, Earl B. had caught up. "Mr. Dupree, please—"

"Look, son," the man said, panting as he stood at the intersection waiting to cross. "Thanks for coming to tell me." He put his hand on Earl B.'s shoulder as his breathing calmed. "But ain't nothing gonna happen. Them Klan—they talk big talk all the time and don't do half the stuff they brag about."

"But my house is on that sheet. They bombed my home!"

"Then I can understand why it upsets you."

"Your wife's sister. What about her?"

The man hesitated before speaking. "But you don't even have a real address. You got to understand, I already lost one job. I can't risk losing another."

"Think of Shirley. This isn't fair to her. She'll be left without a father."

"Nothing's going to happen. Besides, I'm supposed to meet someone there this morning."

"Who?"

"Big Ben. He's gonna help me with a plumbing problem."

His words hammered home, causing Earl B.'s stomach to lurch. "Big Ben?"

"Yeah." The stoplight turned, and Mr. Dupree dropped his hand from his shoulder. "Son, you're making me late to work. I'm sorry, but I got to go." Whipping around, he crossed the street.

Earl B.'s heart slammed inside his chest. Panic and fear turned his voice into a scream. "Mr. Dupree! Please don't go!" A crowd had gathered, but he didn't care.

Shirley's father reached the other side of the street.

"You're being selfish!" Earl B. yelled after him, his voice making odd sounds it hadn't made since he was thirteen. "*Pleeease!*"

But Mr. Dupree kept going and never even looked back.

* * * * *

Earl B. leaned against a telephone pole and tried to ignore people's stares. He needed to think. Mr. Dupree had already turned a corner and disappeared. Why hadn't Shirley told him how stubborn her father was?

Next step—finding Big Ben, who lived in Smithfield, where Grace Redemption Church was located. Earl B. had a choice—head to his uncle's house or intercept him at the church.

Taking off at a jog, he crossed the street and turned at the corner, the same route Mr. Dupree had taken. But Shirley's father was nowhere in sight. Earl B. tried other turns, then backtracked, each time getting more lost. The neighborhood had become a morass, a maze of streets, and Mr. Dupree had vanished. After another block, Earl B. finally found a street he recognized, which meant his uncle's house was nearby. Increasing his pace, he veered out into the street to avoid a man cutting grass. After one more turn, his uncle's house loomed up ahead. Earl B. rushed to the door and knocked.

A couple of kids, carrying school satchels, walked by. He knocked again, harder this time, as his breathing slowed. Nobody answered. Big Ben had already gone.

Back at the sidewalk, Earl B. gazed around, trying to get his bearings. Previously, he had found the church by coming from a different direction. It was definitely close by, but which way? Making a quick decision, he went north. At the corner, Earl B. turned and saw a church steeple up ahead. Grace Redemption. No sign of a bombing, he thought, approaching the door.

Earl B. knocked hard, found a doorbell, and punched it too.

The door opened. It was Big Ben. His forehead creased, and he gave a worried frown. "What's going on?"

"You need to get out of here," Earl B. said.

Mr. Dupree walked up behind his uncle. "You again?" he said. "Will you quit? Nothing's going to happen."

Big Ben glanced at Shirley's father, then back at Earl B. "What's the problem?"

"This kid has some harebrained story about the Klan bombing this place," Mr. Dupree said.

Earl B.'s voice rose. "It's not a harebrained story—"

"It's just another bomb threat," Mr. Dupree said, his voice rising. "It's nonsense."

"If it's nonsense, why has every other place on the list been hit?"

"Hush, both of you," Big Ben barked. "What list?"

"I found a list of Klan bombing sites." Earl B. pulled out the copy and explained everything. As he did, his uncle's face went through a rainbow of emotions.

"And Shirley figured out the date was today?" Big Ben asked, taking the paper from Earl B.'s hand.

"Nonsense," Mr. Dupree muttered.

"You need to get out of here," Earl B. said, his voice faltering.

"We ain't going nowhere," Mr. Dupree said.

Big Ben folded the list, then held it up. "Can I keep this?"

Earl B. hesitated, then nodded.

His uncle slid the paper into his shirt pocket. "Now, you go on and get to school."

"But—"

Mr. Dupree's chin lifted slightly. "You heard him. Go on to school."

"No!" Earl B. yelled, a stubborn edge to his voice. He had been double-teamed. "I'm staying until you two get out of here."

"Go on," said Mr. Dupree. "We got work to do." He started to shut the door, but Earl B. caught it before it closed.

"Let it go, son," Big Ben said, under his breath. "You're making things worse."

Earl B. answered with a wide-eyed, pleading stare, unable to believe what was happening. Not knowing what else to do, he dropped his hand and let Mr. Dupree close the door. Feeling deflated, Earl B. turned and walked uneasily to the edge of the porch. There was a crawl space under the stoop, just the kind of spot the Klan liked to plant a bomb. Climbing down to the ground, he peered under the porch. His eyes gradually adjusted to the darkness, but all that came into view were some old candy wrappers and an empty bottle. Nothing suspicious at all. But he knew there were a hundred other places they could hide a bomb. And sometimes they just drove by and hurled explosives from an open car window.

Backing away, Earl B. couldn't take his eyes off the church, where dynamite might blow up at any time, with Big Ben and Mr. Dupree still inside.

Chapter 33

Going to school was out of the question. By now, Grammaw was already at work, so Earl B. headed home, hoping the empty house would give him some space to think things through. Arriving there, he stomped inside, slammed the door, and charged toward the kitchen. His insides were about to explode. "Damn!" Earl B. shouted, then picked up one of the chairs and threw it toward the front room. It hit an easy chair and crash-landed just short of the window, with one of its legs flying off in another direction.

Collapsing on the couch, he grabbed a pillow and buried his head inside. His shoulders convulsed as he sobbed like a three-year-old. Everybody was so stubborn. Mr. Dupree. Big Ben. His own father. Yes, Earl B. *knew* what could happen to pigheaded people.

Today's ordeal had taken him back to the nightmare of the bombing of his house. Except this time, he knew what was about to happen and couldn't stop it. Just like his mother, Shirley's dad and Big Ben were about to die in a bombing. Earl B. threw the pillow aside and let out a primal scream.

Getting up from the couch, he grabbed his key, glanced at the wall clock, and started toward the door. In fifteen minutes, Ray and Rex would be at High Point, waiting for him. Earl B. needed them now—he needed to strike out, even if it was in the wrong direction. Breaking into a Klansman's house would feel good.

The phone rang. With his hand on the doorknob, he hesitated, then headed back and answered a little louder than intended. "Hello?"

"Hey . . . uh . . . could I speak to Earl B. please?" The man's voice had a nasal quality to it.

"Speaking."

"Hey, this is Cornell." He paused, perhaps expecting a response, then continued. "I need some help, man. Can you come to the ARC office?"

"Right now?"

"Yeah," Cornell said. "I wouldn't ask, but I can't find nobody else around. They must have marched."

"Sorry," Earl B. said. "I've got to meet somebody in fifteen minutes."

"But I can't reach Larry. And nobody else is back from jail. I really need help."

"What's up?"

"I got attacked," Cornell said. "Klan."

Uneasy thoughts drifted through Earl B.'s mind. This wasn't making sense. "Why didn't you march? Why aren't you in jail?"

"I was busy in the church the whole time organizing the kids. It won't take long."

"But I can't. Like I said, I've gotta be someplace at nine."

"Where?"

"I've . . ." Earl B. couldn't exactly tell him he was going to commit burglary.

"My brother's coming down from Gadsden," Cornell said. "But he won't be here for a while." A scraping noise came through the line. "My nose is . . . I can't get it to stop bleeding."

Earl B. looked at the wall clock again. Now it was ten minutes till nine. The seconds ticked by as he came to a decision. "All right. I'll be there."

Chapter 34

By the time Earl B. got to the ARC office, a thunderstorm was in full swing. Still feeling uncomfortable about the whole thing, he crept up the wet stairs, opened the door a crack, and peeked inside. Cornell was sitting in a chair, his face swollen and his shirt bloody. Earl B. opened the door the rest of the way.

Cornell looked up, holding a blood-soaked rag to his nose. "Hey—thanks for coming."

"You need to lie down, man." Earl B. slipped into the room, grabbed his hand, and helped him to the floor. "What happened?"

"Klan attacked me," Cornell said. "Beat me up."

A crash of thunder startled Earl B. "Here? At the ARC office?"

"No. You know that car repair shop up near High Point?"

Earl B. nodded, knowing exactly where it was. His dad had once taken his car there but sensed the owner was trying to rip him off.

"It was in the alleyway behind that building." Cornell took the rag away from his nose and a stream of blood flowed. "I was taking that shortcut to Brother Jack's."

"We need some ice." Earl B. looked around but knew perfectly well there was none in the place. "Pinch your nose together real tight. I'll try to find stuff to clean you up." Scrambling around the office, he gathered a bucket of water, towels, and a handful of rags, then washed Cornell's face. "So what were you doing up at High Point?"

"Meeting Larry." His voice sounded even more nasal than before. "He was going to give me something Shirley wanted me to have."

"Shirley?" Earl B. paused, holding a towel in mid-air.

"Yeah." A boom of thunder rattled the building.

"She marched on Friday. She's in jail."

"That's what I'd heard. But I thought it might be something she'd . . ." Cornell's voice trailed off. "I don't know. I didn't understand it either."

Earl B. dried his face with a towel. "Okay. You were near High Point. Then what happened?"

"Heading down that alleyway, I had the feeling someone was following me. But every time I looked behind, nobody was there." Cornell's fresh rag was already crimson. "Then this guy came out of nowhere, jumped me from behind, and knocked me out cold. I woke up on the ground with my whole body aching and blood pouring out of my nose. He must have beaten me after he brought me down."

"Just one man?"

"I think so."

"And you think he was a Klansman?" Earl B. switched rags with him and dropped the old one in the bucket, which instantly turned the water red.

"I *know* he was a Klansman. I woke up and saw a big 'KKK' painted on the wall of the building next to me."

The lights flickered. "Did you notice his hands at all?"

"Not really. Why?"

"One guy is missing the index finger on his right hand." Earl B. emptied the bucket of bloody water into the sink, then started refilling it. "I just wondered if it was him."

"I'm not sure. I didn't really notice."

He put the bucket of fresh water next to Cornell and sat down. "So you were meeting Larry? Did you see him?"

"No, the guy jumped me before I ever got there."

"So you never found out what it was Shirley wanted you to have?"

Cornell shook his head, then winced in pain. "No."

"When was the last time you saw Larry?"

"Yesterday. He's been here at the office almost every day."

Earl B. rose and paced back and forth a couple of times. "Something's not making sense."

"What do you mean?"

"Shirley went to jail a week ago. Why didn't Larry just give you whatever it was earlier?"

"I don't know. It's Larry." Bitterness and sarcasm laced his words. "Do you really need another reason?"

"The Klansman who attacked you. Could that have been Larry?"

Blood spurted out of Cornell's nose as he laughed. "I don't like Larry, but no I don't think he's a Klansman."

"You sure?" Earl B. said, handing Cornell a fresh rag.

"I really don't think it was him." Another thunderclap sounded, and rain blew against the window. "A lot of people have been getting hurt lately," Cornell continued. "I figured it was just a matter of time."

"Speaking of that, how's Gwen?"

"About the same." Cornell frowned. "Doctor said she probably won't ever see again."

Thinking back to the hospital visit, Earl B. remembered Gwen's swollen face, then shook his head. "It's not fair."

"No," Cornell said, readjusting his rag.

Earl B. glanced at his watch. Ray's gang had probably gone on without him.

Cornell noticed. "If you need to leave now . . ."

"No, I don't mind staying." Earl B. looked out the window. The rain had let up a little, but it was still steady.

"Appreciate it, bruh." His attitude had clearly changed since the day they had worked on repairs at the ARC office. He seemed more relaxed.

"You guys did a good job on this place," Earl B. said, gazing at the ceiling and wall. The new windows still had stickers.

"Thanks, man." Cornell pulled the rag away and glanced around the office. The bleeding from his nose appeared to have almost stopped. "It wasn't easy. I didn't have much help, but Shirley put in a lot of hours." The look on his face made it clear he had enjoyed that time with her, and Earl B. felt a twinge of jealousy. Cornell continued. "Heard you've had run-ins with the Klan."

"You mean the guy with the missing finger?" Earl B. shrugged. He didn't want to get into that story. "He's hassled a few people."

Cornell looked confused. "Shirley said your house was bombed. Were your parents involved in the movement or something?"

"A little." Earl B. didn't feel like discussing his dad either.

"Of course, it ain't like the Klan needs a reason. Nothing they do makes sense. That's part of their game. Keeps people on their toes." He pulled the rag away from his nose, refolded it, then put it back. "It don't matter if you're carrying a picket sign or not. If you're the wrong color or the wrong religion, they're after your ass."

"That's for sure."

"One time, my family was driving to Louisiana. My little sister had to pee. She was about thirteen. We were in Mississippi, and the sun was going down. If you're black, it's against the law to pee in that state. There ain't no place. All the restrooms say, 'White Only.'"

Cornell sat upright, still holding the rag to his nose. "Dad stopped by the side of the road, and she squatted in the grass. From out of nowhere came these rednecks, and they charged toward her. Genuine Mississippi rednecks. My sister screamed and ran back toward the car. By then, me, my father, and my two brothers had jumped out. Some of them white boys ran off when they saw the four of us storming at 'em." His voice faltered. "But the rest fought."

"What happened?" Earl B. asked when he didn't continue.

For a moment, all was silent except for the raindrops hitting the window. Cornell swallowed. "One of 'em had a knife." He pointed to his face. "See this here scar?"

Earl B. saw it. It was hard to miss.

"The Klan gave me that."

Chapter 35

During a lull in the conversation, Earl B. listened to the pellets of rain hit the roof and the occasional boom of thunder. A knock sounded on the door of the ARC office, and he answered.

"I—I'm Calvin Huff," a young man on the stoop said. He carried an umbrella and looked downward except for a few timid glances.

"Come on in." Earl B. introduced himself and they shook hands.

Calvin closed his umbrella, then stooped beside his brother. "Wha—What happened?"

As Cornell told the story, Earl B. wondered how these two could be brothers, one so brash and the other so meek.

"You can come to—to my place till you get better," Calvin said, helping him stand.

Earl B. took the rag from Cornell's hand. "I think the bleeding's stopped. I'll give you a fresh rag, just in case."

"Thanks, man," Cornell said. He glanced at the mess on the floor. "We need to clean this up."

"I'll get it," said Earl B. "You can go on."

"You sure?"

"Yeah. No problem." Earl B. wanted a chance to look around the office a bit. Something about Cornell's story still bothered him.

"Okay. Make sure you lock up as you leave." Cornell and his brother headed toward the door.

"I will." Earl B. tried to keep the irritation he felt out of his voice. Cornell's comment reminded him of his grandmother's nagging.

The brothers left. Earl B. rinsed the bloody rags in the bucket, still mulling over the story of the attack at High Point. According to Cornell, Larry hadn't marched either.

After the cleanup, Earl B. wandered around the office. He picked up a handful of papers from Larry's desk, then threw them back down. On Cornell's side of the office, huge piles of newsletters lay against the wall, undelivered. Glancing at one of them, Earl B. realized they were the ones printed right before the marches began. Apparently, the "direct action" folks were too busy practicing what they preached to deliver them.

At one end of these stacks were two large metal cans. Earl B. walked closer. Gasoline. Perhaps Cornell kept them available for newsletter runs? Or grass cutting?

Back at Larry's desk, Earl B. systematically sifted through papers. They seemed to be routine bills, invoices, flyers, and letters. After tossing them on the floor, a handful at a time, he opened the drawers. The top one on the right held a tray with pencils, pens, paper clips, tape, and other small odds and ends. There were more papers and letters in the left one—nothing unusual.

The bottom drawers, both file-cabinet sized, wouldn't open, no matter how hard he yanked. Earl B. went into the closet and found the toolbox they had used during the repair work. He pulled out a big, strong hammer and tried to pry one of the drawers open with the claw, but it wouldn't budge. Returning to the closet, he found a crow bar. It finally surrendered.

The drawer was stuffed to the brim with four-by-six cards, overflowing out the sides and back. Earl B. knew what they were before examining them—completed voter registration forms. He pulled out another handful and thumbed through them. More of the same. The drawer was chock-full of them.

"Oh my God," he muttered. "Larry never turned them in." Earl B. emptied the drawer, dumping the cards on the floor. Nothing else was inside.

Grabbing the crowbar, he pried the other drawer open. It was nearly empty, with only a black leather-bound book and a folded sheet of paper lying on top of a white cloth.

A roll of thunder reminded him of the outside storm. Picking up the black book, Earl B. thumbed through its pages. It was nothing but a date book with appointments, times, and names of people. A business card slipped out and fluttered to the floor. He retrieved it and read the name, "Ronald Slade, Special Agent, Federal Bureau of Investigation." Switching his gaze to the date book, he skimmed through the pages. His eyes locked on an entry—R. S. He turned the page and saw the same initials. And on another page.

Earl B. picked up the sheet of paper from the drawer and unfolded it. It was identical to the one he had been staring at for several months—the bombing list. Except this one had names written next to the addresses:

59	*35th Ave. N.*	*Roy and Frank*
321	*2nd St. S.*	*Larry and Stubby*
109	*Jefferson Ave. SW*	*Roy and Frank*
30	*Court G Alley*	*Larry and Stubby*
81	*7th Ave. N.*	*Larry and Stubby*
130	*4th Ct. N.*	*Larry and Stubby*
348	*29th Ave. N.*	*Roy and Frank*

His breath caught as his eyes honed in on two things. First, his own street name, Second Street South, with the names *Larry and Stubby* scribbled next to it. And second, the street with the church where Mr. Dupree worked, Fourth Court North, with *Larry and Stubby* next to it also. At the bottom of the sheet, Larry had handwritten Earl B.'s name and phone number.

Still reeling from his discovery, Earl B. remembered the white cloth. Reaching into the drawer, he picked it up and let it fall open—a Klan robe. The hood, which had been tucked inside, fell to the floor, and its empty eyeholes stared menacingly at him.

"You came at the wrong time," a voice said.

Chapter 36

Larry stood in the doorway, holding a can of gasoline in each hand. A rumble of thunder shook the walls of the building.

Still clutching the Klan robe, Earl B. felt his knees quiver. And it wasn't from fear. Every fiber in his body was furious about what he had just found in the desk. "You ain't no civil rights worker," he spat out.

"No kidding," Larry said, setting the gasoline cans on the floor. "Took you long enough to catch on." After opening one can, he carried it to where knee-high stacks of newsletters lined the wall and poured the gasoline onto the papers. "How nice of Cornell to provide tinder for the fire."

Earl B. ignored his comment. "And the man who's been stalking me. The man with—"

"Stubby." Larry chuckled. "Yeah, he's my right-hand man. He'll do anything I tell him to."

"You bombed my house," Earl B. barked, throwing the Klan robe on the floor. "Killed my mother."

There was a subtle change in Larry's expression. Was it surprise? "Earl B. Peterson," he drawled. "The only son of James E. Peterson. Yes, I knew your father. Unfortunately."

"What's that supposed to mean?"

"We worked at the same place. In fact, he got a job that was supposed to be mine." Larry pulled out a book of matches and walked closer to Earl B. "He was one of those uppity niggers. Did I mention I can't stand uppity niggers?"

"You killed him, didn't you?"

"He was in my way." Larry's face contorted into a sneer. "You really want to know what happened?" He faked a laugh. "Yeah, I killed him. Castrated him, too. Me and a few friends. But you'll never be able to prove it. The body—what's left of it—is a long way from here."

"Where?" Earl B.'s voice cracked.

Larry's chin lifted. "At the bottom of a river. And there it'll stay. I made sure of that." He put his right hand in his pants pocket.

Earl B. watched, wondering if it held a weapon. Scanning the room, he sized up the situation. Even if he was fast, the Klansman could easily block his way to the door. Earl B. was trapped. His heart pounded. Surely Larry could hear it.

Outside in the rain, footsteps padded softly. Four Fingers showed up in the doorway, holding more gasoline cans. "Say boss, you want all of—" He abruptly stopped when he saw Earl B.

"Bring 'em in, Stubby," Larry said, then continued. "Your friend's here. You'll finally get your chance to do away with him. He can go up with the building."

Stubby put the cans on the floor. Now, Earl B. had an added complication.

"Keep an eye on him," Larry said, opening another can.

Stubby moved toward Earl B. as Larry poured the contents on the stacks of newsletters along the opposite wall.

Using his peripheral vision, Earl B. saw the crowbar lying on the floor. But the hammer lay within his reach, on top of the desk. "What time's the bombing?" he asked, stalling for time.

"So you finally figured it out, huh?" Larry called over his shoulder.

"Shirley did."

"I got a lot of information out of her. Especially about you. People say she's a hot-shot math student." He laughed. "She was clueless. I figured that monkey wouldn't have the intelligence to solve it."

Earl B.'s temper was just beneath the surface. He took some deep breaths, trying to calm himself. Stubby crept closer.

"What time's the bombing?" Earl B. repeated.

"Tell him, Stubby." Larry dropped the gasoline can and sauntered toward them. A distant roll of thunder sounded.

Stubby moved his shoulders back in a smug gesture. "Well, I'd say"—he looked at his watch—"at least an hour ago." He cackled.

Earl B. felt his tongue pressing on the roof of his mouth. He wanted to hit the man—hard. In one quick movement, he picked up the hammer and hurled it at Stubby's head. A sickening thud sounded as it hit its target. The man collapsed to the floor—out cold. Earl B. lunged toward Larry, who pulled a revolver from his pocket. The teenage fullback reached him before he could shoot, grabbing his arms and pinning them to the wall. Larry's leg strained against him. Earl B. leaned in harder, at the same time shaking the Klansman's right arm, trying to dislodge the gun. But it was no use—the pistol might as well have been glued to his hand.

With his muscles trembling, Earl B. tried to maintain his hold. His arms finally gave out, and the two fell to the floor. Now the teen was trapped underneath, with Larry's body weighing him down. Twice the Klansman tried to lift his gun, but Earl B. thwarted him. Then a click near his left ear made him freeze. Startled, Larry lost his balance, and the teen shoved him away.

Both scrambled to their feet. Earl B. rushed toward Larry, who was backing up and raising his revolver, about to pull the trigger. The fullback caught his arm in mid-swing. They struggled, with Earl B. advancing until they reached the wall. As they slammed against it, the pistol fired. Three yards away, a small fire broke out. Larry's maniacal face was flushed scarlet as he strained to break free. The teen's arm throbbed—he couldn't hold on much longer. Gathering his strength, Earl B. slammed Larry's gun hand against the wall once, twice, three times. Finally, the pistol fell out of the Klansman's grasp and onto the floor.

Earl B. still held Larry pinned to the wall. The next instant, the fire exploded into big flames. In one motion, the teen dropped his hold on him and lunged for the revolver. The Klansman pounced on Earl B., trying to stop him, then reached for the weapon himself. For a moment, both had a piece of it as they rolled on the floor, then Earl B. slammed their hands onto the wooden boards, dislodging the pistol and sending it flying into the fire. The flames, now even bigger, lapped dangerously close to the two, chasing them out the open door. On the porch, Larry rushed toward him, and the tussle continued in the rain.

Gaining the advantage, the Klansman pushed Earl B. steadily back toward the office. The teen felt the heat of the fire behind him. Smoke enveloped their faces. Earl B. coughed, shook his head, shut his eyes. He felt more and more lightheaded as they got closer to the fire. In a last-ditch effort, the fullback shoved his right hand forward, breaking free of Larry's grip just long enough to draw his hand back and deliver a forceful, brutal uppercut to his jaw. The Klansman immediately crumbled. Earl B. let his body drop in the doorway, then stumbled over him, onto the porch.

Another explosion from the fire rent the air, this time shaking the building. It made Earl B. think of Stubby, who was by now—no doubt—toast. The drizzle continued. Standing on the stairs, with his sides heaving, Earl B. glanced back and saw the Klansman's leg rise, flail a little, and fall again. With raindrops running down his forehead and into his eyes, Earl B. started to move toward him, then hesitated. Larry stirred again, trying to raise his body, but then he collapsed.

Leaning forward against a tree trunk, the teen gripped the rough bark with his fingers, while a thousand thoughts swept through his mind. This man was an FBI infiltrator. Klan. Larry had brutally murdered his father, bombed his house, killed his mother. And less than a minute ago, Larry was trying to kill *him*. Earl B. could leave him here to die with Stubby, who had tried to lynch him up on Red Mountain. They'd both be engulfed by the flames, a fire that Larry himself had planned. If Earl B. simply walked away, everything would take care of itself, nice and neat. No one would ever know. For months, he had wished for this. The life of the man who had bombed his house—the monster who had also tortured his father— was now in his hands.

Larry's leg rose again, then fell back down. Earl B. wanted to leave. But he couldn't move, his muscles had turned to stone. The bombing list flashed before him, the one he had just found, with the names of the attackers spelled out. Larry seemed to be the big shot, the one in charge of it all, but he had also been personally involved in four of the strikes. Two of them closely affected Earl B.—his own home and Fourth Court North, the one that had probably injured or killed Mr. Dupree and Big Ben that morning.

Earl B. looked into the distance, as if he could see Grace Redemption Church. He wanted to go there now and see if it had been hit. But something held him here, something that seemed important. Right in front of him, a life hung on the line. A Klansman's life, true. The life of a bigot and killer. A life of poison and hatred. But a life.

Gwen's words ran through his head: *An eye for an eye only makes the whole world blind.* Larry's leg rose and fell again, weaker this time. Flames licked the edge of the doorway.

"Damn!" Stomping toward the Klansman, Earl B. grabbed his legs and dragged him off the porch across the street to a tree. Leaning him against the trunk, he stooped down and looked into the man's unfocused eyes. Larry honed in on the teen and they stared at each other for a moment. Then it was over. Earl B. stood, splashed through a puddle, and staggered his way down Fourteenth Street. Halfway down the block, a wave of nausea came over him, and he leaned against a building and retched.

Chapter 37

Earl B. walked. He wasn't sure where. His body was on autopilot. The rain slacked off to a sprinkle. Sirens screamed in the distance. People passed by, not bothering to hide their stares. His body was filthy—covered in soot, then soaked with water. He trudged along, on sidewalks, in the grass, and alongside buildings. If he went to the church to find out if Shirley's father and Big Ben were still alive, it wouldn't change a thing. What happened was history, and his bed at home seemed awfully inviting. His mouth was dry as paste. A coughing jag sent him hobbling into an empty lot, bent over double, and ended with him spitting out thick, black mucous. The rage that had consumed him a few minutes ago seemed a distant memory. All that was left was exhaustion and an empty feeling in the pit of his stomach. Why hadn't he been able to walk away and leave Larry? Was he weak and spineless? The Klansman's words kept mocking him: *Took you long enough to catch on. . . . He was one of those uppity niggers. . . . I figured that monkey didn't have the intelligence to solve it.*

Reaching his house, Earl B. stumbled up the stairs to the porch, dug out his key, and opened the door. Making a beeline for the kitchen, he downed a glass of water. Another wave of fatigue came over him, and he teetered to his bedroom and fell on top of his bed, with his filthy clothes and shoes still on. For months, he had ached for revenge. Today, Earl B. had the life of the bomber in his hands, and he didn't kill him. He was a complete and utter failure. His mother and father would have been ashamed of him. The phone rang, but he ignored it and fell asleep.

Later, the phone rang again and woke him up. He didn't answer. Earl B. had been dreaming that his father was in a burning building, but he couldn't get to him. His muscles were still tense from the nightmare. Sitting up on the side of the bed, he ran his fingers through his hair and rubbed his forehead, trying to ease his pounding headache, then examined his hands. His fingers were caked with a layer of oily grit and soot. Heading to the bathroom, Earl B. grabbed a washcloth, made a halfhearted attempt to clean up, and looked in the mirror. All he had done was smear dirt all over his face. "I don't even care," he mumbled to himself, throwing down the washrag.

Still thirsty, Earl B. went to the kitchen and gulped down another glass of water. Walking out on the stoop, he locked the door behind him. It had quit raining. The sun, now poised above a neighbor's house, shone into his eyes. He must have slept for several hours. Grammaw would be home soon.

Reaching the sidewalk, Earl B. glanced right and left—Grace Redemption or Shirley's house? Going to her house might force him to deal with bad news. Not yet ready for that, he opted for the church. Maybe the bombing at Grace Redemption hadn't been too destructive—most of them didn't end up killing people. Just because Stubby had confirmed the attack didn't mean Shirley's father and Big Ben were dead.

At the end of the first block, he turned the corner. A young mother came toward him pushing a buggy. Drawing closer, she eyed him nervously and gave him a wide berth. Maybe he should have made a better effort at cleaning up. Too late now.

Earl B. made his way through a residential section, then through a field and over a bridge. Approaching another field, he could tell, on closer inspection, that it had once been paved. But grass and weeds had taken over, cracking the asphalt. Yes, plants might be discouraged by blacktop for a while, but they eventually won out.

Entering Smithfield, he walked more purposefully. Shrubs were in full bloom, parading their pinks, purples, and maroons. Droplets of water clung to the petals. Earl B. caught a whiff of their flowery scent. A woman weeding her rose garden looked at him but didn't speak. Life went on, its beauty and good spirits mocking his broken little world. He turned at an intersection and kept going, squinting into the distance.

Earl B. was close now. He plodded forward a few steps, then stopped. Up ahead was the cross, perched on top like a beacon. It, at least, had survived.

Then he saw the church. Or the absence of one. A skeleton stood in its place, with the cross guarding a pile of charred rubble. Earl B. drew near, then slowed his pace. Yellow tape surrounded the deserted site. Yes, he thought bitterly, even the cops had been forced to acknowledge this one. At the boundary, he stopped and stared. Mr. Dupree's words came back to him: *Them Klan—they talk big talk all the time. They don't do half the stuff they brag about.*

Earl B. turned and walked away, his body feeling empty and exhausted. One thought dominated his mind—nobody could have survived that bomb blast. Now, Mr. Dupree and Big Ben were dead. Earl B. had failed them. Surely, he could have said more, tried harder, convinced them somehow.

Questions kept tormenting Earl B. as he zigzagged his way toward home. What could he have done differently? Told the police? No, they were Klan. In fact, he thought bitterly, it was hard to tell a Klansman from a civil rights worker anymore.

Chapter 38

The sun slipped down and peeked out between buildings. Earl B. was now in his own neighborhood, but instead of turning to go back home, he headed toward Shirley's house. After a few blocks, he entered a business section. A woman walked out of the meat market holding a big paper bag in her arms. Passing Franklin's on the next corner, Earl B. remembered the taste of their wings. When had he last eaten? Maybe yesterday at suppertime?

Earl B. trudged along for a few more blocks, and it became residential again. He wondered who would be at Shirley's house. If Mrs. Dupree was there, would she blame him for not stopping her husband?

And when Shirley got out of jail, would she even talk to him? Before the visit at the fairgrounds, she had already been plenty mad at him because of Ray. This was a hundred times worse. Her last words came back to him: *You've got to do something Earl B. . . . Please. You've got to stop my daddy from going to that church tomorrow.* Turning onto her street, he slowed down. Someone was approaching from the opposite direction. A few more steps, and Earl B. realized it was Shirley. He paused in front of her house and waited as she came closer. Her dress, hair, and body were caked in mud. She stopped, and her gaze swept over him.

"Sorry," Earl B. said, gesturing to his clothes. "I kinda got into a tussle. I haven't had a chance to clean up." A white lie.

Shirley forced a laugh. "I look a lot worse."

"I wasn't expecting to see you."

"They just let us out. Nobody came to pick me up, so I had to walk back." As if suddenly remembering something, Shirley turned and stepped toward the house, then whirled around and faced him. "My dad . . . ?" She left the question unfinished.

"I haven't heard," he said.

Shirley looked at the house again. "The car's gone." Rushing toward the front door, she knocked, then hastily unlocked it.

Earl B. followed, slowing momentarily at the foot of the stairs. Could it have been this morning that he had stood in this very same place? It seemed eons ago. He entered the house behind her.

She called out for her parents. No response. Except for the sound of their own breathing, it was dead silent.

They both kicked off their shoes. Shirley disappeared down the hall, still calling for them. Earl B. waited. She returned with tears in her eyes. "You don't know?"

How could he explain this to her? There seemed to be no good way, and the pained look on her face wasn't making it any easier. "No," he finally said.

She covered her face with her hand for a brief moment. "Did you even find him? Were you able to tell him?"

"I told him."

"And?"

Now for the hard part. The words came out in a rush. "I tried to stop him, but he insisted on going anyway."

A tear escaped and ran down her cheek.

Earl B. moved closer. "I just went by the church."

"And . . . ?"

"It got bombed, all right."

"How bad?" Her voice cracked.

"It's gone. A pile of rubble. Course that doesn't mean . . ." His voice trailed off.

A clock ticked in the background. Shirley's hand was over her face again.

Earl B. squeezed her shoulder gently. "How about a drink of water?"

"Sure."

He wandered through an adjacent small dining room to the kitchen, with Shirley following. Earl B. found a glass in the cabinet and filled it with ice and water.

She took a couple of long drafts. "I was thirsty the whole time we were in jail. I never got enough."

Outside the kitchen window, pink petals from a tall flowering shrub fluttered to the ground in the spring breeze.

Ice cubes clinked as Shirley set her glass on the counter. "Earl B., while I was walking home today from the fairgrounds, I ran into a girl from school who said some kids had broken into a house. The police caught them, and it was those friends of yours." She lowered her gaze to his clothes. "Were you . . . is that the tussle you're talking about?"

"No, I wasn't there." *Thanks to Cornell's phone call,* he thought.

"But it was those guys. The ones you hung out with."

"They wanted me to do it with them, break into some Klansman's house. For revenge. But I didn't."

Shirley gave a short nod and let out a shuddering sigh.

A noise came from the front of the house, startling them both, then they heard the sound of a key entering a keyhole and a doorknob turning. Shirley rushed toward the front door just as it opened. Mr. and Mrs. Dupree walked in, followed by Big Ben. Everyone appeared to be fine.

"Look who's here!" Mrs. Dupree held her hands out toward her daughter. "Lord have mercy, they let you out. My baby!"

"Yeah, they released us today." Shirley drew close, ready to give a big hug, but her mother abruptly stopped and pulled away.

"Ooh, child!" Mrs. Dupree pinched her nose together. "I'm gonna have to take the hose to you." Her expression made it clear she was teasing, and everyone laughed.

Shirley shifted her attention to her father. "Daddy, you're okay!"

"I'm fine." Mr. Dupree chuckled and embraced his daughter. "I don't mind a little dirt."

Earl B., who had been watching the spectacle from the entrance to the dining room, locked eyes with his uncle. Big Ben's glance didn't last long, but it was loaded with meaning. Relief. Kindness. Gratitude. Perhaps even admiration.

Mr. Dupree noticed Earl B. "I see we have company."

"Daddy," Shirley said, "this is—"

"Earl B. Peterson," he said, grabbing his hand. "We don't need an introduction."

"How did you make it home, child?" Mrs. Dupree asked her daughter.

"Walked."

Her mother shook her head. "That's a long way." She took her hat off and held it in her hands. "I asked Bessie DuBose if they could pick you up, but she and her husband had to go to Montgomery. Her sister died. Any trouble getting here?"

"No, ma'am."

Earl B. leaned against the wall, trying his best to stay out of the way and not intrude on the reunion. Big Ben edged over toward him and patted him on the back.

"We been up to the police station," Mrs. Dupree continued. "They brought these two up there for questioning."

"Questioning?" asked Shirley. "For what?"

"The bombing," her father said.

"They think you . . . ?"

He shook his head. "Not really."

"Course they don't," Mrs. Dupree snapped. "They're just trying their best to blame it on a colored person. The cops hassled both of 'em something awful. But it's all over and done with now. They let 'em go."

Shirley looked at Big Ben. "They questioned you too?"

He nodded. "I was with your daddy."

"Get Big Ben some water, child," Mrs. Dupree told her daughter. "He was thirsty, and they wouldn't give him nothing."

Shirley headed to the kitchen. Earl B. watched her parents shuffle toward the table, looking dog-tired. A moment later, she returned with a glass of ice water for his uncle, who immediately took a big gulp.

"I'll get dinner after a little bit," Mrs. Dupree said, laying her purse and hat on the table. "But I gotta rest first." She turned her gaze to Earl B. and his uncle. "You two are welcome to stay and eat if you want."

Big Ben set his empty glass on the table. "No thanks. I need to head out."

"I do too." Earl B. headed to the front door and started putting on his shoes.

"So tell me what happened, Daddy," Shirley said. "I mean, the church got bombed, right?"

Mr. Dupree shrugged. "It did, just like your friend said it would."

Earl B., who was crouched down, tying his shoelaces, looked up, curious to hear the story.

"You weren't in it?" Shirley asked.

"No, sweetheart," her father said. "Big Ben finally talked some sense into me."

"And not a minute too soon," Shirley's mother said, putting her hands on her hips. "Lord knows how stubborn that man can be."

Mr. Dupree shot a pretend look of disapproval at his wife.

"So you got out of the building?" Shirley pressed.

Big Ben answered. "Went off about five minutes after we got out. Felt the blast through the sidewalk. If I hadn't known better, I'd have thought we were having an earthquake."

"He almost got both of you killed, being so bullheaded," Mrs. Dupree said.

"I finally changed his mind." Big Ben waved as he headed out the door. "See you folks later."

Earl B. almost followed, then hesitated as he heard Mrs. Dupree's trembling voice. He glanced back.

"Five minutes," she said, walking toward Shirley with a tear running down her cheek. "Only five minutes after they got out of the building." Embracing her daughter, she laughed and cried at the same time. "Oh, baby. If that young man hadn't warned 'em, they would've been in that blast."

Slipping out, Earl B. silently closed the door behind him.

Chapter 39

Sometimes geography works in a person's favor.

After leaving the Duprees', Big Ben walked Earl B. to his house, since it was on the way to his own place. It gave them a chance to rehash the events. His uncle told him about the moment he and Mr. Dupree had first entered Grace Redemption Church. A squirrel had scampered out of a dark corner, scaring the living daylights out of both men until they realized what it was. The story gave Earl B. a good belly laugh, something he needed after all they had been through.

There was only one drawback to their time together. During the stroll, his uncle mentioned his bedraggled appearance a couple of times, fishing for an explanation, but he never asked outright what had happened. And Earl B. didn't volunteer any information. His brawl with a Klansman wasn't anyone else's business, and besides, it was water under the bridge.

At his doorstep, they closed out their conversation, and Earl B. went inside. Radio static hissed from the kitchen area.

"Is that you, Earl B.?" Grammaw hollered. She appeared in the doorway of the living room and laid eyes on him. "Lord, have mercy," she gasped. "What in the world happened to you?"

"Had a little disagreement," he muttered.

"Looks like more than a little disagreement to me." Approaching him, Grammaw placed her hand along the side of his face. "You okay?"

"I'm fine."

She looked over her glasses at him. "You in trouble?"

"No, Grammaw." He heard a noise behind him and realized Big Ben hadn't left—he was coming inside.

"Hello, Esther."

"I didn't know you were here," Grammaw said.

"What's going on?" Big Ben asked. "What's that noise, Esther?" The radio static still hissed in the background.

"Oh, come on back here."

Earl B. kicked off his dirty shoes, and he and his uncle followed as she hobbled into the kitchen.

"I was trying to get the news on this gadget." She fumbled with the dial. "Addie Thomas from church just called and told me they made some big-time settlement and the kids were released." The static was as loud as ever.

Big Ben took over and turned the dial, bringing in the local news. They listened for a few minutes, but the reporters only talked about two things—a woman who had been missing for a week and a car crash that had just happened on Decatur Highway.

"Don't surprise me none, them not covering it on local news," Big Ben said. "The white businesses got the reporters on their side."

"I'll find a station." Earl B. dialed it to WENN, and Shelley the Playboy's voice boomed out.

"And you kids went up against them dogs, fire hoses, and even Bull Connor's tank," the deejay was saying. "Made the national news. It looked like a war zone out there."

"He's right about that," Big Ben said.

"You filled the jails and brought them bigwigs to their knees," Shelley the Playboy continued. "The great city of Birmingham has finally agreed to desegregate lunch counters—within ninety days— and hire Negro clerks and salesmen in the stores. This afternoon, Reverend King called it a moment of great victory!"

"Ain't that something?" murmured Grammaw. "I never would have thought . . ."

"Now," the deejay said, "here's a special dedication to Mr. Bull Connor from Mr. Ray Charles hisself."

The opening strains of "Hit the Road, Jack" began playing.

"Hard to believe," Grammaw said, turning the radio off.

"Yep," Big Ben said. "In Bombingham, of all places."

Earl B. eased away and tried to slip into the hall toward his bedroom, but Grammaw called his name.

"Yes, ma'am?" he answered.

Her eyes bore into him. "You never did tell me what happened."

Big Ben laid a hand on her arm. "Esther."

Grammaw shifted her gaze to his uncle.

"Let it go," he said gently. "He's had a rough day." Big Ben looked at Earl B. "You go take a shower. I'll talk to her."

Chapter 40

Springtime in Birmingham, Alabama. Trees were in full bloom. Delicate, white petals drifted to the ground like fresh, falling snow, filling the air with their fragrance. A shrub was adorned with a blanket of yellow blossoms. Earl B. took a deep breath in, enjoying the mixture of scents.

It was the next morning, and he was crossing the main road, walking to Shirley's house. Now, there was a different smell— someone was frying breakfast, perhaps bacon or sausage. Earl B. entered her neighborhood. This time, finding her street was easier. Drawing closer to the house, he saw her sitting on the stoop outside, with her head in her hands, in a sleeveless, yellow dress. The outfit was vaguely familiar, but he hadn't remembered it being so bright. Earl B. liked the way it looked on her. About ten feet away, he stopped walking. She looked up.

"Hi." He took another step closer.

Shirley nodded. "Hey," she said softly.

"I need to talk to you about something."

Her expression changed slightly, but he couldn't read it. "What?"

"The ARC office—"

"Burned to the ground," she said. "Yes, I know."

"You do?"

"Yeah." Shirley stood and leaned against the hand railing. "Rachel came over last night, frantic because she couldn't find Larry. We both found Cornell, and he told us about it. The police think the Klan did it."

Earl B. shrugged. "I guess you could say that."

"You know something?"

He told her the whole story, about Larry, Stubby, the fight, the fire.

After he finished, Shirley stared at him for a few moments without speaking. "So Larry was Klan?" she finally asked.

"Yeah."

"I can't believe it," she said, shaking her head.

"It makes sense now," Earl B. said. "That's why Stubby was talking to Rachel. He was probably looking for Larry that day."

Shirley heaved a sigh. "Yeah, I'm sure she had no idea who he was."

"So what did Cornell tell you?"

She shrugged. "The police investigated and asked him a ton of questions."

"They thought he had done it?"

"I don't think so. The cops found Larry lying on the ground across the street when the building was still burning. Took him to the ER."

"He survived? Did they question him?"

"Yes, Larry told 'em he was in there working with that other guy—Stubby, you called him?"

Earl B. nodded.

"They smelled smoke. Next thing he knew, the place was on fire."

"So he didn't try to blame someone else?"

"Apparently not," said Shirley. "I was surprised he didn't try to pin it on somebody like Cornell. Or you."

A chill went through Earl B.'s body.

"Said he breathed in a lot of smoke," said Shirley. "And his face was all bruised and swollen. I guess you're responsible for that." She smirked.

"Is he still in the hospital?"

"No, disappeared after he was treated."

"Disappeared?"

"Nobody knows where he went," Shirley said. "When Rachel got home from jail, it looked like he'd moved out of the apartment." Her expression changed slightly. "Wonder what she'll say when I tell her Larry was Klan."

"He was just using her to infiltrate the group."

"But she'll flip out when she learns about him. She's Jewish. I'm surprised he didn't kill her."

"Well, anyway, he's gone."

"And I say, good riddance." Her gaze wandered to the side of his face, where his nine stitches had been. "I guess all of us got a few new scars out of this experience." She sat back down on the stoop. "Oh, I got other news. My daddy found out who got him fired. You'll never guess."

"Who?"

"Stewart Owens, Carolyn's father," Shirley said, with a look of disgust. "He did it to get a little extra vacation time."

"Seriously? A black man?"

She nodded. "But Daddy's talking about getting one of those new jobs they're talking about."

"I heard about those."

"People won't recognize this town. Who knows? By the time I get out of college, they might be hiring Negro scientists."

"Hmm. They'll let you into college?" Earl B. teased. "A jailbird like you?"

She snorted. "Believe me, I've thought of that. It's been on my mind all morning."

The dark look on her face made Earl B. regret his words. "Look, a slew of kids went to jail," he said, his tone now serious. "Something tells me they won't count those as real arrests. They'll let some of them into college."

"Maybe. Even so, I feel like I helped a lot of people. Some things are more important than my own piddly, little problems. Gwen taught me that." She looked off into the distance.

Earl B. sat beside her on the stoop. "Wonder why Larry didn't blame the fire on me."

"Maybe because you saved his life, pulling him out."

"I had the chance to let him die and I couldn't do it." His eyes began stinging, and he covered his face with his hands.

She touched him on the arm. "If you had let him die, you'd be as bad as he is."

Dropping his hands, he let out a cynical laugh.

"I mean it, Earl B.," she said earnestly. "You were angry with Larry, right? The easiest thing you could have done was to let him die. But if you had done that, the cycle would never end."

A woman carrying two grocery bags walked by and nodded at them. She kept going down the sidewalk, then disappeared around the corner.

Earl B. stood up. "You want to go somewhere and eat?"

Shirley looked uncertain. "I just ate breakfast."

Hesitating, he put his hands in his pockets. Maybe she didn't want to go out with him, and this was her excuse. Earl B. decided to try one more time, then quit pressuring her. "How about lunch?"

"Sure. What time?"

He shrugged and glanced up at the sky. It promised to be a sunny day. "Noon?"

"Where?"

"Nelson Brothers? Green Acres?" He paused, trying to think of more black-owned restaurants.

"Loveman's?" she suggested.

He did a double take. "Loveman's?"

She answered with a mischievous smile.

"They won't desegregate until after ninety days." Earl B. remembered how unpleasant the last time had been. "Let's go to a place we can sit down."

"We could always try."

"You know something?" he asked, laughing. "You got a little devil in you." Earl B. fingered the moss agate pendant in his pocket. "Okay. I'll meet you under the clock at Loveman's at noon."

"Sounds good," she said, rising from the stoop.

He backed away slightly, but something kept him there. Pulling the pendant from his pocket, he held it out for her to see.

"You did it!" she gushed, gazing at the necklace. "It's beautiful, Earl B."

"Will you wear it?" he asked.

A tender look came over her face. "Thanks, but . . . I really love it, but I couldn't take something like that, since it belonged to your mother."

"I'd like you to have it." He held the stone just below her neck. "Besides, it'd look nice on you." Without waiting for an answer, Earl B. took the ends of the chain in his fingers and clasped them together behind her neck. He hesitated a moment before drawing back, enjoying the feel of her hair touching his cheek and the scent of her perfume. Tears had formed in her eyes. He smiled. "I was right. It looks good on you."

"Thanks, Earl B," she whispered.

He leaned over and kissed her. It didn't last long, but it was tender and warm, like a caress. "See you at noon." He backed away. She waved, then went toward the front door.

Earl B. turned and left. Heading down the sidewalk, he looked back once, but she had already gone inside. He glanced at his watch. Nine thirty. Two and a half hours, and they'd be together again.

Bits and pieces of their conversation came back to him as he walked. So Larry was alive. *The easiest thing you could have done was to let him die. But if you had done that, the cycle would never end.* Maybe she was right.

The sky was deep blue, with only a few white, fluffy clouds thrown here and there. The sound of a child laughing drew his attention. In the next yard, a man bounced a plastic ball to a kid. Earl B. paused on the sidewalk and watched, remembering his own dad doing the same thing. The little boy stopped the ball, then tried to throw it back to his father. It was a wild pitch that went toward the road. Earl B. automatically reacted by catching the ball, dribbling it twice, and tossing it to the father.

"Thanks," the man said, smiling.

"No problem," Earl B. said, continuing his walk. Rounding the corner, he passed by Franklins, then backtracked and went inside.

"A dozen take-out," a woman shouted as he walked in the door. Earl B. knew her voice—Big Booty Judy, his mother's friend. She hung up the phone. The place smelled so good he could already taste the food. Earl B. walked up to the counter.

Judy stood poised with a pencil. "Can I help you?" Her expression changed. "Hey, ain't you the Peterson kid? Lillian's son?"

"Yes, ma'am."

"Earl B." A tender smile came across her face. "It's been a while. I bet you came for some wings."

"Yes, ma'am."

"A dozen? Half dozen?"

"Dozen." Earl B. decided to stash a few in the refrigerator and take them to Big Ben. He paid, then wandered around the store, looking at the groceries—miniature versions of cereals, cracker boxes, and snacks, along with bread and milk. Two kids came in, bought candy bars, and left.

"Here it is, Earl B.!" Judy held out a greasy paper bag as he approached the counter. "I put an extra one in there," she whispered.

Outside, Earl B. munched on a wing as he walked down Sixth Avenue, the main business drag. After a few blocks, he turned, heading into his neighborhood. A woman was stooped over, weeding around a row of shrubs with bright purple blooms. She looked up and said hello.

A good feeling swelled up inside him, an awareness and excitement he hadn't experienced since . . . when? Actually, Earl B. didn't remember ever having this particular feeling before.

He turned on his street and went past a lady pushing a baby carriage. She smiled and spoke. Approaching his house, Earl B. slowed his pace, then stopped to take it in. It was a small home, but it was theirs. The gaping hole was gone, and any damage was no longer visible. Okay, there might be some wood here and there that didn't match, but nobody but him—and Big Ben—would notice. The windows were decent. Yes, the color of the house was weird, but when he saw the place now, Earl B. saw the work that had gone into it, and not only his own sweat and toil. His uncle had taken him to the lumberyard and helped cut boards. Asa had been willing to paint alone until Earl B. quit acting the fool and decided to join him. Maybe he would write Asa a letter tomorrow. Shirley's parents would have his address.

The flower garden in front of the house reminded him of his mother, who never got to see the tulips she had planted last autumn. Now, there were all kinds of crazy colors—reds, yellows, oranges, and purples. Earl B. slipped one hand into his pocket—more out of habit than anything else—but then remembered the gemstone wasn't there anymore. It was now hanging around Shirley's neck, and that made every muscle in his body tingle.

This afternoon, Earl B. would pull some of the weeds in his mother's tulip garden. Then he would pick a bouquet and put it on the kitchen table to surprise Grammaw.

Yes, there were some bad people in the world. But there were some really good ones too, and they made it all worthwhile. People like Big Ben and Asa and Grammaw. And now Shirley. With people like that pulling for him, Earl B. was lucky. And glad to be alive.

Author's Note

Many of the characters and events in this historical novel are fictional. However, bombings like the one at the beginning of the book had become commonplace by the early 1960s in Birmingham, Alabama. In fact, the city had earned the nickname "Bombingham" because of about fifty racially motivated bombings that had occurred since the end of World War II. With the exception of Bethel Baptist, I invented all the sites on the Klan list in this novel. In reality, many of the targets were homes, especially those in the community known as Dynamite Hill. However, plenty of churches were attacked also.

In those days, segregation was the law in Birmingham. African Americans had to sit in the back of the bus, drink from separate water fountains, and attend separate schools. After ordering food at a downtown lunch counter, they were not allowed to sit down and eat. They were forced into low-income jobs in factories, if they could find work at all.

Groups of committed protesters sprang up, both locally and nationally. The one in this novel, the Alliance for Resistance and Change (ARC), is fictional, but it represents the alphabet soup of organizations that rose during these years. Activists disagreed on the best way to bring about social reform. The most conservative wing preferred voter registration and legal proceedings. The "direct action" folks had become frustrated with this route, and they organized nonviolent boycotts, sit-ins, and marches. In 1963, the most militant movement, inspired by Malcolm X, was in its infancy. These people shunned the principle of nonviolence, insisting they had the right to defend themselves if attacked.

Rev. Fred L. Shuttlesworth emerged as a charismatic leader in Birmingham, using both litigation and direct action to force change in the city. His home and his church, Bethel Baptist, had been repeatedly bombed. In 1962, local African American college students organized boycotts of white stores. Because of an Alabama statute banning boycotts, they called them "selective buying campaigns." Profits were slashed, but businesses still refused to budge on desegregation policies. Shuttlesworth convinced Rev. Dr. Martin Luther King Jr. to come to town and help crack Birmingham.

In early 1963, King joined the effort in Birmingham—along with Rev. Dr. Wyatt Tee Walker and other activists—to map out a strategy of sit-ins and marches to provoke mass arrests. The protests were scheduled to begin after the March mayoral election. Eugene "Bull" Connor was running against Albert Boutwell and Tom King. In an earlier vote, citizens had chosen to alter the city government, eliminating the position Connor had occupied for over two decades—the Commissioner of Public Safety. Boutwell won the mayoral race, but the combative Bull Connor refused to leave office while attorneys fought the legitimacy of the new government.

The demonstrations finally started in April, with protesters holding sit-ins at lunch counters throughout the city. Marches typically began at Sixteenth Street Baptist Church, which hosted many mass meetings and served as headquarters for the campaign. The goal was to pack the jails and twist the arms of businesses, forcing the government to negotiate. However, many African American adults were afraid to participate. Whites in town found many ways to intimidate them, threatening to take away their jobs, home mortgages, and car loans if they took part in the protests. In an attempt to embolden more demonstrators, King and others were arrested and jailed on Good Friday, April 12, 1963. During his incarceration, he wrote his famous essay, "Letter from a Birmingham Jail," which defended the strategy of nonviolent resistance. He was released on April 20.

By this time, Rev. James Bevel, a firebrand veteran of the Nashville Student Movement, had begun recruiting young people to protest. Since children had no jobs, mortgages, or car notes, they were immune to the threats of white businesses. They also had the most to gain, since they were inheriting a world of segregation and injustice. In workshops, students were educated in nonviolent tactics. Flyers were distributed in African American schools and communities, urging kids to demonstrate. Popular local disc jockeys, including Shelley the Playboy and Tall Paul White got the word out about the marches.

It worked. On "D-Day," May 2, 1963, hundreds of students left their schools and headed for Sixteenth Street Baptist. About one o'clock, wave upon wave of young people, ranging in age from six to twenty, departed from the church in organized groups, carrying signs and singing freedom songs. A bewildered Bull Conner, still clinging to his lame-duck commissioner post, watched as hundreds were arrested and loaded into paddy wagons. By nightfall, the jails were nearly full.

But the marches continued the next day, and a frustrated Bull Connor ordered fire hoses to be turned full force on the demonstrators. The high-pressure barrage of water lifted children off the ground, propelled them down the street, and even hurled some over parked cars. Next, Conner commanded police dogs into action, and the German shepherds viciously attacked and injured several protesters. Graphic images of Birmingham's brutal assaults against unarmed children were displayed on television's evening news, the *New York Times*, and *Life* magazine. Ironically, Bull Connor's tactics called national attention to Birmingham's civil rights problems and sparked a dramatic turnaround in public opinion across the country.

The protests continued, and by May 6, the jails were so packed that children were being locked up in the stockade at the fairgrounds. On May 7, another thousand people were arrested, but many more flooded the downtown streets, making it impossible to conduct business. Political leaders were stubborn, however, and it was not until May 10 that the city government finally agreed to a few improvements, including the desegregation of lunch counters, restrooms, fitting rooms, and drinking fountains within ninety days.

There was immediate backlash. Unlike in the novel where there's an idyllic calm, the next day, vigilantes bombed several sites—

including the Gaston Hotel, where King had been staying only hours earlier. Unrest continued over the following days and weeks, as leaders puzzled over how to implement some of the allowed changes in Birmingham. The transformation was slow. Lunch counters were not desegregated until the end of July.

Violence occasionally still reared its ugly head in the city. In September, Pres. John F. Kennedy called in the National Guard to help desegregate the schools. A few days later, Klansmen bombed the Sixteenth Street Baptist Church, killing four young girls and injuring many others.

In spite of these setbacks, however, the Birmingham Children's March had injected energy and momentum into the civil rights movement. By putting their lives on the line, these brave activists set the stage for the March on Washington in August and the Civil Rights Act of 1964. Moreover, they showed the world that one is never too young to make a difference.

Rhonda Lynn Rucker
October 2018

Acknowledgments

A book needs more than an author to come alive, and this one is no exception. I want to extend my heartfelt gratitude to all the following people:

My husband, James "Sparky" Rucker, who gave me a feel for what it was like to be an African American teenage boy in the South in 1963. You were also my first reader, and you provided help around every turn. I appreciate your love and support.

Marvin Smiley, my brother-in-law, who participated in the Birmingham Children's March and told me about his experience. He and his wife, Winifred "Penny" Smiley, also hosted me for several days while I wandered around Birmingham doing research. Love and thanks to you both.

Dorothy Smiley, Marvin's gracious mother, who described living and working in Birmingham in those days. She also helped me understand what it was like having a child arrested for demonstrating. Unfortunately, she passed away in 2014. I miss her. She was an inspiration to all who knew her.

Dick Willey, Terry Carruthers, and Ann Schwarz, my writing colleagues who painstakingly trudged through several revisions of this novel. No words are enough to express my appreciation for your patience and talents.

James Rucker, my son, who has a keen sense of plot and doesn't mind telling me things I don't want to hear. My stories are always stronger because of you. Also, a special thanks for your ideas about the book title and cover.

Greg Gratton, who owns Green Acres Café and graciously granted me a phone interview.

All those who work at the Birmingham Public Library, where I spent hours doing research. Librarians are priceless. Be nice to them.

My editor, Devinn Adams, and also Nina Kooij and all the folks at Pelican for their hard work.

My parents, Darrell and Elizabeth Hicks, who taught me the importance of love and social justice.

Finally, thanks to all of you who marched. By facing police dogs and fire hoses, you did what adults failed to do—fill the jails and transform your hometown. You helped our country come closer to its dream of liberty and justice for all. Hats off to you.

Bibliography

Aldridge, Jane. "Legal Tussle Ahead On City Hall Issue: Legal Move is Likely: Either Side Could Act." *Birmingham Post-Herald,* 4 April 1963.

American Studies at the University of Virginia. "Birmingham's Racial Segregation Ordinances: May 1951." American Studies Accessed 29 November 2015. http://xroads.virginia.edu/~public/civilrights/ordinances.html.

Atlanta Constitution. "135 Cases Cited of Mistreatment to Negroes Here." 24 April 1921.

Badger, Edward. "Question: When Will Lame Ducks Fly Out of City Hall?: Three Judges Say April 15; Council Seeks Court Order." *Birmingham News,* 4 April 1963.

Baker, David Victor. "Female Lynchings in the United States: Amending the Historical Record." *Race and Justice.* Vol 2, Issue 4 (October 2012) pp. 356-391.

Bennett, James. "Legal Tussle Ahead On City Hall Issue: Boutwell Meets With Councilmen, Attorney Today." *Birmingham Post-Herald,* 4 April 1963.

Birmingham: A. H. Parker High School. 1962. *Bison 1962 (Yearbook).* Birmingham Public Library. Accessed 4 October 2015. http://bplonline.cdmhost.com/digital/collection/p132001coll0/id/6130.

Birmingham Historical Society. Jun 2006. "Birmingham Historical Society Newsletter: Celebrate the 50th of the Movement." Birmingham Historical Society. June 2006. Accessed 10 May 2012. http://www.bhistorical.org/pdf/BHS_Newsletter_05_06.pdf.

Birmingham News. "10 More Negroes Arrested in Sit-Ins." 5 April 1963.

Birmingham News. "City Seeks to Hold Mixers in Contempt." 13 April 1963.

Birmingham News. "Commission Appeals to High Court." 25 April 1963.

Birmingham News. "The Faces of Bethel Baptist Church." 20 Jan. 2008.

Birmingham News. "Failure to Play Race News in Headlines Draws Ire of Wallace, Shuttlesworth." 5 April 1963.

Birmingham News. "Fire Hoses, Police Dogs Used to Halt Downtown Negro Demonstrations." 3 March 1963.

Birmingham News. "Library for Negroes Will Be Dedicated at Smithfield." 6 April 1956.

Birmingham News. "New Marching Groups Jailed." 2 May 1963.

Birmingham News. "White Clergyman Urge Local Negroes to Withdraw From Demonstrations." 13 April 1963.

Birmingham Post-Herald. "20 Negroes Sit In, Face Trial Today." 4 April 1963.

Birmingham Post-Herald. "Boutwell, Connor to Vie – April 2 Runoff Will Decide New City Government." 7 March 1963.

Birmingham Post-Herald. "Boutwell Elected City Mayor, Calls Council Together Today: Wins Over Connor By 8000 Votes: Largest Vote Ever Recorded Here Cast in Election." 3 April 1963.

Birmingham Public Library. "History of the Branches." Birmingham Public Library Database. Accessed 12 Dec. 2011. http://bpldb.bplonline.org/cm/HistoryOfTheBranches.

Birmingham Record Collections. "Shelley Stewart." Accessed 13 October 2016. http://www.birminghamrecord.com/brc/hall_of_fame /shelly-stewart/.

Birmingham World. "Birmingham Grid Forecasters." 3 November 1962.

Birmingham World. "Birmingham Is Shamed By Bombing!: 12 Children in Church Narrowly Escape Death." 22 Dec. 1962.

Birmingham World. "Carver Meets Carver; Parker Tackles Western." 3 Nov. 1962.

Birmingham World. "Explosion Rips Two Block Area As Family Watches TV." 27 March 1963.

Birmingham World. "JCAA Football Standings." 7 Nov. 1962.

Birmingham World. "Parker Defeats Abrams, 13-0." 3 Nov. 1962.

"Birmingham's Racial Segregation Ordinances: May 1951." American Studies at the University of Virginia. http://xroads.virginia.edu/~public/civilrights/ordinances.html/ordinances.html (accessed 29 November 2015).

Boutwell, Albert. "Boutwell Bids to Weld Unity: New Day Dawns for Birmingham." *Birmingham News,* 3 April 1963.

Branch, Taylor. *Parting the Waters: America During the King Years 1954-1963.* New York: Simon and Schuster, Inc., 1988. 673-802.

Brown, Jeannette. *African American Women Chemists.* New York: Oxford University Press, 2012.

Carawan, Guy and Candie Carawan, comp. *We Shall Overcome!: Songs of the Southern Freedom Movement.* New York: Oak Publications, 1963.

Carpenter, C. C. J., Joseph A. Durick, Hilton L. Grafman, Paul Hardin, Nolan B. Harmon, George M. Murray, Edward V. Ramage, and Earl Stallings. "Statement by Alabama Clergymen." Estate of Martin Luther King Jr. 12 April 1963.

Carson, Clayborne, Charles R. Branham, Ralph David Fertig, Mark Bauerlein, Todd Steven Burroughs, Ella Forbes, Jim Haskins *et al.* Foreword to *Civil Rights Chronicle: The African-American Struggle for Freedom,* by Myrlie Evers-Williams. Lincolnwood, IL: Publications International, Ltd., 2003.

Cinema Treasure. "Lyric Theatre." Accessed 1 May 2012. http://cinematreasures.org/theaters/20211.

Cleek, Ashley. "The Route of Division." *Al Jazeera America,* 31 May 2015. Accessed 4 June 2015. http://projects.aljazeera.com/2015/05/birmingham-bus/.

Collins, Sarah. "'The Fifth Little Girl': Birmingham Church Bombing Survivor Still Seeks Compensation 50 Years On." Interview by Amy Goodman. Democracy Now, 17 September 2013. Accessed 8 June 2015. https://www.democracynow.org/2013/9/17/the_fifth_little_girl_birmingham_church.

Columbia University. "When the South Said, 'No,' Teachers College Said, 'Yes.'" Teachers College; Columbia University. Accessed 11 August 2013. http://www.tc.columbia.edu/articles/1999/february/when-the-south-said-no-teachers-college-said-yes/.

Cone, James H. *Martin & Malcolm & America: A Dream or a Nightmare.* Maryknoll, NY: Orbis Books, 1991.

Cook, George. "Mayor-Council City Rule Wins: But Court Case May Be Ahead." *Birmingham Post-Herald,* 7 November 1962.

Dean, Charles J. "Smithfield Library Closing is End to Worn Building." *Birmingham News,* 18 August 1986.

Escovedo, Alejandro. "Shelley Stewart, Radio and the Birmingham Civil Rights Movement." *Counterpunch,* 12 June 2002. Accessed 22 November 2011. http://www.counterpunch.org/2002/06/12/shelley-stewart-radio-and-the-birmingham-civil-rights-movement/.

Eskew, Glenn T. *But for Birmingham: The Local and National Movements in the Civil Rights Struggle.* Chapel Hill: University of North Carolina Press, 1997.

Foscue, Lillian. "Boutwell Elected City Mayor, Calls Council Together Today: Urges Start to Carry Out Voters' Wish: New Official Has Open House as Votes Counted." *Birmingham Post-Herald,* 3 April 1963.

"Gestetner 180, running..mpg." YouTube video, 0:48. Posted 29 November 2008 by "terryview." Accessed 30 January 2013. http://www.youtube.com/watch?v=E5klsvETCAs.

Gibson, Robert A. "The Negro Holocaust: Lynching and Race Riots in the United States, 1880-1950." Yale-New Haven Teachers Institute. Accessed 18 February 2016. http://www.yale.edu/ynhti/curriculum/units/1979/2/79.02.04.x.html#b.

Glionna, John M. "Birmingham's Vulcan Statue, Often the Butt of Jokes, Remains Well-loved." *Los Angeles Times*, 12 April 2015. Accessed 18 March 2017. http://www.latimes.com/nation/la-na-birmingham-vulcan-20150412-story.html.

Gratton, Greg. Phone interview by Rhonda Lynn Rucker. 20 June 2012.

Gray, Jeremy. "Loveman Village, Titusville Residents Discuss Redevelopment Proposal." *Birmingham News*, 22 March 2012. Accessed 28 May 2012. http://blog.al.com/spotnews/2012/03/loveman_village_titusville_res.html.

Grooms, Anthony. *Bombingham*. New York: One World/Ballantine Books, 2001.

Hack, Dan. "Mimeograph Machine, IPRC." YouTube video. Accessed 30 January 2013. http://www.youtube.com/watch?v=u0wUcCInJ2o (video removed).

Hailey, Foster. "Dogs and Hoses Repulse Negroes at Birmingham: 3 Students Bitten in Second Day of Demonstrations Against Segregation." *New York Times*, 4 May 1963.

Hailey, Foster. "U.S. Seeking a Truce in Birmingham; Hoses Again Drive Off Demonstrators: Two Aides Meeting With Leaders – Negroes Halt Protests Temporarily." *New York Times*, 5 May 1963.

Hansen, Jeff and Chanda Temple. "Faith Under Pressure." *AL.com*, 16 July 2000. Accessed 6 March 2012. http://www.al.com/specialreport/?bombing/97-look.html.

Hevesi, Dennis. "Abraham Woods, Civil Rights Pioneer, Dies at 80." *New York Times*, 13 November 2008. Accessed by 22 November 2011. http://www.nytimes.com/2008/11/13/us/13woods.html?pagewanted=print.

HMdb.org: The Historical Marker Database. 21 January 2010. "Brock Drugs Building." Accessed 6 June 2012. http://www.hmdb.org/marker.asp?marker=26723.

HMdb.org: The Historical Marker Database. 11 December 2011. "Rev. Fred Shuttlesworth Bethel Baptist Church." Accessed 7 March 2012. http://www.hmdb.org/marker.asp?marker=50398.

Huntley, Horace. "The Lyric Theatre and Birmingham Segregation." *C-Span Video Library*, 10:47. Posted 31 Oct. 2011. Accessed 1 May 2012. http://www.c-spanvideo.org/program/302713-1.

Huntley, Horace, John W. McKerley, and Robin D. G. Kelley. *Foot Soldiers for Democracy: The Men, Women, and Children of the Birmingham Civil Rights Movement.* Birmingham: Birmingham Civil Rights Institute, 2009.

Internet Archive. "U.S. Telephone Directory Collection." Accessed 6 June 2012. http://www.archive.org/stream/usteledirec00022/usteledirec00022_djvu.txt.

Isaacson, Lou. "Mayor-Council To File Litigation." *Birmingham News*, 4 April 1963.

Jackson, Cyrondys. "Historic 1963 Prom Planned During Civil Rights Commemoration." *AL.com*, 4 April 2013. Accessed 11 August 2013. http://www.al.com/opinion/index.ssf/2013/04/historic_1963_prom_planned_dur.html.

Jones, Adam. "Riley: Show School Spirit." *TuscaloosaNews.com*, 31 August 2007. Accessed 28 May 2012. http://www.tuscaloosanews.com/article/20070831/NEWS/708310335?p=4&tc=pg.

Kennedy, Stetson. *The Klan Unmasked.* Boca Raton: Florida Atlantic University Press, 1990.

King, Martin Luther Jr. "Letter from Birmingham Jail." Estate of Martin Luther King Jr. 16 April 1963.

King, Martin Luther Jr. *Why We Can't Wait.* New York: Signet Classics, 2000.

Klibanoff, Hank. "How the Civil Rights Movement was Covered in Birmingham." Interview by Audie Cornish. *All Things Considered*, NPR Radio, 18 June 2013. Accessed 4 June 2015. https://www.npr.org/sections/codeswitch/2013/06/18/193128475/how-the-civil-rights-movement-was-covered-in-birmingham.

Kuettner, Al. "Marchers Go Undoused In Sunday Demonstration." *Birmingham World*, 8 May 1963.

Levine, Ellen. *Freedom's Children: Young Civil Rights Activists and Their Own Stories.* New York: Puffin Books, 2000.

Logue, Mickey. "Boutwell Bids to Weld Unity: Victor By 7982 Votes, He Calls Council to Meet Today." *Birmingham News*, 3 April 1963.

Logue, Mickey. "Negro Church, Homes Bombed; Infants Hurt." *Birmingham News*, 15 Dec. 1962.

Long, R. R. "Alabama Christian Movement for Human Rights Meeting." Birmingham Police Department Inter-office Communication. 15 January 1962.

Longley, Neil, Todd Crosset, and Steve Jefferson. "The Migration of African Americans to the Canadian Football League During the 1950s: An Escape from Discrimination?" International Association of Sports Economists/ *North American Association of Sports Economists Working Paper Series,* Paper No. 07-13. June 2007. http://web.holycross.edu/RePEc/spe/Longley_CFLDiscrimination.pdf

Manheim, James M. "Fred Shuttlesworth Biography – Invited to Give Sermons, Outfoxed Segregationist Police Commissioner, Injured by Fire Hose." Accessed 28 May 2012. http://biography.jrank.org/pages/2372/Shuttlesworth-Fred.html.

May, Gary. *The Informant: The FBI, the Ku Klux Klan, and the Murder of Viola Liuzzo.* New Haven: Yale University Press, 2005.

McGuire, Danielle L. "It Was Like All of Us Had Been Raped: Sexual Violence, Community Mobilization, and the African American Freedom Struggle." *The Journal of American History,* Vol. 91, No. 3 (December 2004), pp. 906-931. Organization of American Historians. Accessed 31 August 2013. http://www.jstor.org/stable/3662860.

McWhorter, Diane. *Carry Me Home: Birmingham, Alabama: The Climactic Battle of the Civil Rights Revolution.* New York: Simon and Schuster, 2001.

Meaders, Daniel. "Black Women Who Were Lynched in America." The Henrietta Vinton Davis Memorial Foundation. 1 August 2008. Accessed 20 February 2016. https://henriettavintondavis.wordpress.com/2008/08/01/black-women-who-were-lynched-in-america/.

Mendelson, Mitch. "Collegeville has Essence of Small Neighborhood Life." *Birmingham Post-Herald,* 7 Nov. 1980. Accessed 13 December 2011. http://bplonline.cdmhost.com/cdm/singleitem/collection/p4017coll2/id/191/rec/1 (accessed 13 Dec. 2011).

Mighty Times: The Children's March. DVD. Directed by Robert Houston. Montgomery, AL: Teaching Tolerance Project of the Southern Poverty Law Center and Home Box Office, 2004.

Mobley, Bill and Ted Bryant. "Tornado Hits Bessemer, Damage in $Millions." *Birmingham Post-Herald,* 6 March 1963.

National Association for the Advancement of Colored People. "Record of Lynchings in the United States and Newspaper Clippings." Papers of the NAACP, Part 07: The Anti-Lynching Campaign, 1912-1955, Series A: Anti-Lynching Investigative Files, 1912-1953.

National Association for the Advancement of Colored People. "Reports on Lynchings, 1919-1936." Papers of the NAACP, Part 07: The Anti-Lynching Campaign, 1912-1955, Series A: Anti-Lynching Investigative Files, 1912-1953.

National Park Service. "Four Little Girls." Accessed 4 August 2018. https://www.nps.gov/articles/fourlittlegirls.htm.

National Park Service. "National Historic Landmark Nomination: Bethel Baptist Church." National Park Service. 2005. Accessed 7 March 2012. http://www.nps.gov/nhl/designations/samples/al/Bethel%20Baptist%20Church.pdf.

National Park Service. "National Register of Historic Places Multiple Property Documentation Form." 2004. Accessed 18 December 2011. http://www.nps.gov/nr/publications/sample_nominations/CivilRightsBirminghamMPS.pdf.

New York Times. "Outrage in Alabama." 5 May 1963.

"No Easy Walk: 1961-1963," *Eyes on the Prize: American's Civil Rights Years, season 1, episode 4.* DVD. Directed by James A. DeVinney and Callie Crossley. Blackside, Inc., 1986.

Nossiter, Adam. "Murder, Memory, and the Klan: A special report; Widow Inherits a Confession to a 36-Year-Old Hate Crime." *New York Times,* 4 September 1996. Accessed 30 January 2016. http://www.nytimes.com/1993/09/04/us/murder-memory-klan-special-report-widow-inherits-confession-36-year-old-hate.html?pagewanted=print.

Patterson, Homer L. *Patterson's American Education, Volume 59.* Mount Prospect, IL: Educational Directories, Inc., 1962.

PBS. "Claude Neal Lynching." PBS—Freedom Never Dies: The Legacy of Harry T. Moore. Accessed 21 February 2016. http://www.pbs.org/harrymoore/terror/cneal.html.

Poole's Funeral Chapels. "History." Accessed 6 June 2015. http://www.poolefuneralchapel.com/about-us/history.

Powell, William. *The Anarchist Cookbook.* Secaucus, NJ: Lyle Stuart, Inc., 1971.

Ramos, Kara. "Remembering a Dark Page of History." *Valdosta Daily Times,* 15 May 2010. Accessed 21 February 2016. http://www.valdostadailytimes.com/news/local_news/remembering-a-dark-page-of-history/article_9ed9cbab-3059-520d-a7b0-e20af458556a .html.

Red Mountain Park. "Red Mountain Park Trail Map." Accessed 18 March 2017. https://redmountainpark.org/activities/trail-map/.

Rieder, Jonathan. *The Word of the Lord is Upon Me: The Righteous Performance of MLK.* Cambridge, MA: Belknap Press of Harvard University Press, 2010.

Ronk, Liz. "The Girl Who Lived: Portrait of a Birmingham Church Bombing Survivor, 1963." *Time,* 6 August 2013. Accessed 8 June 2015. http://time.com/3877750/16th-street-baptist-church-bombing-victim-sarah-collins-1963/.

Rucker, James Jr. Personal interviews by Rhonda Lynn Rucker. Maryville, TN, various dates between 2011 and 2018.

Schudel, Matt. "Joe Perry, Football Star of the 1950s and First African American MVP, Dies at 84." *Washington Post,* 26 April 2011. Accessed 24 November 2015. https://www.washingtonpost.com/joe-perry-football-star-of-the-1950s-and-first-african-american-mvp-dies-at-84/2011/04/26/AFHkMttE_story.html.

Shook, Phil H. "The Loveman's Years: Curtain Closing on Lifetime of Memories." *Birmingham News,* 3 April 1980. Accessed 13 September 2012. http://www.birminghamrewound.com/features/farewell_lovemans.htm.

Shuttlesworth, Fred. "Danville Demonstrations, Reverend Fred Shuttlesworth Speech (WDBJ Television, Danville, VA)." Filmed 1963. Television News of the Civil Rights Era: 1950-1970 video, 1:06. Accessed 5 December 2011. http://www2.vcdh.virginia.edu/civilrightstv/wdbj/segments/WDBJ04_17.html.

Sloat, Bill. "The Lion Still Roars." *Plain Dealer,* 11 April 2004. Accessed 28 March 2012. http://blog.cleveland.com/pdextra/2011/10/the_lion_still_roars.html.

Smiley, Dorothy. Personal interview by Rhonda Lynn Rucker.. Birmingham, AL, 24 Nov. 2011.

Smiley, Marvin. Personal interviews by Rhonda Lynn Rucker. Birmingham, AL, 20 Nov. 2011 and 23 Nov. 2011.

Stallworth, Clarke. "For Birmingham Mayor: Boutwell, Connor in Runoff: Ex-Lt.-Gov. Leads; 'Bull' Vows Fight." *Birmingham Post-Herald,* 6 March 1963.

TeachingAmericanHistory.org. "The Power of Nonviolence."Ashbrook Center at Ashland University, Ashland, Ohio. Accessed 15 June 2012. http://www.teachingamericanhistory.org/library/index.asp?documentprint=1131.

Temple, Chanda and Jeff Hansen. "Ministers' Homes, Churches Among Bomb Targets." *AL.com,* 16 July 2000. Accessed 7 March 2012. http://www.al.com/specialreport/?bombing/97-min.html.

Thomas, Kalin, Thomas Dorsey, and Sheila Umolu. "Birmingham." *Soul of America.* Accessed 30 April 2012. http://www.soulofamerica.com/birmingham-guide.phtml.

Threatt, Glennon. "Desegregation Roils Birmingham." By Kimberly Hill. *Documenting the American South,* transcript, 16 June 2005. Interview U-0023. Southern Oral History Program Collection (#4007) in the Southern Oral History Program Collection, Southern Historical Collection, Wilson Library, University of North Carolina at Chapel Hill. Accessed 22 November 2011. http://docsouth.unc.edu/sohp/U-0023/excerpts/excerpt_1177.html.

United States Department of the Interior. National Register of Historic Places Registration Form for the Birmingham Civil Rights Historic District. 19 October 2006.

University of Alabama at Birmingham. "May 2011." UAB University Archives. Accessed 28 May 2012. http://www.uab.edu/archives/image-of-the-month/2011/170-may-2011.

University of Alabama Board of Trustees. "Chronological History of the University of Alabama at Birmingham." University of Alabama at Birmingham. Accessed 26 June 2014. http://www.uab.edu/archives/chron.

Wang, M.Q., G. S. Downey, M. A. Perko, and Yesalis, C.E. "Changes in Body Size of Elite High School Football Players: 1963-1989." *Perceptual and Motor Skills* (1993): 76, 379-383.

Ward, Thomas J. Jr. "Black Hospital Movement in Alabama." *Encyclopedia of Alabama*. Auburn University Outreach. 24 August 2009. Accessed 8 June 2015. http://www.encyclopediaofalabama.org/article/h-2410.

White, Marjorie L. *A Walk to Freedom: The Reverend Fred Shuttlesworth and the Alabama Christian Movement for Human Rights, 1956-1964*. Birmingham: Birmingham Historical Society, 1998.

Woods, Abraham. "Abraham Lincoln Woods Memoir." By Addie Pugh. UAB Mervyn H. Sterne, transcript, 1975. Accessed 22 November 2011. http://oh.mhsl.uab.edu/alw/tr.pdf (site discontinued).

Wright, Barnett. *1963: How Birmingham's Civil Rights Movement Changed America*. Birmingham: Birmingham News and the Birmingham Media Group, 2014.

X, Malcolm. "Malcolm X at Michigan State University - January 23, 1963." Filmed January 23, 1963. YouTube video, 47:23, Posted 6 December 2012 by Donnie Mossberg. Accessed 16 January 2014. https://www.youtube.com/watch?v=bNZDfyJRdLw.

About the Author

For thirty years, author Rhonda Lynn Rucker has performed as one-half of the duo Sparky and Rhonda Rucker. Blending history and storytelling with their authentic, spirited songs, the two activists spread their message of social justice throughout the United States and overseas. Their performance credits include the Kennedy Center, the Smithsonian Festival, the National Underground Railroad Freedom Center, and the Mississippi Valley Blues Festival. Sparky and Rhonda have also led and participated in workshops at the Highlander Research and Education Center, which was instrumental in energizing and organizing people during the civil rights movement.

Rhonda Rucker, standing sixth from left; her husband, James "Sparky" Rucker, standing third from right; their son, James Rucker III, sitting in foreground, far right; and in-laws. She interviewed Marvin Smiley, standing second from right, and Dorothy Smiley, standing fifth from left, about the Birmingham Children's March. (Photograph by James Rucker III)

The Artists of Change Award given to Sparky and Rhonda Rucker.

Sparky and Rhonda Rucker with their MLK Art Award from the Dr. Martin Luther King Commemorative Commission in Knoxville, Tennessee.

Rhonda and Sparky Rucker with their Spirit of Freedom Commemorative Medal of Honor. The duo was presented with the medallions at the African American Civil War Memorial in Washington, DC, after the publication of Rhonda's book Swing Low, Sweet Harriet.

Sparky and Rhonda Rucker lead music on a Southern civil rights bus tour in January 2012 and visit the memorial for civil rights activists Andrew Goodman, James Earl Chaney, and Michael Schwerner at Mt. Nebo Missionary Baptist Church in Philadelphia, Mississippi.

Sparky and Rhonda Rucker sing with Rev. Dr. Bernard Lafayette Jr. during a Southern civil rights bus tour in January 2012. (Photograph by Pam Zappardino)

Rhonda and Sparky Rucker perform with blues musician Nat Reese and singer Ed Cabbell.

Rhonda and Sparky Rucker perform in the late '80s.

Rhonda and Sparky Rucker perform in 2016 at Common Ground on the Hill in Maryland. (Photograph by Betsy Calvert)